"The perfect marriage of strange and wonderful!"

— ELLE BEAUMONT

"With tragic, lovable characters and most excellent music, Lyrics & Curses is a fun ride through my favorite decade!"

— ERIN BEATY, THE TRAITOR'S KISS

"Refreshingly unique and wonderfully nostalgic"

— AMBER R. DUELL

"A deeply romantic and quirky romp."

— KATYA DE BECCERA

D1600833

Lyrics & Curses

Cursed Hearts Duology

BOOK ONE

Candace Robinson

Midnight Tide
Publishing

Edited by Carla Lewis, Brandy Woods Snow, and Jess Moore.

Cover Art and Design © 2020 JRC Designs/Jena R Collins

Inside Artwork provided by Ricky Lee

Interior Formatting by Book Savvy Services

Lyrics & Curses/Candace Robinson — 1st ed.

ISBN print format: 978-1-953238-01-6

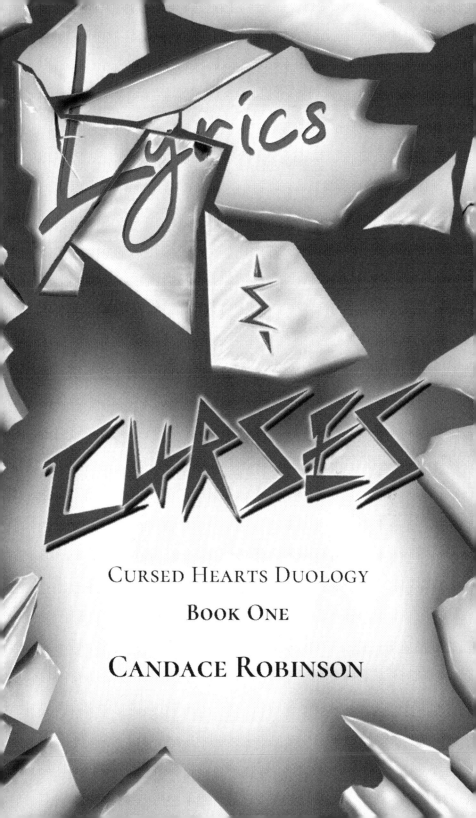

Lyrics & Curses

Cursed Hearts Duology

Book One

Candace Robinson

CONTENTS

For Patricia,

You totally get the eighties like I do

SIDE A: PHASE ONE

 # CHAPTER 1

To Lark:

Lyrics from "Under Pressure" — Queen, David Bowie

"Just One Kiss" pulsed through Lark's headphones as she hopped onto her bike and headed to work. A motorcycle would've been ideal, but her old-fashioned, rusty bicycle worked just as well. She preferred the term *rustic*.

Halfway out of the trailer park, she slammed on the brake pedal and plopped her feet to the cement to keep from tipping. Her mop of curly brown hair swung forward as she reached into her large jacket pocket to pull out her second-hand store Walkman. She pressed the stop button, bringing the band's chanting to an end.

"Sorry, boys, this won't do it for me today."

Lark shifted her backpack, and her cluster of tapes clacked. She performed a mystery grab and quickly exchanged the Cure for the Pretenders.

"Brass In Pocket" drifted through her ears. The singer, Chrissie, knew just how to get Lark in a focused mood. And *focused* was what she needed today since she was going to impress a boy named Auden by wearing something outside of her baggy comfort zone. Besides that, today was her best friend Imani's last day at work.

Maybe "Under Pressure" would've been a better song choice.

She pedaled her way through the scorching heat to the

store—beads of perspiration gathered on her forehead and hands, more so from nervousness than the temperature. It might've only been the end of June, but in Texas, the sun's rays liked to go ahead and start frying people a little early. Lucky for Lark, she didn't get hot so easily.

Her bike wheels vibrated over the uneven parking lot as she pulled up to the gray-and-white painted strip mall. A large black sign with the name *Bubble's Oddities* scrawled across, along with a picture of a skull and bubbles, loomed from in between the other stores. The owner, Jimbo, had originally named the store Oddities when he'd opened it a few years ago, but had thought adding the name Bubble's to the title would draw more people in.

He was right.

Lark supposed people were attracted to the idea of happy, soapy spheres floating majestically through the air as opposed to having zilch—she sure was.

She pressed the brakes once she made it beneath the overhang. With a hard push on the rusty kickstand, she glanced up at her shop's window, catching sight of the Help Wanted sign. The glass was black on the outside, yet clear on the inside. No one could peer in, but whenever she was inside the store, she could see all. A lot of people did interesting things when they thought no one was looking.

Lark stepped off the bike and slid her hands in the pockets of her heavy black jacket. The single piece of cloth was her security blanket, and she felt naked without the thing— whether the world was hot or not, she'd be seen wearing it.

Biting her lip, she avoided glancing at the music store for the time being because she wasn't ready to face a certain boy just yet. Her heart pumped a little harder. "Calm down, you troublesome heart," she whispered.

Before she could head inside Bubble's, something caught her eye from the right. She slowly turned her head in the direction of the laundromat, just past the music store where Auden worked. Her stupid heart accelerating even faster as she thought it could be him. Instead, her brows lowered a fraction when her eyes focused on a man wearing all black—a pork pie fedora hat, ski mask, trench coat, and gloves.

Beside him, a large rectangular object covered in what looked like black crushed velvet, leaned against the store's window. Lark yanked down her headphones and wondered if she needed to call the cops, but she'd dealt with plenty of odd customers at Bubble's before. For now, she'd leave it alone.

He turned his head in her direction—the ski mask was solid with no eye, nose, or mouth holes—and pushed off the storefront's glass. Had he seen her staring?

The blood in Lark's veins sang with warning. Her hand automatically clutched at her backpack and the knife hidden inside. She'd began carrying a knife with her after what almost happened to her sister with Beth's—her mom—ex-boyfriend. Just as she opened her mouth to call him out, he turned his head and moved in the other direction. Lark huffed and shook her head. Scared, and for what? Nothing.

She whirled around and pushed open the door of the oddity store, the cowbell clanging as she entered. A musty smell—*so* her cup of potion—hit her nose, the familiar odor like a second home.

Small animal skulls and bright pink and green tarot cards dangled from the ceiling. Lark shuffled down the aisle, making her way toward the counter in the back. Her hand skimmed over the items covered in a thin layer of dust. Shrunken and stuffed heads of animals, chakrams, Kpingas, and other unusual weapons filled the shelves. She reached the mini guillotine—a perfect fit for Barbie. To test her theory, Imani had brought her sister's Barbie doll to the store. Together, they had experimented and concluded the trial a success as the blade sliced through the neck, cleaner than a knife cutting through butter. It had been a temporary cure for boredom, even though Imani had ended up owing her sister a new Barbie *and* Ken doll.

Speak of the devil, Lark thought when Imani slid into view behind the counter.

"Finally!" Imani sighed when Lark set her backpack on the floor beside the empty stool.

Lark glanced at the Kit-Cat Klock, its tail clicking from side to side. "I'm ten minutes early."

"I've had to keep a conversation going with Jimbo." Imani hiked a thumb over her shoulder, pointing to the partly open storage closet. "You know how that is. It's basically like talking to myself."

"I heard that," Jimbo grunted as he scuttled out from the cracked door, carrying a huge cardboard box that his aristocratic nose was buried in. His head was bald on top, shining under the light like Mr. Clean. In complete contradiction, a ratty black braid fell down his back. Jimbo's skin resembled worn leather, and mostly Choctaw blood ran through his veins.

"I hoped you would, Jim-bo." Imani's eyes were glued to the cardboard.

With careful precision, he set the box of trinkets down on the counter and ducked back into the closet, his feet scuffing along the floorboards.

As soon as Jimbo disappeared from sight, Imani lunged toward the box and rummaged through the goods. Her black locks, pinned on the side of her head with a hot pink bow, framed her face like a dandelion.

Imani's brown eyes snapped to Lark's. "Are you going to remove the jacket so I can see?"

"I'm thinking about it." Lark had been all gung-ho about sporting a different outfit for her impending music store visit. Now, she wanted to rewind those moments of optimism.

Jimbo popped out one more time from the closet with a smaller box, containing a cluster of Native American artifacts and old books. "You girls got it handled?"

"Of course. We're your best employees." Imani issued a Cheshire Cat smile, showing off her white teeth.

"You're my only employees. Now I'll be down to one." His gaze shifted to Lark, then back to Imani. "Seeing as this is your last day here, Imani, you can pick something off the wall to take as a souvenir."

There Jimbo was dredging up gloom and reminding Lark of how much she was going to miss her friend.

Imani had been wanting to work at her family's hair salon for a while, but her mom wouldn't give her the position just because she was her daughter. When the receptionist spot finally opened, Imani jumped at the chance to apply.

Both Lark and Imani's stares slid to the shelf of "miracle" remedies. Lark crinkled her nose because she wasn't sure if she would use any of the contents in those bottles for *anything*.

Her once-hopeful belief in the potions' abilities was shattered when a customer returned to Bubble's pissed off and demanding a refund because her love remedy hadn't panned out. Lark had graciously pointed to the back of the bottle where it clearly read, *Most likely will not work.*

5

"Thanks, just what I've always dreamed of," Imani answered with sarcasm.

"Hey! Those are hot sellers in this store." Jimbo grinned with crooked, yellowing teeth—too much coffee and too many cigarettes.

"Hmm." Imani didn't argue.

Without another word, Jimbo took out an antique ceremonial smoking pipe from the box he was carrying and tossed them both a wave over his shoulder as he left the store.

Once the glass door shut, Imani quickly turned to face Lark. "So? Remove thy jacket."

"Are you trying to seduce me?" Lark arched an eyebrow and batted her eyelashes.

"Only if thou wants to be seduced," Imani teased.

"I'll have to think about that, Shakespeare," she said, unzipping the front of her jacket and exposing the electric blue and black full-body leotard. She pulled the Walkman from the jacket pocket and placed it on the counter, leaving the headphones around her neck.

Imani let out a low whistle. "It's like Pat Benatar meets David Bowie in the 1970s. Vintage."

"I wouldn't necessarily call the seventies vintage. But I did find it for a dollar while sifting through the racks at the thrift store." Lark finished removing her jacket, showing off the tight leotard and feeling slightly uncomfortable. It was like a second skin, and she was used to wearing baggier things.

"You paid a whole dollar for that?" Before Lark could say anything, Imani held up both hands in surrender and shouted, "Kidding! I knew you always had something under that bag of garbage you wear."

Lark looked down at her A-cups. "I think we all have bodies, Imani."

"Yeah, but who knew there was a ballerina body under there without you having to do the work?" Imani frantically motioned up and down the length of Lark's thin frame.

Lark shrugged. She didn't think she could do a lunge without getting a cramp in her thigh. If anyone had a good body it was Imani with all her curviness.

"Don't look at me like that. I'm completely honest to the 87th degree." Imani paused. "Anyway, I have some goodies for you."

Lark fixed her gaze on the trash bag stuffed with clothes. Most of Lark's clothing came from secondhand stores or was passed down from Imani whose parents bought her new clothes all the time. Imani would wear them a few times and then move on. Lark got no such luxuries. Beth was too busy spending her money on alcohol and cigarettes until recently. But to be truthful, Lark liked searching through the vintage rack for old things in need of some love.

Rummaging through the open bag, Imani fished out a pair of yellow heels and a matching belt. "Here, you asked me to bring these." She handed them to Lark. "But keep them, too. I never wear them."

She stared down at the bright heels and belt, the color practically blinding her. Her normal black and gray tones suited her "somber" homelife—still, she couldn't be *totally* morbid, so Lark always paired her style with red lipstick and matching nails.

Removing her headphones, she set them on the counter, so she could take off her boots. She slipped on the heels, then wrapped the belt around her narrow waist.

"So Emilia already left?" Lark asked, clipping the

Walkman onto the side of the belt. She finished by sliding the headphones back around her neck.

"Yeah." Imani let out a sigh.

Emilia was the German exchange student staying with Imani's parents for the school year. Only Lark knew that Emilia and Imani were more than friends—Imani was still waiting to tell her parents.

"Enough of bringing up misery. She'll be back before school starts, so go find your brooding prince. His van was already parked in the lot behind the store when I got here." Imani grinned.

Lark bit her lower lip, hesitating. "Maybe I should put the jacket back on."

Before Lark could touch her security blanket, Imani snatched it from the counter. "I don't think so. Take your time." Still smiling, she looked around the empty store. "I'll take care of the booming business."

"Fine." Bubbles of dread and anticipation filled Lark's chest as she pulled the headphones from her neck and placed them over her ears. She grabbed a twenty from her backpack before walking out of the store.

There were two reasons she went to the music store on Wednesdays. One, she'd buy something new. Her other reason —Auden Ellis.

As she opened the door to Music Revelations, she automatically found him at the back of the store, bent over a cassette rack. The minute she stepped over the threshold, he angled his head over his shoulder. Lark turned away, trying to hide the nervous tapping of her fingers against her Walkman. She didn't always come in *just* because he worked there. When she'd started the job at Bubble's, Auden hadn't been employed at Music Revelations yet and she'd still visited every Wednesday to pick out something.

She probably should've been saving all her money for a car. And she was, with some of it, but music was her escape. If Lark had to ride a decaying bike until she hit forty, then so be it. The little money she did have left went toward helping with the groceries since her sister, Paloma, had chosen not to work over the summer.

When Lark had moved to La Porte halfway through tenth grade, Auden's band shirts at school had drawn her attention. Unfortunately, a girlfriend had already been attached to his hip—until the beginning of Lark's junior year. During their math class together, no talking had occurred, but something better—a musical connection through song lyrics.

Lark didn't know why he exchanged the lyrics with her, but she knew why *she* did. It was a form of expression, where somehow, he got her and understood her like no one ever had.

She headed to the vinyl section, brushing her fingers against the different records on the way. Auden's slicked-back, chestnut-brown head was hogging the cassette tape area, and her nerves were too on edge to walk in that direction.

Black records hung all over the walls, along with framed pictures of famous musicians. It took her a moment to find the "S" category—they must've moved things around. She flipped through vinyl after vinyl until she located Siouxsie and the Banshees. This one she had on cassette, but the LP just gave a completely different sound when she needed it.

Cradling Siouxsie to her chest, Lark glanced down at herself and had almost forgotten she wasn't wearing her safety net of a jacket. Auden had been too much of a distraction when she'd come in. Lark turned her head to the store counter where he'd magically appeared. They might not have talked at school, but over the summer, there had been a couple times where they'd done more than talking. Memories of his hands on her body ran through her mind, and Lark's heartbeat accelerated. She wished she'd talked afterward, but more than anything, she didn't want to tarnish what had happened between them in class with the lyrics.

Today is the day. Lark's determination was enhanced by the siren voice singing in her ears. Before she could change her mind, she clutched the vinyl tighter and strode to the counter, swaying her hips side to side, something she normally didn't do.

When Lark reached the checkout, she placed the vinyl on the purple-and-black checkered counter and tugged down her headphones. She tried to both make eye contact with Auden and avoid it—her eyes probably looked like a silver ball in a pinball machine going haywire.

Auden wore a blue jean vest over a David Bowie T-shirt and tight black jeans. A silver earring dangled from his left ear with the same color stud right next to it, doubling the sexiness.

His hazel eyes met Lark's. With an almost robotic tone, he gave her the price of the record, and she handed him the twenty-dollar bill. He handed her $3.98 back, and Lark felt like an idiot with nowhere to slide the change into. *I need damn pockets on this stupid leotard.*

"You don't have quarters?" she asked, staring at her handful of dimes and pennies.

"Sorry, fresh out," he said with a soft click of his tongue. "Bag?"

Lark's gaze dropped to the counter. Siouxsie's image on the album cover stared back at her with those distinct dark eyes of hers. "Sure."

Auden's gaze moved slowly down her body as his fingers played with his bottom lip, his expression unreadable. "Costume party?"

"Excuse me?" Her eyebrows lowered in confusion.

He flicked his index finger up and down, indicating her outfit. "You going to a costume party today?"

Lark narrowed her eyes. "In June?" A hint of embarrassment was there, but she didn't show it.

"Yeah?" He shrugged a shoulder and placed his hands flat on the counter.

"Is that a question?" She tried to avoid staring at how nice his hands looked because she was annoyed that nothing was going how she'd imagined it would've.

"Just wondering what's going on with the leotard." Smirking, Auden handed her the bag.

"Sorry, I gotta get back to work." She yanked the bag from his hand, tossed the change in, pulled up her headphones, and left the store.

Outside Music Revelations, she let out a defeated breath, running her hands down her face in irritation. She never really went out of her comfort zone, and she should've kept it that way, all while listening to her cassettes somewhere else. Now, she only had one reason to go next door on Wednesdays —music.

As she turned, her body jerked when she noticed the creep with the pork pie hat was back. He hadn't been there when she'd gone into buy the record.

Something sounded over the music of her headphones. She wrinkled her forehead and pulled the headphones down— a melody floated through the air from somewhere behind her. Familiar, too familiar. "Space Oddity" played in the distance... on a flute? David Bowie's song was not a fearful one, but something about the way the music seeped all the way to her bones had her captivated and jittery at the same time. Something didn't feel right about it...

Lark froze. The man's head was turned toward her as if he was gazing at her from underneath the mask. A chill ran up the length of her spine.

"Hey!" she called, wishing she'd brought her knife with her.

He pushed off the wall as if he'd been waiting for her, lifted the bulky rectangular object into his arms, and strode toward her. The music continued, the flute's pulses growing fiercer, harder. No one else was outside.

Instead of stopping in front of her like she expected, he brushed past her, dangerously close, and kept walking toward the music.

Sucking in a sharp breath, she hurried to the door at Bubble's and gave one last glance over her shoulder toward the man. But he was already gone. Had he taken off running? In the distance, an almost-silvery aura flickered—*a strange glare of the sun?*—and faded at the same time the note to "Space Oddity" ended.

She tore open the door and rushed to the back of the store.

Lark placed the bag on the counter next to the cardboard box, where she found Imani's head almost fully submerged as she sifted through the contents.

"Did you see a guy over at the laundromat dressed all in black, wearing a trench coat and a pork pie hat when you came into work?"

"No?" Imani slowly rose from the box, then tilted her head as if in thought. "I think I would've remembered someone besides you wearing a jacket in the middle of June."

"What about a flute playing music outside?" Lark's voice sounded almost desperate.

"I can't hear anything over the radio in here." A slow song from the 1960s played through the store. Lark dropped her shoulders, letting the tension diffuse.

"Oh." Lark threw on her jacket, wanting to just forget about the guy. It wasn't as though she'd been attacked. She changed the subject and asked, "Going fishing in that box?"

Imani lifted her hands in the air like she was holding a fishing rod, winding up the string and yanking it back. Then she studied Lark's face. "Trying." Her hands suddenly dropped, and her eyebrow arched. "What happened next door?"

Lark clenched the front of her jacket and pulled it tighter. "We had a semi-conversation, and he asked me if I was going to a costume party."

Imani scanned Lark up and down. "I can see why he'd ask that. You do normally dress differently—long baggy skirts, black pants, bulky sweaters, heavy jacket. There's a consistency in the things you wear."

"Well, screw this situation," Lark grumbled.

Imani knowingly grinned. "No back seat time again?"

"Whoa, whoa, whoa. Things may not have gone as planned, but let's be rational here. I'd have to think about it." Lark laughed. Imani knew about her crush but not the story behind it. That was Lark's hidden jewel that she kept for herself.

Lark had been sitting in front of Auden for the entire year, trying hard not to turn around to catch a glimpse of what band shirt he was wearing each morning. Auden had passed up his paper for her to grade during math class.

That day, his homework had the usual doodle on it—a

skeleton. Sometimes they'd been punk rockers, horned creatures, or gloomy trees—he was genius. Something had stirred in her as she stared at the skeleton—it was missing something. With her red pen, she drew a speech balloon and wrote Kate Bush song lyrics inside, as if the skeleton was singing them. She didn't think Auden would say anything or even notice. But he had. The next day, instead of a doodle, there'd been a song lyric from Queen where his new drawing should've been, written just for her. The only thing left to do had been to write him a lyric in return.

Months of writing song lyrics back and forth had led to a simple game of spin the bottle. That, in turn, had ended in the back of Auden's van where he sure as hell hadn't acted with the same aloofness she'd just witnessed in the store.

"On to more important matters," Imani said, interrupting Lark's thoughts. "Look at what I found." She pulled out a headless Elvis statue wearing a sparkly white suit, exposing too much chest. The King's neck leaned forward, using his head as a microphone, as he belted out his famous tunes.

Imani sang "Viva Las Vegas."

"Viva Las Headless," Lark sang back.

Imani looked at the ceiling, letting out a witchy laugh, then struck the counter with her palms. "Yes, much better lyrics!"

Lark hovered over the box and sifted through—more junk. "Did Jimbo really buy this crap at auction, or did someone come to the store and sell it?"

Their boss regularly went to auctions to find things to resell or other items for his personal Native American spiritual stash at home. He was leaving again in two days for Las Vegas to explore several huge collections. Lark stared at the

Elvis statue and thought, *what a coincidence*—being Vegas and all.

Other times, people came into the store and tried to sell away their weird goodies. Lark and Imani weren't allowed to let the customers pawn stuff, though—only Jimbo could give an offer.

"No, these are things from his personal collection," Imani replied, producing a small lamp with baby doll legs attached to the bottom, arms at the side, and a dusty lampshade as the head. "I think I may have to purchase this one for myself."

"Not if I buy it first." Lark reached out to grab the prize.

"Too bad—I already claimed it." Imani held it up to the light like a trophy. "This is a hundred times better than the lamp in *A Christmas Story*."

Lark would have to agree, and she'd have actually bought it too. Anything with baby doll parts could spice up a room.

"But, don't worry," Imani continued. "I didn't leave you empty-handed." She pushed two paperbacks in front of Lark. "Jimbo was getting rid of a few books."

Lark picked them up and read the titles, one on paranormal activity and the other a way to get rid of ghosts. "Thanks!" She liked reading about anything different, so she shoved them in her backpack.

To take up time, Lark and Imani dusted off the shelves and found places to put Jimbo's home decorations out for sale. Only four customers deigned to pay them a visit, each one more unusual than the last. But no sight of the creep in black.

By the end of the day, Lark wasn't ready to go home, though she couldn't avoid it. After collecting her things, she turned to Imani who was babying her new lamp. "Don't forget to pick out a *miracle* remedy from the wall."

"Hmm." Imani tapped her chin, browsing the selection on the plastic shelves.

"Wipe away skin?" Lark suggested.

"I think they mean dead skin cells. I'm not sure I want to put this on my skin, though." Imani placed the blue bottle back. Smart choice.

Scrunching up her nose, Lark pored over the other bottles: *Hair Grower*, *Love Potion*, *Stain Remover*, and several other ridiculous "potions."

"What about this mystery beautifying hair shampoo?" Lark asked, tapping the lid with her middle finger.

"I have to watch what I put on my hair, and I don't think anyone should use it unless maybe on a doll's hair." Imani twiddled her fingers in the air. "I think I'm going to go with… this one." She grabbed a pink bottle that read, *Bubbles*.

"For your sister?"

"Yeah, she still hasn't forgiven me for bringing her toys to test out up here, even though I bought her more." Imani unzipped the alligator's mouth of her scaly green purse and stuffed the bottle inside.

They turned everything off and locked up the store. "It's bogus I won't see you here anymore," Lark groaned.

"Don't you worry, we have all summer to hang out, little lady." She wiggled her finger at Lark. "Maybe we'll have a *costume party*."

With the huge bag of clothes in one hand and the new vinyl in the other, Lark puckered her lips. Imani walked away laughing, leaving Lark to face her bike. It only took her a second to realize she hadn't thought about carrying everything while biking. Huffing and puffing, she managed to prop the trash bag as best she could in between the handlebars.

While focusing on the bag, a sound filled the air. Music

notes. She jerked her head over her shoulder, scanning thoroughly yet seeing no one, only hearing the flute. The notes pulled together into a stream as "Space Oddity" formed like it had before, almost melancholic with a deep sadness she could feel under her skin. "Not this again," she whispered.

As she twisted back around, something forcefully struck her shoulder, triggering a small zap against her arm that caused her heart to gallop. The contact was strong enough to push her backward, the bag tumbling off the handlebars to the ground with a crinkly thump.

"Dammit." Lark rubbed her arm and looked up to see the same guy dressed all in black from earlier, speed walking in the direction of the music. He didn't look behind him, just continued his long strides as he carried the same bulky, cloaked object in his hands. "Thanks for that," she mumbled to his back.

As if he heard her clear as day, the creep came to a stop and glanced back. Lark's heart pounded in her chest. Her shaking hands sank to her backpack and partially unzipped it to retrieve her knife.

But as she lifted her eyes back to the guy, he was gone. Another quick exit. Farther down the road, another hazy glow caught her attention. She rubbed her eyes, and it vanished. And so had the music.

She gripped her chest, her breath coming out in uneven spurts. A door banged open, and she jumped, her attention shooting up ahead. "What the hell!"

Auden's tall, lanky frame darkened the doorway to the music store. His hazel eyes fell to the bag on the ground as he came closer, while Lark had her feet planted on either side of the bike.

"Drop something?" Auden asked.

"Yeah. Did you—never mind." She didn't want to quiz him about people vanishing or mysterious music, not when he'd already asked her if she was going to a costume party.

Auden reached down and picked up the heavy bag, then set it in between the handlebars. "Be careful with the bag. Wouldn't want you to get in a wreck."

"Yeah." She let the bag lean against her chest and avoided eye contact.

"I see you're back in your usual," Auden said, staring at her jacket.

"Yeah," she grumbled.

"Shame." He grinned, showcasing a few crooked bottom teeth before turning to head back into the music store.

What the hell did that mean?

# CHAPTER 2

To Auden:

Lyrics from "Running Up That Hill" – Kate Bush

Auden went back inside Music Revelations and peered down at his watch. He had about an hour left before he could close up the joint.

He'd gone outside to meet his friend Darrin, but instead, he'd come into contact with Hell on Wheels. A lovely hell he didn't know if he wanted to encounter again—or did he? Lark Espinoza wasn't the typical girl he went for, but that didn't mean she was any less worthy. She was just *different*.

Lark had taken him by surprise when she'd strolled into the store with her lithe body on display. He'd known she would come in today, as she did every Wednesday, but she probably hadn't caught him side-eying her the entire time. He was good at staying under the radar, pretending nonchalance.

The door opened and Auden's gaze drifted to the store's new guest.

"There's my man," his best friend Darrin yelled, tracking dried mud into the store as he carried in his prized skateboard. The store owner, Jacee, would be pissed, but that wasn't his problem.

"You're late." Auden scanned Darrin's freshly-colored red Mohawk. A few days ago, it had faded to a pale shade of pink, but now it was back to Coca-Cola can red.

"Nah, right on time. I had to pick up a pack of smokes and

a couple of candy bars." He tossed a Twix to Auden, who almost caught it before it tumbled to the floor. "You never were an athlete, were you?"

Auden couldn't say he was, but he could've been if he'd really cared for sports. Most of the time, he hadn't felt like trying.

"I take that as a no." Darrin laughed, propping his skateboard against the counter and taking a seat on the stool behind the desk.

"Jacee's going to throw a shit fit if she catches you behind there again."

"I highly doubt it. She's always staring at my junk," Darrin said, shoving the candy bar in his mouth.

"That's because you always have holes in your pants and your bright ass underwear shows through."

"Really?" He stood up to inspect the fly of his jeans. "I suppose I've been unaware this entire time."

When he realized he was still staring at Darrin's crotch, Auden rolled his eyes and jerked his attention to the cassette rack. "Let me finish putting that last box of tapes up and then we can head out of here."

Darrin took a seat and started back up on his chocolate. "Heather Thomas is having a party tonight, and you can crash at my place after."

Heather Thomas was Scott Price's girlfriend. It wouldn't have meant shit to Auden, except for one thing—Scott Price was Lark's ex-boyfriend. Why she'd been with that moron to begin with, he couldn't understand.

One time the asshole had made a homemade buzzer and without Auden knowing, Scott had shaken his hand and it had shocked the shit out of him. Scott had thought it was the most hilarious thing in the world, so Auden ripped the buzzer from

Scott's hand and crushed it under his shoe. The idiot hadn't tried anything since then.

"I think I'll pass," Auden said, clenching and flexing his fist. He was thinking about the buzzer, but mostly about Scott pressed up against Lark.

"Plenty of booze, man." Darrin threw back a pretend shot glass.

"You have plenty of that at your apartment."

Darrin moved out on his own as soon as he'd hit eighteen five months earlier—Auden wasn't quite that lucky yet. He wouldn't be eighteen until the end of August.

"Come on," Darrin begged. "Don't be like that."

Auden finally gave in, satisfying his friend's desire to see those shitheads. "Yeah, okay, but you're driving after the party."

The rest of the hour, Darrin fiddled with things on the desk, then browsed around the store. Meanwhile, Auden finished unloading the cassettes and organizing the records that had been dropped in wrong spots by careless customers.

Before Auden closed up the joint, he picked up the store phone to call his mom. Well, it wasn't his real mom, but his mom's sister, Janet. She'd adopted him with her husband, Donnie, when Auden was two—after his real dad "accidentally" murdered his mom, blaming it on a bad drug trip and his schizophrenia. His murderer of a dad was now safely tucked away in prison for the rest of his life, and Auden refused to ever visit. He may have not chosen his illness, but he'd chosen to do drugs.

His mom answered after two rings. "Hello."

"Hey, Mom"—Auden pressed his shoulder against the wall—"I'm going to be staying the night at Darrin's tonight."

"Again?" She sounded sullen, as if he'd never return home.

"Yeah, you know, another *Star Wars* marathon. Watching movies all night, we will," Auden grunted in his most God-awful Yoda voice.

Darrin's eyebrow rose as he slowly chewed a piece of gum. Auden lifted his own eyebrow right back at him.

"All right"—his mom laughed and that was what he'd wanted to achieve—"but I want you home for dinner tomorrow after work."

"Sure."

"I love you," she said, sincerity laced in those three words.

"Okay, I'll see you tomorrow," he rushed the statement out and quickly hung up the phone. His mom and dad were great parents, but with his past and baggage, he didn't trust in happily ever afters. Things could easily be broken or taken away, so it was best not to want or enjoy them. A morbid philosophy, but it kept his heart safe.

When he was eight, he'd uncovered the truth about his parents by overhearing his mom and dad talking. The things kids find just by pressing a careless ear to a door in hopes of discovering some sort of buried treasure isn't always the case. Auden's mom had been crying. He'd known his real mom had died and that his father was locked away in jail, but he hadn't known that his dad was the one to do it. He hadn't questioned his mom about his real dad until he was twelve—by then he'd bottled it up for so long that there was no turning back. Auden wished she'd told him sooner. He knew why she hadn't. She loved him and worried it would affect him. And yet, maybe it wouldn't have scarred him if she'd told him from the begin-ning. But the thing was, if he hadn't overheard, then she probably never would've told him and that bothered him more than anything.

"*Star Wars*?" Darrin asked, chewing his gum a bit faster.

"Isn't that what you always put on?"

"I was thinking more like the Romero movies tonight. Night and Dawn to prepare for *Day of the Dead*."

"Too bad that one looks shitty." Auden folded his arms across his chest.

"It really does, but hey, it's Romero, right?"

Auden did have a soft spot for the violence—maybe he was more like his real dad than he wanted.

Once outside the store, Darrin switched out his gum with a half-smoked cigarette from his pack and lit it. The smoke surrounded Auden, and he missed the nicotine. He'd quit six months ago when it was another thing in his life that he'd felt too addicted to. And now, he was better off ridding himself of it completely.

Darrin blew a smoke ring in the air as he hopped on his skateboard. He flew down the cement path that led behind the building to where Auden's van was parked, then disappeared from view.

Auden shoved his hands deep in his pockets and kicked at loose pebbles as he stared at the ground, following the rumbling sounds of the skateboard when another noise filled the air. He stopped, cocking his head, and craned his neck for a better listen. It grew louder and took him a moment to recognize the song coming from a flute. "Space Oddity"—one of his favorites.

Something struck his shoulder, a bite of electric shock

zinging through his arm. He shook it, trying to alleviate the residual tingle, and twisted sideways, catching a glimpse of a person walking past him wearing black clothing. The stranger was dressed like he'd just come straight out of an old gangster film with his trench coat.

"Watch where you're going next time!" Auden yelled.

The man stopped in his tracks, slowly angling his ski-mask-covered face over his shoulder.

Auden inhaled sharply and waited for the man to turn around and keep on walking, but the stranger remained planted, staring at him. Something was off—besides his wearing a trench coat in the hell-hot of June. Lark wore jackets in the summer as well, so maybe Auden *was* the odd one out. Another few flute notes floated in the distance, the song dancing wickedly in his ears. The stranger's hands fidgeted at his sides as he continued to stare, and Auden took a deep swallow. Something was about to happen—something big and life changing.

From the side of the building, the whir of skateboard wheels caught his attention. Quickly, Auden glanced behind him, then back to the man with the pork pie hat, but he was nowhere in sight. Only a bright beam of silver light remained, blinking rapidly before fading into nothing, as though it was never there. It had to be the reflection of the lights from the parking lot. *Life changing indeed.*

Darrin wove back around from the side of the building, drawing closer, and circled around Auden with his cigarette dangling from his mouth. He wobbled, then stumbled, almost eating the pavement. "Fuck."

"That's why you don't smoke and ride." Auden chuckled, but then stopped when he noticed the music no longer playing.

"Like you could do better." Darrin pushed the skateboard forward and backward with his right foot.

Softly, Auden shoved Darrin off the board. "Hey, did you hear that? Someone was playing 'Space Oddity' on a flute."

Darrin tilted his head and closed his eyes, listening.

"No... not now. Like a few moments ago."

Opening his eyelids, Darrin shook his head. "I didn't hear anything, but I wish I had. You already know I can't hear that great out of my left ear from popping those damn firecrackers when I was nine."

Auden searched around the mostly empty parking lot. "What about a man dressed all in black? Did you see him? He bumped in to me and ran off or something."

"Sounds like several people at our school, Auden."

Auden gave a half-hearted shrug and hopped on the board, skating his way to his beat-up van, not being able to get the flute melody out of his head.

He performed a quick kickflip with the board and shoved it upward, catching it in his right hand before handing it back to Darrin.

"I eat my earlier words." Darrin took another drag of his cigarette and flicked it into the parking lot. Pulling out the pack of cigarettes from his shirt pocket, he opened the lid, yanked out the chewed gum from inside, and plopped it back into his mouth.

"I could've given you a new piece." Auden had several packs in the glove compartment inside his van—Jenny. He named the van after the song "867-5309/Jenny," even though the tune was horrendous. It was ironic that people believed Jenny was actually out there in the world—well, here she was now embodied as Auden's van. After he'd turned sixteen, his parents had offered to buy him a new car, but when he'd seen the black van, it was the only thing he'd wanted. If he ever got the guts to finally leave and road trip across the country, it would be perfection and have enough room to sleep in. But to date, he'd never left—he was still here, even though he'd graduated a little over a month ago.

"Gotta conserve." Darrin patted his back pocket where his wallet was. "I'm on a budget with the bills and all."

Auden fished out his keys. Darrin went to yank them from his hand, but Auden was too quick. "No, not yet. I need to be drunk before I let you drive Jenny."

"All in due time then."

"Co-rrect." If Auden was going to go with Darrin to the party, he knew he'd have to drink to get through it. "So are we going straight to this shindig or your place first?"

"Party." Darrin pointed in what Auden assumed was the direction to Heather's. He had no clue where she lived since she'd never had a get-together that he knew of. Auden had actually been partied out lately, but before he quit going to them after summer ended, he'd live a little a few more times.

As he was about to turn right onto the street from the parking lot, he caught sight of a man standing at the edge of the street, holding a large object. Auden blinked and then blinked again, but the person was still there—the same stranger who'd bumped into him earlier. Whatever the object was, it was hidden underneath a sheet of black cloth. Auden turned to Darrin. "See that's the—" He stopped mid-sentence when he flipped his head back to the side and saw only a silvery light in the stranger's place. And then it was gone.

"The what?" Darrin asked over the music in the van.

"Nothing… only the street." Something in his head was playing tricks on him. "Just give me the directions to the party."

Darrin told him how to get to Washington Street as he smacked his gum. If he started blowing bubbles again, Auden would have to throw him out of Jenny and make him walk the rest of the distance to the party.

The van didn't have anything but a radio to listen to. In the back, he kept a portable record player with loads of vinyl for when he wanted to park somewhere and have some quality music time.

"This is it!" Darrin shouted, punching Auden in the bicep.

They turned onto Washington, newly constructed homes lining the road. Rows of cars were parked up and down both sides of the dimly lit street. Heather was going big with this one, and he wasn't a fan of huge parties. They always led to increased drama.

He parked half a block from the house in a spot that must've recently opened. Feeling a bit nervous, Auden chewed on the nail of his middle finger as he walked around the front of the van to meet Darrin.

"You all right?" Darrin asked, juggling his lighter.

"Why wouldn't I be?" Auden shoved his hands into his pockets and stared straight ahead at the two elm trees, with recently cut branches.

"I don't know, maybe because you start doing weird things with your nails when you're anxious about something. Sometimes you run the tip of a pencil so hard over them in class, I think you're going to make permanent craters."

"It's nothing." It *was* something. He wasn't sure if Lark would be here, and if so, would she still be wearing that leotard? She'd had it covered with her oversized jacket and black boots in the parking lot, but the image of the leotard painted on her lithe body would forever be ingrained in his mind. He should've said something better when he'd seen her.

Darrin lit up a new cigarette and blew smoke at the two flecks of stars in the night sky. "She's not going to be here, man. Heather didn't invite any of the juniors besides Scott."

"I don't know what you're talking about." The nerves slipped away, but in its place was—what? Disappointment?

"For fuck's sake," Darrin groaned. "Just admit it. I saw the two of you come out of your van at Shannon's last party."

"We were talking."

Darrin squinted an eye at him. "Mm-hmm."

They had been—sort of, among other things.

Through the dark, they approached a large two-story house covered in off-white brick. In front of it was a long, cracked driveway. A few familiar people from school were standing outside in the front yard beneath the light from the porch—most of them with red cups in hand.

Just as Auden and Darrin were about to pass a group of guys whose faces Auden recognized—but not their names—a large beefy hand plopped down on his shoulder. "Hey, Auden, where've you been?"

He stared at the broad shoulders of one of the football players from school, the guy's eyes already glazed and red.

"Work." Auden tried to back up to go inside but Darrin had already joined the group of guys.

"Did you see Stella's titties tonight? They looked bangin'." The nameless football player held out his hands in front of his chest as if holding two oversized watermelons. "I'm gonna get me a slice of those tonight."

Auden quirked a brow and Darrin shook his fist in the air in agreement, even though neither one of them had seen Stella yet.

"Okay, well, I'm going to go and find Felisa," Darrin said, turning to Auden. "I'll look for you a little later."

"I'll be where the beer's at."

Felisa wanted to be more than whatever she and Darrin were, but he wasn't cool with that. Darrin said he had too much to live for to be tied down, which meant he'd still have a wandering eye. But at least he was upfront with her about it.

Auden, on the other hand, just didn't want to feel that addiction, like he needed someone when they weren't around. *Been there, done that.*

Inside Heather's house, they walked down a long hallway leading to the living room. Several paintings of cats hung on the walls. In one corner, a large grandfather clock's pendulum tick-tocked back and forth with the music. People were crushed against one another—too many elbows rubbing together. Darrin found Felisa, a tall girl with bronze skin and a hungry smile, awaiting him.

"My girl!" Darrin called, smiling back with a goofy grin. Sometimes Auden wasn't sure how his friend picked up all the ladies.

Auden brushed past several sweaty people, stopping for moments of small talk when someone would halt him from passing. Finally, he made it out the back door to the keg and grabbed two red plastic cups, filling them to the brim—one for now and one for later.

He turned around and bumped into Scott and Heather. Scott, his shaggy dark hair flopping over one eye, leaned forward and softly punched Auden in the bicep. Auden looked down at the guy's small hand—Scott had ridiculously tiny hands. And because he was almost as tall as Auden, it came across as odd.

"I can't believe you came!" Scott exclaimed, head banging the air. "One of the coolest guys in school, or was, now that you're gone."

"I'm still here." In town, anyway.

Scott wrapped his arm around Heather's curvy waist. "You know what I mean."

Did he? How Lark had ended up with this goofball, Auden wondered even more now as Scott rattled on and on *and on* about shitty music and how they should jam together sometime.

Auden used to fiddle around on the drums, but last year he'd lost most of his passion for it—like a lot of other things.

While listening to Scott rave about the upcoming party on Friday night at Shannon's and how he had to be there, Auden chugged his entire first cup of beer.

"Yeah? Let me check with Darrin about it later." Now having a chance at escape and to try and relax, Auden headed into the kitchen to where a group of guys were doing shots. As he scanned the large living room crowd, he checked to see if maybe Darrin had been wrong. Maybe he would catch a glimpse of Lark or even her sister Paloma, but neither were there. Because when Paloma was at a party that generally meant her sister had tagged along with her.

After finishing the second cup of beer, an easy, floating sensation gripped Auden, and he was oblivious to everything except his very full bladder. He beelined to the downstairs bathroom, but when the line was too long, he headed up the narrow staircase to take a leak. If there wasn't one upstairs for some reason, he would find somewhere outside to piss. But it was his lucky day—a door was wide open.

After relieving himself in the Clorox-smelling bathroom, he opened the door and was staring at the floor when voices caught his attention. Farther down the family-portrait hallway, a tall rectangular object rested against the wood-paneled wall, a black crushed-velvet fabric enveloping whatever was hidden beneath. The object appeared incredibly similar to the one the man with the trench coat had been carrying.

The hallway was vacant, but whispers circulated in the small space, the hushed voices suddenly halting when the first familiar music notes sounded from beneath the cloth. He paused. Rapid breaths escaped him as he closed his eyes and gripped the sides of his skull while counting to five. When he opened them, the object was gone, along with the over-dramatized sounds of "Space Oddity." *Get a grip, Auden. Get a fucking grip.* His chest heaved, as he inched forward to where the object had been, hands shaking.

He had drunk way too much.

Someone grabbed him by the bicep and yanked him into a bedroom, then shut the door.

His body tensed, head spinning, in the dark room. A soft body pushed him against the backside of the door, wet lips meeting his neck, making him forget about his drunken images.

He groaned when the warm lips moved against his skin. After the nights with Lark in his van, he knew this would inevitably happen again. He'd been yearning to have her lips against his like before. "All you had to do was ask," he whispered, while wanting to repeat one of the lyrics he'd scribbled to her during math class or possibly recite what she'd written down of "Running Up That Hill" that first time.

Auden's hand reached up, tangling his fingers in Lark's bob of loose brown curls, hoping to get trapped there. Instead, he fisted tight thick curls, falling to someone's mid-back—and he knew who those red curls belonged to.

Drew.

She had been his girlfriend for two years until the beginning of his senior year when she'd switched schools. After the move, she hadn't wanted to be tied down any longer, though at almost every party, they would find the nearest place of interest to have sex.

But he hadn't seen her in months.

Auden leaned sideways, pulling away from her suction, but she held on like a leech as she reached for the top button of his pants. The overwhelming scent of her hairspray invaded his nostrils. He couldn't deny she felt good, but he was over it. Over *her*.

"Hey, not now." He clamped down on her wrists, slowly withdrawing her fingertips from the button on his pants.

Drew shifted back and flipped on the light switch. As the light cascaded across the room, she glared at him. "And why not?"

Pressing his head against the door, he blinked a couple of extra times to let his eyes try to focus on her. "Just not now. It's been a while since I've seen you." He stared down at her blue crop top hanging off her shoulder and the tight pink mini skirt that showed off every curve she had. Yet all he could think about was Lark in the store today, wearing the one-piece.

"You've never had a problem before." Drew backed up and placed her hands on her hips.

"Well, maybe I do now. I don't just want to fuck and not talk after, okay?" Wasn't that what he'd done to Lark, though? It wasn't as if the fault was his alone—she hadn't tried to talk to him afterward either. The most talking they'd done since then was the minuscule conversation they'd had in the music store and then outside when he'd picked up her bag.

"You know what?" Drew huffed. "Screw you, Auden. I'll find someone else."

"You always were good at that, even when we were

together, right?" He didn't give one damn about it now, but a year ago, he sure would have.

"We're done."

"I'm sorry, are you breaking up with a non-existent boyfriend?"

"You're such a scumbag." Drew flung open the door, causing Auden to move out of the way for her to scurry out. *So I'm the scumbag, even though I'd never cheated on you. Right...* He closed the door behind him and slid to the floor, slamming the back of his head against the wood. The slight throb felt good—his head wasn't spinning as much anymore.

He looked around at what must be Heather's younger sister's room. A *Muppet Babies* comforter covered the mattress, and a cluster of about thirty stuffed animals sat on top, all judging him. This was somewhere he wouldn't have felt comfortable screwing, anyway.

Outside the bedroom, a cacophony of notes coming from a flute poured out. Auden hurried and yanked the door open, anxiously looking both ways down the carpeted hall, but all remained silent, not a single music note floated through the air. Only the laughter and bass line from downstairs.

Another beer was something he needed in that moment, and then he'd find Darrin to drive Jenny back to his apartment. He hoped to God he wouldn't draw up any more drunken imagery or have another run-in with Drew on the way to the alcohol. Before she ended things with him, he thought they'd been completely in sync. But she'd been just another piece of an addiction-filled puzzle. And he'd chosen to toss that particular puzzle piece away, along with the cigarette one. Once he'd done that, Auden had felt lighter without them, especially added with the progress he'd made by working with the school counselor for years. Even when he was younger, addiction had always been there, such as the need to collect every action figure he could.

But the lyrical notes with Lark were ones that were different, they made him feel worthy because they didn't take from him, they gave.

As he stumbled down the stairs, the shitty party music played on full blast. "Hungry Like The Wolf" blared through the speakers, making his head pound even harder. At the last party he'd gone to, he remembered Lark saying, "We get it. You have a large appetite, Duran Duran."

He chuckled to himself at the memory as Darrin strolled up and handed Auden a beer. "The music's great, isn't it?"

"No." Grabbing the plastic cup, he guzzled it down. Last one of the night.

Darrin reached up to wrap an arm around Auden's tall frame. "Lighten up."

"Like a light bulb?" Auden said, filled with sarcasm.

"Sure. Why not? I don't carry light bulbs, though, but I do have a flashlight." He tugged out a miniature blue one from his back pocket.

"I don't even want to know *why* you carry that." Auden shook his head, regretting his decisions of the night. "Are you ready?"

"If you are."

"Yeah, I was going to grab another beer, but you must've read my mind." He stared at the empty cup for a moment and set it down. Next time, he wouldn't slip into the old Auden.

On the way out, Auden's shirt clung to his back and stomach in the humid air. Darrin kept staring at Auden's neck. "Found you some action?"

"No." His mind drifted to Drew, and he cringed about the

incident. What bothered him even more than his cheating ex-girlfriend was the fact he'd thought it had been Lark.

"Ah. Unwanted attention then." Darrin grinned.

"I fixed it." One problem anyway. Yet a particular girl with musical lyrics continued to be a pestering gnat buzzing around inside his head.

"Drew was dancing in the living room all over some guy I'd never seen before."

"Good for her."

"Normally, you'd be more down in the dirt about that." Darrin's gaze fixed on Auden as if he thought his friend might punch something right then and there, but he didn't.

"Things change."

With a smirk on his face, Darrin clasped Auden's shoulder and gave it a tight squeeze. "That they do."

Auden tossed the keys to Darrin, entrusting him with Jenny. If Darrin messed with her too much, he would have to protect himself from Auden. But when Darrin slipped into the driver's seat, he massaged the steering wheel with an awed expression. That alone let Auden know she was in good hands.

Out the passenger window as Darrin drove, something moved from the corner of Auden's eye. His head spun as he turned and focused on the same fucker with the trench coat who'd bumped into him at the store. He stood on the sidewalk, holding the rectangular object, and staring right at Auden. Auden wondered what his expression was beneath the mask.

"Stop!" Auden shouted, right when Darrin was almost at the end of the street.

Darrin slammed on the brakes, jolting them both forward.

"What? Did I almost hit someone?" He threw the van in park, studying the street with his mouth hanging open.

"No." Auden looked back out the window at the man still standing there. In a flash, the stranger disappeared, a silvery light faded in and out. "Di-did you see that?" With wide eyes, he hurried and faced Darrin. "The man, he was right there, holding something and then just poofed into some silvery shit."

Darrin squinted his eyes and leaned over Auden to get a better view out the window. After a moment, he started chuckling. "Man, you're so drunk. No one was there."

Auden's head was spinning, but he could've sworn...

Darrin relaxed back into his seat. "We'll start that movie marathon when we get to my place to get you back into shape." Then he sang the wrong lyrics spewing out from the upbeat song playing on the radio.

"I guess so." Auden pulled the lever to recline the seat back and zoned out the world. The confusion over what he thought he'd seen left him feeling like his grip on reality was slipping. Much like his real father's had before him.

# CHAPTER 3

To Lark:

Lyrics from "People Are People" — Depeche Mode

When Lark got home from work, she parked her bike behind the trailer. The trailer was actually in semi-decent shape, not dilapidated like a lot of the other ones around the park. The bicycle, on the other hand, was practically garbage, but that didn't mean it wouldn't get stolen. Two kids had already attempted thievery in the past—she wasn't about to risk someone trying to jack it again.

Lark slung the heavy trash bag of goods from Imani over her shoulder like she was Santa *fucking* Claus. In the other hand, she carried her Siouxsie vinyl and listened to a little "Love Is A Battlefield" through her headphones. Pat Benatar had all the right answers in life. Thoughts of Auden still crept through her head, though she tried not to dwell on the "costume" comment. She pushed the thoughts aside as she shuffled up the wooden steps, each one groaning.

Something silvery flashed in her periphery and she paused on the steps, hesitantly turning her head in the direction from which it came. "Hello?" she said, her chest heaving.

A stray dog darted out from the other side of the trailer, barking as it ran across the street, practically giving her a heart attack. Lark let out a sigh. With the creep at the store, the strange flute music, and the stress with Auden today, she tried to hold it together.

The front door was already unlocked, and the inside of the trailer reeked of cigarette smoke, burnt cheese, and bad perm. Grunting, she dropped the bag in front of her feet and shut the door with the heel of her boot. Lark slid the headphones down and took a deep breath.

Beth's freshly curled head poked up from the stove, a beer and cigarette in one hand and a spatula in the other. That answered Lark's questions on the smells, and it was an accurate portrayal of her mother, who she refused to call "Mom." Throughout Lark's life, Beth had never felt like one, not when she'd forgotten to pick Lark and her sisters up from school or when she'd left them sleeping in the backseat of her car while she went inside the bar.

"Made it just in time. Supper's ready." Beth's raspy voice boomed against the thin walls.

"What is it?" Lark maneuvered herself across the cluttered living room to get to the kitchen, passing the ratty recliner and useless junk. Months-old newspapers and magazines that never got thrown away—because Beth claimed she hadn't read them yet—covered the coffee table and patches of the stained carpet.

"We're embracing you girls' culture tonight. I made *enchiladas*." Beth said the last word with a terrible Hispanic accent.

"You are aware Dad's heritage was from Spain, and enchiladas are more Mexican?" Lark peered over Beth's shoulder and stared at the glass container with burnt enchiladas drenched in queso dip, resting on top of the stove. "Also, I don't think the people of Mexico drench their enchiladas in chile con queso, but I could be wrong."

Beth swung her beer to her mouth and nursed it for a long minute before slowly dragging it back down, pursing her thin lips. "Are you being a smartass? After I just slaved around in the kitchen for you and your sister."

Lark didn't understand why Beth was even trying to embrace Dad's "heritage?" They never married, and he hadn't been around to help raise Lark and her sisters—too concerned about hanging out at the bar and picking up hookers.

She figured misery did love her dad's company as he'd driven home drunk one night and hit another drunk driver. In the end, they'd both died. If it would've been an innocent family, maybe Lark would've been more sympathetic. Scumbag Syndrome. Her dad had left them with Beth, and she was still angry about that, but living with him could've potentially been worse.

"Thanks, Beth. I love ash with my enchiladas," Lark said, rolling her eyes.

Beth tapped the cigarette in a glass ashtray on top of the counter. "I lit the cigarette after I pulled the food out."

Lark's gaze zoomed-in onto the cooking utensil where Beth's fingers gripped it tightly. "But you have a spatula in your hand and are digging them out with a lit cigarette in the other."

Beth shook the cooking gear in the air as if she were a nun and wanted to slam it down on Lark's fingers like a ruler. "You're about to get none, missy."

Could I only hope for such a miraculous thing? she thought.

Turning on her heels, Lark shuffled back through the living room and picked up the bags to bring them into her room. She might've been acting like a twat to Beth, but even with her being Lark's birth mother and raising them all these years, Beth had checked out a long time ago. Then last month,

Beth came around and acted like she could slither her way back in and win Mom of the Year. It would take a lot longer than that. Beth may not have been Faye Dunaway in *Mommie Dearest* going crazy with a coat hanger, but sometimes no mom at all was worse.

When she opened the door to her room, her sister, Paloma, was there, browsing through Lark's drawers as if her life depended on it.

"What are you doing in here?" Lark asked, tossing the two bags on the floor beside her twin mattress. She hurried and shut the door, so the smoke wouldn't drift in from Beth's cigarette.

She and her other sister, Robin, had shared a bed, but that got taken with Robin when she left for college. Thanks to a scholarship, she made it out of this shithole— Lark didn't think she was going to be as lucky. Since then, Lark only had a mattress on the floor. Not that she minded —it made her feel closer to the earth anyway, even though the trailer sat above ground level. After learning more about Jimbo's Native American ways, she respected the world a bit more than she had before working at the oddity store.

"I was looking for those loop earrings with the silver crosses hanging that Imani gave you," Paloma said, not looking at Lark as she continued to sift through the dresser drawer of underwear. She wasn't sure why Paloma would think there would be earrings in there.

Lark's Siamese cat, Lucy, made a soft purr as her sky-blue eyes fixed on her. Softly, she rubbed the little heathen's head. Lucy was the one individual in the trailer who seemed to actually truly care about her.

"Are you practicing religion now?" Lark asked, taking off

her backpack and headphones, then setting them on the mattress across from Lucy.

Paloma's head whipped over her shoulder. "No, I'm practicing Madonna."

"Attempting carbon copyism?"

Paloma practically slept in the Madonna-esque white lace gloves—she was wearing them now, paired with a loose green tank top, pink skirt, and black leggings.

"Is that even a word or something you made up again?" Paloma stared at Lark's black jacket. "It's better than training to be Morticia from *The Munsters*."

With a loud snort, Lark's grin spread across her cheeks. "Do you mean Morticia from *The Addams Family* or Lily from *The Munsters*?"

As usual, Paloma hid her lazy eye behind a lock of hair. She should show off that thing—it was awesome. "You're seriously a jackass."

"I've been called smartass and jackass within the past five minutes," Lark started. "I'm not sure which word I prefer. However, I do like donkeys."

Paloma rolled her dark brown eyes, shut the drawer, and caught sight of the trash bag from Imani on the floor. "What's in there?" she asked, rushing headlong to the bag and peeling back the plastic. Why did she even bother asking? She was already searching through the clothes.

Paloma was her twin sister, fraternal twin to be exact. Lark couldn't say that they had any secret bond or twin-dar. Her sister looked more like their dad with jet-black hair and brown complexion, while Lark was paler with crazy curls and light brown eyes. Her sister's hair was naturally straight, but she had a perm and used way too much hairspray. She was sure Paloma would have it dyed blonde soon to match her idol

—Madonna. Lark and Paloma were not friends in the slightest, but they definitely understood each other.

A collection of bracelets rattled on Paloma's wrist as she picked through the garbage bag. If her sister went back to her babysitting gig, then she'd be able to afford more things.

"You can take a few pieces out of there, but leave all the black stuff," Lark said and took a seat on the mattress. Lucy curled up on her lap as Lark stroked her soft fur.

Her sister's eyes shifted to the yellow heels in the bag, and Lark quickly crushed the pop-up memory of the music store catastrophe.

"Whoa. Whoa. Whoa. These are rad." Paloma held them up, her eyes glowing with want.

"Sorry, those are off limits." Lark leaned sideways and snatched them from Paloma's hands before she ran off with them. The shoes already had a nostalgic moment attached to them with Auden—a shitty one—and she wanted them. "And those earrings you're looking for are in the second drawer of my dresser, inside the shoe box."

"Perfect." A few skirts and a neon pink top dangled from Paloma's arm as she headed for the earrings. She dug through the box and proudly held them up to her—as if Lark gave a damn about their glistening sheen.

"Now, go prove to the world that you're officially like a virgin," Lark said in a sarcastic tone.

Her sister's eyes narrowed at Lark. "I *am* a virgin."

"That's too bad." Lark smirked.

Paloma grinned devilishly in return. "Scott called."

Her twin knew Lark couldn't stand Scott. She let out a string of curses, and Paloma laughed, exiting the room.

Scott Price was a guy Lark had "dated" for about a year, until five months ago. When he started talking about what college they would be attending together, she had to sink that ship quickly. Especially since they were only in their junior year of high school. She could practically see him dropping down to one knee their senior year with a quarter-machine ring in hand.

It must not have been that big of a deal to him when she cut the string with a chainsaw because the next week Scott was dating Heather Thomas. And with Scott, anyone could fill the "girlfriend void," including Lark. She was just relieved he wouldn't be bugging her anymore, but he still called every week to keep the friendship going. They weren't friends before, and they sure as hell weren't friends now.

"Supper, girls!" Beth yelled, her voice sounding too sweet.

Lark removed her boots and scrambled to change into something more normal—a pair of black jeans and an over-sized black T-shirt.

"See you in a bit, Lucy." The cat didn't pay attention as Lark headed out of the room and came face to face with Beth and Paloma in the kitchen. Lark slumped into one of the chairs at the two-person table. Beth had "found" the extra seat somewhere—a fold-up lawn chair with frayed fabric. Paloma studied her two enchiladas and Beanee Weenees on the side, while Lark suspiciously eyed the food right along with her sister.

Not being able to hold back any longer, Lark's left eyebrow quizzically flicked upward. "I'm not sure Beanee Weenees qualify as part of our *heritage*."

"It's beans, ain't it?" Beth grunted while pouring tea into glasses filled with ice.

Paloma picked up her fork and stirred tiny circles in the beans. "I'm not really sure if they are."

Lark cracked a smile, taking a shallow sip of the overly sweetened tea.

Beth's cigarette was no longer in attendance, but a bottle of beer was proudly displayed in front of her. "Come on." She held out her hands to Lark and Paloma, gesturing them forward. "Grace."

Paloma and Lark stared at Beth's séance hands in confusion. Lark was tempted to grab a few candles for what was looking to be more of a witchy occasion than prayer time.

Beth shot Lark a glare. "Families pray before eatin', don't they?"

"Some?" Paloma said, mostly a question.

"Okay, forget the hand holdin' nonsense." Beth clasped her hands in front of her. Lark watched in amusement as Beth began, "God, thank you for this glorious food. Amen."

"A to the men," Lark drawled. The last time she and her sisters had gone to church was when she was twelve. Beth would drop them off to repent for their sins, while she went off to commit new ones of her own. Lark had preferred the crucifixes to being around Beth's strange men. Thankfully, Beth hadn't brought a man home in a long time. Lark tried not to think about those past days because she had grown away from being that scared and shy little girl. Music had saved her —it still did.

"Well, don't just look at it. Dig in." Beth air-poked at the two of them with her fork.

Lark struggled as she tried to cut the partially blackened enchilada, but when she finally got a piece in her mouth, it actually wasn't half bad. She wasn't sure if the tortilla was supposed to have the crunchiness to it, but it worked.

"Beth. I mean… Mom"—Paloma was at least attempting

to use the "M" word—"can I go to Shannon's party Friday night?"

Lark watched her sister in confusion. Why was Paloma suddenly trying to be Daughter of the Decade? And was she going to award Beth with a blue ribbon for being Mom of the Day because she cooked a burnt enchilada? Lark could go shove some tortillas in the oven right then and watch them burn. Maybe she would be awarded a trophy for Best Darkened Food. Paloma had always been closed off from Beth and had remained more distant from her than Lark. But her sister seemed to be wanting to give Beth her thousandth chance, while Lark just couldn't...

"Your sister going?" Beth's gaze shifted to Lark's. She hadn't even known about Shannon having another party.

"Yeah." Paloma played with the cross dangling from the hoop earring she was already wearing. Lark would've remembered agreeing to go to this so-called party.

"Then, all right." Beth started coughing and patted her chest. She really needed to give up the cancer sticks.

Despite wanting to leave the room, Lark finished up the rest of the enchiladas and drank the cup of sweet tea until it was gone. However, she left the beans along with the weenies. She rubbed the roof of her mouth with the tip of her tongue, trying to swallow the sugar that wouldn't go away.

"Uh, thanks... Beth." Lark couldn't say "Mom," no matter if she was pretending to be polite to stay on her good side. The *thanks* part was good enough.

Holding back her annoyance, she headed straight into Paloma's room to where her sister had slithered off—the little viper. Hundreds of posters and pictures covered her entire wall—mostly Madonna, the Go-Go's, Michael Jackson, and

Cyndi Lauper. Lark would let Cyndi slide because she could rock out to her when she needed to.

"What the hell was that in there?" Lark whisper-shouted as she closed the door behind her, throwing a hand in the air.

"What?" Paloma glanced up from her magazine while lying on her stomach. She had paused flipping through an old *Rolling Stone* issue as if she hadn't just been the biggest suck-up to exist.

"Permission about the party? And then saying I'm going?" Paloma could've at least asked her first. She didn't even know why her sister bothered checking with Beth—she never had before.

Paloma rolled onto her back, still clutching the magazine, and stared up at the popcorn ceiling. "You know she's trying, so I thought I'd ask instead of having to sneak out."

Lark snatched the magazine out of her sister's hand to look at the cover—Madonna—she should've known. "Even if she would've said no, you still would've gone."

"I know, but we need to meet her halfway." Paloma was starting to piss Lark off because her sister knew how shitty Beth had been for their entire lives, and Robin had it the worst.

"Robin isn't meeting her a millimeter of the way." Or even microscopically for that matter. But Robin seemed to have put Lark and Paloma in her distancing box, too. Lark supposed they were reminders and something Robin wanted to be rid of. Like trash.

Paloma ripped the magazine from Lark's hand. "Robin only cares about herself. She barely even calls, and when she does, it's only to argue with Beth."

The part that bothered Lark the most, though, wasn't even the fact her mother had been shitty her entire life. It was how close Lark had been with her older sister. She hated to admit it, but it hurt like hell.

"Besides," Paloma continued, "I think you'll have fun." If this had been during the school year, Lark would've called BS on that, but the past two parties had been interesting, to say the least.

"The last two times I went with you to a party, I couldn't even find you."

"You mean, *I* couldn't find *you*." Paloma pointed a finger. "You wandered off somewhere." So Lark had. But afterward, she couldn't find Paloma.

"Remember when we played spin the bottle?" Paloma asked.

Lark rolled her eyes. "You act like that was five years ago. It was a month ago."

"Just because you didn't enjoy it doesn't mean I didn't." Paloma sucked on her bottom lip and Lark wanted to hurl. She knew Paloma was imagining the kiss with Craig and how she'd gone right to town with it.

Lark mainly hated the spin the bottle incident because it had been in front of everyone. Her sister bringing up that night had Lark thinking about Auden following her outside after the game had ended.

"So?" Paloma drawled, her face pleading, preventing Lark's thoughts from going in that direction.

"Yeah, fine. As long as Shannon doesn't play shitty music the whole time." Last time she kept rewinding "Every Breath You Take" over and over and over and *over*. She got it—Sting had a few issues with obsession. Could he be any more obvious?

The phone rang and Paloma snatched it up before Lark could—she always did that. "Hello? Yeah, she's here." She looked at Lark and started to hand her the phone. "It's Imani."

"I'll get it in my room." When Lark closed the door behind her, she picked up the phone. "You can hang up now," she said.

Imani started to talk right away. "So I thought about what happened today at work with your brooding prince, and—"

"Wait a second." Lark opened the door a crack, so she could see into Paloma's open room, who was still listening on the phone. "I said, hang up!"

Grinning ear to ear, Paloma finally hung up. "Brooding prince, huh? You have a new boy toy who isn't Scott? Tell me more!"

"Go listen to Madonna or something," Lark grunted and slammed the door.

Picking the phone back up, Lark lay on her mattress and punched the pillow a few times to make it somewhat comfortable. "Sorry about that, Imani." Lucy scampered forward to curl up beside her.

"Don't worry. Sheena does the same thing to me."

"Yeah, well, your sister's eight, not seventeen—she can do stupid shit like that," Lark said, laughing.

Imani changed the subject. "So I was thinking about Shannon's party on Friday."

"Have you been talking to Paloma?" Imani hadn't mentioned anything earlier at work about Shannon having a party.

"No, why?" she asked, sounding confused.

Lark twirled the phone cord in her hand while staring at the record player, and the Depeche Mode vinyl beside it, on the floor. "She's going to that party, too."

"Oh good"—Imani chuckled—"we can now start our own

48

group, like in *The Breakfast Club*. Can you guess which one *you'd* be and which one *she'd* be?" Lark automatically knew Paloma would be Molly Ringwald, and she'd be Ally Sheedy. But if she ever met John Hughes, she'd tell him he'd stolen her style for that movie because Lark had it first.

"I know which one you'd be," Lark said. "The one who lights his boot on fire."

"Oh! That gives me a fantastic idea. I might try that tonight, actually." She heard Imani smiling through the phone. "But I was thinking, since Auden was at the last two parties we went to, he'll probably be there."

"I don't care if he's there." She *so* cared if he was there.

"Third party should be the charm, right?" The last two parties were a charm. She just wasn't sure if they made a difference.

"Imani, I swear I'm going to miss you at work."

"Me and my humor?"

"All of you."

"I'm not dead, Lark."

Lark clapped her hands together. "So if we were to design our funerals, how would they be?"

A faint humming from outside interrupted Lark from paying attention to what Imani was saying. The phone slid halfway down Lark's ear. Music. It couldn't be, could it?

"Imani," Lark said hurriedly, "let me call you back." She hung the phone up before Imani responded and yanked the mushroom-printed curtain covering her window to the side. In the distance, a form was walking away, draped in a dark cloak. "Space Oddity" played from a flute, a darker tone to it than she'd ever heard from her vinyl. The person looked small and lithe, most likely feminine. As she went to lift her window, a flash of silver light flickered and the person was no longer there. The silver aura and music evaporated, causing her heart to clench in her chest before rapidly striking her ribcage over and over.

Lark let go of the window with shaky hands and stumbled backward. Something strange was going on. Ghosts. She'd never seen ghosts before, didn't know if she believed in them until right then. People didn't just turn into silvery light and disappear for no reason.

# CHAPTER 4

To Auden:
Lyrics from "Shadows of The Night" – Pat Benatar

Auden pushed up from the bed and gripped the side of his head. His vision wavered as he fought the swells of pain pounding on his skull. He'd drank too much and now he was paying for it.

Thankfully, the sheets were fresh since Darrin rarely slept in his own bed. Auden didn't understand why his friend always slept on that ratty pull-out couch.

Pressing two fingers to his temples, the previous night came back to him in a whirlwind, his drunkenness, his hallucinations. He *wasn't* going to become schizophrenic like his father—he only heard and saw the things because he'd been too drunk. That was all.

Tossing back the covers, Auden slipped on his red Converse and headed into the living room. He found Darrin lying on his stomach, snoring lightly. His stiff red Mohawk was folded to the side.

With a light nudge, Auden kicked the back of the pale-yellow sofa. "Hey, do you have any aspirin or anything?" The throb felt like it was hitting a vein directly behind his left eye socket.

Darrin's eyelids flickered open. "What, Dad?" His voice came out groggy.

Sighing with a smile, Auden cooed, "You've been a very,

51

very naughty boy. Do I need to get the belt?"

His friend's eyes widened into full moons and Darrin released a loud yawn. "I might have to use the belt on you if you say something like that again."

"Seriously, do you have something to take?" Auden scanned the room as if he could find the magical Ibuprofen pill bottle. "My head hurts like hell after last night."

Darrin sat up and stretched his arms as though he'd just come out of hibernation. "Yeah, there should be Tylenol in the cabinet next to the fridge."

Tylenol was like drinking water. The magical cure for nothing, but he'd take it to try and clear his head. "Thanks."

Auden sorted through the wooden cabinet, past a pack of bandages and Pepto-Bismol, where he found the Tylenol. He grabbed a glass from the other cabinet and went to the sink, filling it with water. The water was lukewarm, but he swigged it down with the pills regardless.

The TV was still on from Auden and Darrin playing Atari after watching *Night of the Living Dead* the night before, but the volume was off.

Auden glanced at the circular clock above the pantry and it was already noon. "Shit." He stilled as if he could laser in on the clock and turn back time. His shift had started two hours ago.

"What?" Darrin asked, turning the volume on the TV back up.

"Where are my keys?" Auden set down the glass and frantically patted his jean pockets. "I gotta get to work. Since I'm really late, I'm pretty sure I can expect a merciless yelling from Jacee." He knew he'd have to calm her down as soon as he strolled in like the last couple times he'd been late—by promising he wouldn't do it again.

"They're on the counter. Just tell her you overslept or felt sick." Darrin shrugged.

Auden had used excuses a few times lately. He'd never been late most of the months he'd worked there, but then recently a couple things had interfered, such as car troubles and traffic. In this case, a brutal hangover.

Snatching the keys from the chipped countertop, he flew out the door and caught a glimpse of Darrin picking up the game controller. Auden wondered how Darrin didn't get fired from his job. *Oh, that's right, he works for his grandma, grooming dogs.*

Once inside Jenny, Auden sped his way to the music store —or at least attempted to. He hit every damn stoplight on the way, and each one felt like four minutes before it turned green. Red, red, red, *red*!

Auden flicked on the radio. "Space Oddity" had just started, reminding him of the flute he'd heard the night before. He quickly changed the channel and let "Shadows Of The Night" fill the van.

Since it would be a shorter walk, Auden swung into the front parking lot, though it was doubtful a couple of saved minutes would erase how late he was. He scanned himself in the rearview mirror, realizing he looked like complete shit. His brown hair was no longer combed back and a lock fell into his eyes, so he ran his hand through it as best he could.

As much as he needed a shower, there hadn't been time for one. He lifted his arm, then took a whiff and cringed. His clothes reeked of the night before, but that would all have to wait until after work.

He stepped out of the van, catching a glimpse of the busy street where he'd thought he'd seen someone when Darrin hadn't. The man with the trench coat and the flute music were *not* real.

Swallowing the thought, he hurried toward the music store. The heat blared down on him as he prepped himself for Jacee's yelling. He rubbed his hands together in anticipation as he glanced at the Help Wanted sign outside of Bubble's Oddities. By now he figured someone would've already been hired since the sign had been up for a few weeks.

Inside Music Revelations, nobody sat at the desk—there was only one customer in the store. *Perfect. I'll just pretend as if I was here the entire time. Maybe it's possible she'll never even know.*

Creeping behind the counter, Auden signed in on the clipboard and stood there like he hadn't just arrived two and a half hours late. A squeak from the back of the store signaled the door opening and out walked Jacee. Her muscles flexed as she brought in a large box brimming with vinyl. When her gaze met his, a scowling expression formed on her face. Jacee could take any guy down if she needed to—she could kick his ass for being late. As she lowered the box, her purple ponytail swung to the side, revealing the other half of her head, which was shaved.

Before Jacee had a chance to make it to the counter, a customer in his mid-thirties, who was trying too hard to look like John Lennon's duplicate, strolled up with four records. Auden's head throbbed as he rang up the man, then handed him the bag with his merchandise.

As soon as the glass door closed behind the John Lennon impersonator, Jacee yelled, "You're fired!"

"What do you mean I'm fired?" Auden shuffled around the counter and stopped directly in front of Jacee, staring down at her. He couldn't believe it.

She studied the ticking clock above the cassette tapes for a long five seconds, then back at him, her dark eyes narrowing. "I mean… you're late, and now… you're *fired*."

This couldn't be happening—he needed this job. "Come on, my alarm didn't go off, and then I woke with a massive headache." He rubbed his temple and squinted his eyes to prove his point.

"Why did you wake with a massive headache?" Jacee eyed him with suspicion.

"Because I get migraines?" It was a good excuse and honest since he did get them when he drank too much. Maybe it would help if he confessed that he wasn't feeling like himself the last couple of days and had been seeing things. But that was something which would have to remain behind lock and key.

"Don't care." She flicked her hand at the door. "You're. Fired. You can pick up your last check on Friday."

Auden held up his index finger. "One more chance." Then he puckered his lips into a pout and held up his other index finger, pleading.

"Do I need to call the cops?" Jacee spat.

"Jesus, Jacee, get a grip." Slowly, he backed away from her with his hands held up.

Her expression hardened. "Let's see how far you make it in life with that attitude."

If he knew he wouldn't be arrested, he'd knock down all the cassettes he'd just set out the night before. Instead, he stepped outside and just stood there, thinking. The few times he'd been late before had only been about five or ten minutes, and even though he knew it was his fault this time, he was still ticked off. He preferred this mood over his panicked one from earlier, though. At least this one distracted him for a bit.

Auden needed the money, and he didn't want to take any of his parents' cash. They wanted him to begin college in the fall, and he didn't want to do that right away. He intended to just take one year off and then start the following year. He wanted to get away for a little while, but how could he do that if he was broke?

The white paper taped on the dark glass of Bubble's Oddities caught his peripheral attention, and he turned his head to the Help Wanted sign.

If Jimbo was already at work, he'd most likely give Auden the job. Every time he came into the music store, Jimbo would shoot the shit and talk about obscure music that even Auden hadn't heard of.

One problem—Lark.

Straightening his jean vest as best he could, he walked into the oddity store, welcomed by the cowbell. Animal heads, lots of skulls, doll parts, Venus fly traps, and a section of old magician posters were on display as he followed an outside aisle leading to the counter. He looked up at the animal skulls and the artwork on each tarot card dangling from the ceiling. There was so much bizarreness there, and if he got the job, he wouldn't mind having the unique scenery. He would relish in it.

Jimbo didn't even glance up as he read a tattered newspaper. The lines on his forehead deepened as he intensely scanned the paper, his dark braid falling over his shoulder.

"Hey, Jimbo," Auden began, "I was wondering if you're still hiring. I saw the sign on the door."

Jimbo's half-bald head jerked up as if he hadn't heard Auden's heavy footsteps. After setting down the paper, he pulled off his reading glasses. "I am." He squinted at Auden. "Don't you work next door?"

"I did, but not anymore." Auden slouched forward and propped his forearm against the counter.

"I think you're the longest one Jacee's been able to keep over there." Jimbo folded up the newspaper and set it aside.

"Seems like it." Auden chuckled. The other employees who had worked there had lasted less than a month.

"I'm assuming she fired you. So, what happened?"

"I was late." Might as well be honest. Jimbo could always go next door and ask Jacee if he really wanted to verify it.

"Are you going to be late here?" Jimbo gave Auden a pointed stare and blew specks of dust from his glasses.

"No." He'd make sure every day the damn alarm clock was set two hours before he had to go to work.

"Then you can have the job." Jimbo shrugged. "I was going to hire someone when I got back from Vegas and could go through the applications. But since no one has applied yet, and I only have one worker at the moment, I can give you a shot."

"Really?" No hoops to go through? Balls to juggle? Jacee had made him do three interviews.

"Yeah, but you won't get a key to the store or work alone until Lark deems you worthy."

Lark—he groaned inside his head. "All right."

"I'm leaving tomorrow evening, but can you start on Saturday?" Jimbo tucked his glasses into his shirt pocket. "The store's gonna be closed on Sundays as usual, but also Mondays until I get back so you two aren't overworked. So, for now, you can also work the following Friday and Saturday ten 'til six. But if you do well enough, I'll tell Lark to let you work the following week Tuesday through Saturday. Does that work?"

It would for now, and if he found something better later, he'd take it. "Yes."

"Let me get the paperwork for you to fill out and you'll be all set. When I get back in a couple of weeks, I'll make an official schedule."

The paperwork wasn't a huge stack like Jacee had given him—there were only two forms. Quickly, he filled them out and handed the papers back to Jimbo. Last time Auden searched for a job, it had taken him ages to get one. This was a piece of cake.

"Hope I see you when I get back, if Lark doesn't work you too hard."

Auden's head felt a hundred times better when he left the store, but he stared at the gravel of the parking lot to avoid the sun's glaring rays just in case his migraine decided to come back. He'd slap on his shades as soon as he hopped back in Jenny.

Brakes squealed and he looked up just in time to catch a familiar set of wheels almost making contact with his shin.

He knew those wheels like the back of his hand since he saw them almost every day outside Bubble's.

"I guess you did almost get in a wreck on that bike." Auden thought back to the night where he'd seen her outside the store with the big plastic bag that had been on the ground in front of her. He held up his hand to his forehead to shield his eyes from the sun as he glanced down at the handlebars. "No trash bag today?"

"You could at least look up from the ground when you walk, you know," Lark grumbled not meeting his gaze. Her hair was a windblown mess of curls.

"So I've been told. Apparently, I haven't learned my lesson yet. You want to teach me?" His gaze finally met hers when her light brown eyes angled upward, appearing a dark caramel underneath the blazing sun. Even though it had to be eighty-something degrees, her body was all bundled up in her usual black jacket. The back of his neck was already sweating, while she didn't look bothered by the heat at all.

They stood staring at each other, silent for what felt like the span of an entire length of a music album. Lark's hand fidgeted back and forth over the handle grips. Her eyes shifted away from his, first squinting, then widening in the direction behind him.

Turning his head over his shoulder, Auden could see what she was looking at. Outside the laundromat stood the same man from the day before who'd bumped into him—black trench coat, pork pie hat, ski mask—the one he'd drunkenly imagined at the party. The man had his booted foot pressed up against the glass storefront window, appearing to be watching them. Was his imagination playing tricks on him like before? *Not that shit again.*

But maybe he wasn't hallucinating since Lark was also looking in the man's direction.

"Do you see that man over there?" Auden finally asked, prepared for her to say no, the way Darrin had. He focused on the large rectangular object, draped in black material and propped against the glass. He wondered what that was—he'd wondered last night too.

"Yeah, I see him." Lark scowled in the direction of the guy, and Auden had never seen her look sexier.

Lark was seeing him too—it wasn't just him. But that didn't explain the strangeness, the vanishing. Had that part been in his head?

"I'm going to call the cops when I get inside the store,"

Lark continued. "I think…" Her words stopped when her eyes lifted to the side of his neck. "Guess you had fun last night."

Auden didn't know why it bothered him so much, but his stomach sank at the thought of her seeing that. He hadn't had a good look at the hickey on his neck, but it must've been noticeable since her gaze was glued to it.

"Not really." What he really wanted to say was how he'd thought it was her at first, but that would only lead to that need. And he missed their lyric notes—he thought he wouldn't, but he did more than anything.

With a crestfallen expression, Lark propped her foot back on the pedal and started toward Bubble's. "I've gotta go to work."

Something in him didn't want to see her vanish. Swiftly, he reached out and grabbed her handlebars, causing her to stop. "Are you going to be at Shannon's party tomorrow?"

"Maybe." She shrugged and avoided looking at his face and neck.

Clasping both of her handlebars, he leaned forward, close but not close enough. "Well then, maybe I'll see you there."

Frowning, she removed his hands from the bike with her soft fingertips, and he almost groaned aloud at the thought of having her hands on his skin beneath his shirt, wishing they could go back to that night.

"Maybe," she said and pedaled away toward Bubble's, but not before glancing several times to the stranger outside with his object.

He wondered how she would feel when Jimbo let her know he'd be working with her.

After watching Lark park her bike and head into the store, Auden turned around and faced the laundromat again.

The man with the pork pie hat was still there, silently

watching him. What was strange was the fact that Auden knew the man was studying him with intensity, even with the ski mask having no eyeholes.

As if the man could hear Auden's thoughts, he held up a black gloved hand and with his index finger, slowly ticked it back and forth at him.

What the fuck?

Lark had told Auden she was going to call the cops, but he wanted to warn Donna over at the laundromat what was going on. Jaw clenched, he crossed the parking lot until he stood a few feet from the man and his mystery object.

"Why are you here?" Auden asked in a serious tone.

The man cocked his head, expression hidden under the black mask. Staying silent, the man slipped a gloved hand inside his pocket.

Auden balled his hand into a fist, preparing for a punch, and remembered what had happened the last time he'd gotten in a fight. One of the guys at school had been teasing a younger kid, and Auden wasn't having it. He'd promised his mom it wouldn't happen again. *Well, sometimes shit happens.*

The man lifted a small yellow Post-it note from his pocket and showed it to Auden. It read, *Can't speak.*

"You can't speak?" Auden dropped his fists, a bit of sympathy washing over him as he waited for some sort of acknowledgement. There was none. "You need to go. The cops are being called." He turned and walked inside the laundromat where swishing washing machines and clothes spinning in dryers echoed through the store.

The manager, Donna, worked at the counter, dumping rolled change into the register. Her hair was hidden underneath a scarf, and wrinkles and age spots covered her arms. She glanced up at Auden. "Hey, honey."

"Hey, Donna. Lark from Bubble's is calling the cops because some man has been loitering around in front of your store. He also claims he can't speak. I doubt you do, but just in case, do you know him?"

"I haven't seen anyone, but this is my first week back from vacation. How long has he been out there?" She leaned over the counter, her already wrinkled forehead folding into more creases. "I don't see anyone."

Auden spun around, but the guy was already gone. "Maybe a few days."

"Okay, honey, I'll keep a lookout."

Shaking his head to himself, Auden opened the door and searched up and down the strip mall. *Good, he must've listened and left.*

A sound struck his ears, toying with the insides. The music. He halted, stifling the shout in his throat. Music slow and deep from the flute drifted into the store. Where was it coming from? It sounded like it was directly across from him, but no one was there. He whirled around to look back at Donna. "Do you hear that?"

She looked up from the register and tilted her head. "Hear what?"

He strained his ears, now hearing nothing except for passing cars. "Nothing, Donna. I heard nothing."

Auden walked inside his house and found his mom, Janet, in the kitchen hovering over the stove. The scent of freshly baked cookies caressed his nostrils. His nerves were still on edge from the music outside the laundromat, and maybe he should've stopped by Lark's work to ask her about it, but he just felt too stupid to bring something like that up if Donna and Darrin hadn't heard it. He didn't want her to see him differently.

His mom strolled out of the kitchen wearing an apron covered in heart cookies, her hair in a high ponytail with fluffed bangs.

"You're home early," she said, kissing his cheek.

"Yeah, I'm starting a new job on Saturday." Auden was already prepared for her questions—the worry, the caring, the lack of scrutiny when she should've gotten rid of him a long time ago. He'd been in fights, been late, not called her, drank way too much. But he couldn't help being grateful that she never gave up on him.

She examined him for a moment. "You were fired?"

"I was late."

Her gaze fell to his neck where he should've flicked up the collar of his jean vest. "So I guess you did more than watch movies at Darrin's."

A tense silence filled the room. He didn't know what to say—when she wanted the truth, he never lied to her about it. But he couldn't tell her that something strange had started happening to him the day before or she would call up his old counselor. "Yeah, but don't worry, Darrin drove."

His mom let out a deep sigh, swiping a hand down her cheek. "Despite you almost being eighteen, you still live under this roof and have so much to learn. You have two little brothers who look up to you, and you need to be responsible enough around them."

Nick and Zach were eleven and thirteen, and they were headed down a good path but they weren't in high school yet. High school could easily change things.

"At least I got a new job right away at Bubble's." There

was always a part of him that believed he didn't deserve his mom, and he never wanted to be a burden to her, especially if it was possible he could inherit his father's disorder. His face had to remind her at least a little of his birth father. Sometimes, he believed it was better if she didn't have to see his face—a job helped with that.

"That oddity place?"

"Yeah, the owner seems real chill."

Rubbing her hands over the front of her apron, she nodded. "Well, okay, but please don't go back to being as wild as you were a few years ago. I love you." She placed an arm around his shoulders. "Now, go eat a couple of cookies and take a shower because you smell like cow dung."

He wasn't as wild as she thought. She mostly believed he was because he'd failed to call or tell her where he was. He tried to do that now. "I don't smell *that* bad." Taking another whiff of himself, he choked on his defenses.

"I've smelled worse"—she laughed—"but you still reek."

Auden snatched a peanut butter cookie from the pan on top of the stove and shoved it into his mouth, savoring the sugary sweetness as he swiped an extra three. He headed to his room before his shower, then stopped to stare at the posters all over his walls: bands, movies, and other meaningless stuff.

An emotion struck him then, he'd used these *things* to take away the pain. Why couldn't he just *not* blame himself? He wasn't his father. He cared about his parents and brothers, but he just wanted to get away from everything, possibly leave the town for a little bit if he could. Maybe somehow that would heal him and he could be normal like everyone else.

His gaze fixed on his desk where the shoe box, filled with the shreds of lyrics that he and Lark had written back and forth in class, sat. He wasn't sure why he'd collected them at first, except for the fact that someone seemed to understand music the way he did. Drew, his ex, never got music—or him. Sometimes it was easier to put his feelings into lyrics and use the music to do the talking. Then the notes became an addiction, because he'd wanted them each day. He *needed* them.

When the school year ended, he'd thought the addiction would subside since he'd graduated, and Lark hadn't.

But it wasn't gone.

He ripped a Sex Pistols poster down from his wall, followed by a picture of Joey Ramone and on and on and on. He wanted his room to feel like it didn't belong to him, so he didn't feel anchored here anymore. He could pile up all his music in his van and leave like he'd always wanted. *What's really keeping me here?* He couldn't control the image of Lark on her bike from slipping into his thoughts.

Outside his window, a rift of music floated through the air and into his room. His heart pounded. "No, no, no," Auden whispered. If his mom wasn't home, he would've shouted it. Pressing his hands tightly over his ears, he could still hear the flute's melody. Something flashed by his window, as if someone had barreled past.

With labored breaths, Auden stalked closer to the glass and shoved the curtain aside. The black-covered object rested against the fence. *Why is it here?* The music picked up speed, that same "Space Oddity" song, only it was more sinister. A silvery light flashed by the object, and it vanished, along with the music. Auden dropped to his knees, closed his eyes, and crushed his hands to his ears anyway, as though that would keep it from happening again.

CHAPTER 5

Lark finished watering the Venus flytraps then straightened the seed packages—dwarf banana tree, monkey face orchid, and egg tree—on the wire rack.

She set the empty watering can behind the counter and pulled her headphones off, halting the Beatles from singing to her, and exchanged it for a cracked-spine copy of her V.C. Andrews' book—*Flowers in the Attic*. The story was odd, but she read it over and over again.

Despite her best efforts, she couldn't concentrate. The stranger in the trench coat with his weird flute accompaniment paraded through her thoughts. There was an intense need to understand what she'd seen—what she kept seeing. It clawed inside her. Who was the man? What was up with that ski mask and the silvery glow that followed him? Why did he prefer an uber-creepy flute version of a David Bowie song? The only scenario she could come up with was that the flute player was definitely some kind of ghost, but what about the man in black? When she'd called the local police department, they hadn't cared—they barely questioned Jimbo and her when they'd come out. Jimbo had shrugged it off because he was used to strange people coming in and out of the store.

Thinking of the strange guy reminded Lark of her

encounter with Auden the day before when he'd seen the man too. She couldn't believe she'd almost hit Auden with her bike. He'd appeared more than a little rumpled from a late night out. And with his hair forward, she'd thought he looked almost irresistible. *Almost.* Because she had seen the beastly pink blemish on his throat. Vampire bites would've been more appealing. And she couldn't help but think about their lyric exchanges… It had been too long without having a new note from him to read.

She was still contemplating whether to meet up with him that night at the party, when she glanced out the window and a small squeak escaped her.

The guy with the trench coat stared straight into the store, watching her again. But she could only see out. He couldn't see in because of the tint. At least she hoped he couldn't. But then the creep pressed something to the window, a yellow sticky note reading, *I'm sorry.*

Sorry for what?

Lark was going to find out, but she wasn't taking any chances. She hurried to her backpack behind the counter and pulled out her knife. The cowbell clanged as the glass door opened. She had the knife flicked up and ready.

Jimbo strolled in with two plastic bags full of food. His hair was down and flowing with pride. He'd always said he was relieved to still have hair at all.

"Be right back." Lark hurried past him with her knife in her jacket pocket. She pushed open the door, but the creep was no longer there. Folding the knife back, she turned around and slowly padded down an aisle to the front counter. Maybe he had been apologizing for freaking her out? Still, it seemed… off.

Her eyes met Jimbo's when she sat back on her stool.

"Did you see the guy outside wearing all black and a pork pie hat before you came in?" she asked, her voice uneven.

"No, but I wasn't really paying attention." Jimbo rubbed a beaded necklace at his throat. "You saw him again?"

"Yes." Her thoughts turned to the previous day at her trailer, and she glanced over at Jimbo. "Do you believe in ghosts?"

"Sure. As you know my ancestors were part of the Choctaw tribe. I inherited a second sight from my grandfather who was very attuned to spiritual things." Jimbo slid a cardboard Happy Meal box toward her. "I have several spirits who live at my place. Leave them alone, and you'll be fine."

Maybe that was the best choice—ignore the strange.

"You got me lunch?" Lark asked, clasping the cardboard *M* handle at the top. "I said I didn't want anything."

"You say that, but every time I'm eating my burger, I can see you secretly salivating." Jimbo set the kid's drink beside her Happy Meal box.

Her stomach sank. He'd spent money on her when she could've walked over there and bought her own meal. She'd been taking care of herself for as long as she could remember and hated putting anyone at a disadvantage. "Thanks. How much do I owe you?"

"It's on me. You have to run the store while I'm gone, so my treat." He shot her a look that left no room for argument.

She shrugged and opened the box, taking out a cheeseburger and a pack of fries, followed by the toy. It was one of those pull cars that one drags back and releases to make it go. Ronald McDonald's clown head peeked from behind the yellow car's steering wheel.

Creepy, she thought. But not any creepier than the other toy car that had a Big Mac driving it. She lifted her head to peer out the window, wondering if she'd catch another glimpse of the man to try and show Jimbo. But he hadn't come back.

"Oh, I think I forgot to tell you yesterday," Jimbo started. "There's a new hire coming to work with you tomorrow, and he'll be here Fridays and Saturdays. If he does well next Saturday, you can go ahead and let him work Tuesday through Saturday the following week."

She glanced up from the toy car that she was dragging backward on the counter. "Oh? I thought you were waiting until you got back to hire someone."

"Well, I figured you might need some help on the busier days, but you're the only one with a key." He paused and started for the front door. "That reminds me, I need to take down the Help Wanted sign."

"All right." She didn't think the new coworker would be as cool as Imani. Really, she would've preferred to work by herself, but if the new person was annoying, she could easily slip on her headphones. Before Lark could question it further, the store phone rang and Jimbo answered. He rattled on to the customer about what goes into taxidermy while she started to eat.

For the remainder of the shift, Lark stayed busy with customers while Jimbo went outside for numerous smoke breaks and cleared out boxes in the back room.

"I'll close up, so go ahead and live life," Jimbo said. "See you when I get back, hopefully with plenty of treasures."

"I think we have a different opinion on treasures, so I'll have to see." She grabbed her backpack of cassettes from the carpet and headed outside to her bike, exchanging the Beatles tape for the Clash. She lifted her head but stopped mid-motion when the stranger appeared again outside the laundromat.

His head rotated toward her.

"Hey!" she called. "What were you sorry about?"

He didn't reply, only continued to watch her. Almost methodically, he ran the tip of his gloved hand across the top of the rectangular covered object, leaning against the glass window. *What's under there?* As if he could read her mind, he reached down, tugging at the fabric covering the object. She caught a glimpse of dark wood.

The guy then motioned toward himself as if he was calling her over to see what was hidden beneath the black velvet. Curiosity blossomed in her chest, but she didn't move forward. As she hurriedly pulled out her knife from her jacket pocket, he held up a hand and lightly shooed her away as though he was bored. She needed to get Jimbo. But as she turned to go back in the store, a whistling noise sounded and the familiar melody played, hitting a crescendo. She spun around, trying to pinpoint its location, but it emanated from behind her, in front of her, all around her, and all at once. The song touched each and every one of her nerve endings, lighting them aflame.

Lark froze when the man in black straightened, grabbed the object, and took off running, not toward her but away from her before coming to a sudden jerky stop. As though the music had made him halt.

"What the hell?" She tore open the glass door to Bubble's and yelled, "Jimbo, hurry! I think you might need to try one of your spiritual techniques out here because I swear on all that is holy, something weird is going on."

"What do you mean?" he asked, moving faster than she'd ever seen him move.

When she looked back over her shoulder, the "Space Oddity" melody fizzled to an end. The stranger in black was no longer there, but she caught a glimpse of the cloaked figure holding a flute. The cloaked figure's curves were more distinctive now and confirmed her suspicion that it was, in fact, a woman. Before Lark could decide to move toward her or away, the woman vanished into a flash of silvery light.

"Did you see that?" she asked Jimbo, who was standing beside her, peering outside. "The song—it was almost beautiful. And the man with the hat, possibly possessed by another spirit with an instrument, left again. Did you see the cloaked woman holding a flute disappear?"

Jimbo strained his eyes as he searched around outside. "I didn't see or hear anything, Lark. But that doesn't mean I don't believe you. Wait here." He left her standing there and came back a few seconds later with a selection of items in his hand. "I got you some salt. A friend into the paranormal once showed me this, and it works. Use it at the entrances of your home and ignore them. In the meantime, I'll keep an eye out before I leave." He handed her a couple paperbacks along with the salt. "Also, here are a few books you can read while I'm gone. Don't bother with the cops anymore. They wouldn't be able to help with something like this anyway."

She slipped the things into her backpack. "Thanks."

"Remember what I said," he called after her. "Leave them alone."

She strode toward the laundromat, slowing as she approached to peer into the windows. Five people lingered inside—a woman with two toddlers, an elderly man, and a younger woman with headphones on. No person dressed in black—she glanced down at herself—besides her.

Brush it away. Ignore it as Jimbo had said.

As she pedaled home to the trailer park there was still

plenty of light out, but it had started to fade when she parked her bike at the back of the trailer.

"Hey, baby doll," Beth called when Lark opened the front door. The TV was on and Beth clasped her usual cigarette in one hand and a beer in the other, watching *Mama's Family*. She had started calling Lark and Paloma nicknames over the past few days. Paloma was "sweetie pie."

"Hi." Lark closed the door, her body still jittery from work.

Beth's gaze angled back to the TV. "God dammit! I'm tired of this piece of junk." She stood from the recliner, stormed to the TV, and struck the top with her hand.

Rolling her eyes, Lark pulled down her headphones and rotated the TV's antenna. Then she crushed the parts covered in aluminum foil, causing the fuzzy lines to clear.

"You're a lifesaver, baby doll." Beth inhaled the nicotine and sat back down in the recliner.

"We've only been doing the same thing since forever." What they really needed was a new TV. Sadly, as long as this one worked, they wouldn't be getting another unless Lark bought it. And she wasn't going to waste her money on that.

"Why do you always gotta have a smart-alecky comment, huh?"

"I'm just saying."

"Well, sometimes it's better to keep your trap shut. Be more like your sister." Beth pursed her lips and tilted her head to the side.

"Robin?" Lark knew Beth was talking about Paloma, but she wanted to rile her up anyway.

"Don't even speak that name to me," Beth spat. Then her face took on a look of guilt because it wasn't Lark who had caused the tension there. Beth must've gotten into another argument with Robin. It was a frequent thing, yet tomorrow, Beth would probably have a nice nickname for her too.

"Okay."

The phone rang, only once. Paloma must've answered it from the other room.

"Lark, it's for you! Imani!" Paloma shouted.

She turned away from Beth, who was now scowling at the TV, probably thinking about whatever happened between her and Robin.

As soon as Lark was about to open her door, Paloma said, "And don't take all day—I'm expecting a phone call from Shannon before the party."

They didn't have call waiting, and almost every time Lark was on the phone, Paloma was there, hovering.

Ignoring her sister, Lark grabbed the phone off the floor beside her mattress. Lucy hopped down and wove her furry body through Lark's legs in figure-eight movements.

"Got it," Lark yelled and waited until she heard the other phone receiver being set down. It took longer than necessary.

"Hello."

"Hey, it's me," Imani rushed.

"I assume you're on your way over to pick me up." Lark took a seat on the mattress, scooping up Lucy and placing the cat in her lap. "I need to talk to you about something."

"That's the thing. I have some pretty bad news for you. Mom's dead-set on going to some hair show this weekend in San Antonio that she literally just found out about fifteen minutes ago."

"And?"

"And... that means she has to drag me with her. Since it starts bright and early in the morning, she wants us to leave tonight."

Bad news. Lark groaned and fell back on her pillow. "Now I'll have to hang out with Paloma or talk to the wall. On second thought, the wall it is… or I could just stay home." Maybe she should stay home—it wasn't as if Beth would really forbid Paloma from going.

"I'm sure the boy next door will be there," Imani purred.

"You mean the boy from the store next door?"

"Same difference," Imani purred again. But based on the conversation outside Bubble's the other day, she knew he'd be there too.

"Stop acting like a cat. You're not Lucy." Lark snorted. "When are you coming back?"

"Sunday evening."

"Fair enough."

"How about next Saturday we do *The Rocky Horror Picture Show* midnight showing? Dress up and all." Lark could practically hear Imani beaming over the phone.

"Yeah, okay. I'll do Magenta this time."

"That's a step up from Riff Raff."

"Can't help it. He's seriously rad and on the sexy side," Lark replied. Imani may be in love with Columbia from Rocky Horror, but Riff Raff was a thousand times better.

"Be safe at the party. Talk to you when I get back."

"Will do."

Lark wanted to talk to Imani about what she'd seen, but she didn't want to do it on the phone with Beth and Paloma around. Disappointed that her friend in crime wouldn't be going with her to the party, Lark stroked the top of Lucy's white and gray head. "Sorry, girl, it'll just be you and Beth for a while."

She contemplated telling Paloma she wasn't going, but a part of her needed the distraction after the things she'd seen. Besides, the other part wanted to see if Auden would show up. She wanted to say she'd ignore him, but she'd be kidding herself. Nothing could prevent her thoughts from going back to that night.

It was the first party of the summer and Lark sat there, watching Shannon drink beer after beer, until she was drunk as a skunk.

Shannon stood in the middle of the room, swaying a bit and giggling. "How about a game of spin the bottle?" she yelled like they were at the ripe age of thirteen.

Lark looked around the room, searching for Imani, but she must've already snuck off somewhere with Emilia. That left Lark on the outside, stuck to observe Paloma and her friends, rather than be a part of their inner circle.

The night had already been awkward with Scott and his girlfriend trying to talk to her earlier. Lark decided it was time to leave, before things got even more awkward with the kissing game. Right as she pivoted on her heels, Lark's eyes came into contact with the one boy who could make her want to stay. Auden ran a hand through his hair as he entered the house with his friend Darrin.

She scanned people's faces, trying to calculate a percentage for when the bottle might land on Auden. She wasn't that good at math. Foolishly, she took the risk.

Shannon drunkenly barked out her orders. "Everyone line up in a circle." Lark pretended to be nonchalant, even though her heart was bouncing—one of the rare times she ever felt nervous anymore. If the bottle landed on anyone besides Auden, she would walk out of the room and not give a shit who she left waiting for a kiss. If the tip of the bottle pointed at Auden, she'd show him what a kiss was like. Lark had all the experience she needed from Scott—not that it was a good experience.

Turn after turn, she waited impatiently, praying the bottle wouldn't land on Auden at another girl's hand and wishing to God that no other boys' turns pointed at her.

"Your turn!" Paloma cheered to Lark, handing her the bottle.

Blowing out a breath, she spun that glass bottle like there was no tomorrow, already prepared to shrug her shoulders and make a hasty exit. Then the almighty power from the sky answered her wish—the tip slowed to a stop and pointed directly at Auden.

Lark's heart was attempting to beat out of her ribcage. Her confidence dropped as she crawled forward, taking her back to her scared and shy younger days. Then her eyes met Auden's beautiful hazel ones.

She had imagined every kiss in the book possible with this guy. Holding her breath, she pressed her lips to his, not long enough to gather any of the warmth, before she quickly thrust herself backward.

Paloma patted Lark's back in an "aww that's so cute" way.

As the music played through the speakers, Lark just wanted to leave, leave the circle, leave the room, leave the house. She hadn't glanced at Auden, not once, and when the game was finished, Lark hurried outside and relaxed her shoulders, in failure, against the side of the house. She didn't know Auden had followed her until he leaned against the brick beside her, tilting his head in her direction.

The way he was looking at her in that moment was a way she would always want to be looked at by him.

Auden was the first to break the silence. "I think we can

do better than that without an audience." After the pitiful kiss that'd taken place inside, she desperately wanted to prove the point too.

Lark nodded, too afraid she would say something stupid. His body turned to face her, pressing her up against the side of Shannon's house. With a soft touch, his lips connected to hers, molding together perfectly, and this time the warmth came. He kissed her deeper and deeper until a kiss could go no further, and she didn't want him to ever stop.

Auden was the first to pull back, lips swollen.

Lark grabbed his wrist. "Do you want to go to your van?" She meant to say inside, but the thought of going into his vehicle electrified her, so she didn't correct herself.

A look of surprise crossed his face, but then his expression matched hers—a wanting of something more.

Without words, because none were needed, he tugged her in the direction of his vehicle and tapped the door with his knuckle. "Her name's Jenny."

Cracking a smile, she sang the phone number from the song.

"Mmm, I'll give you a kiss now for that."

Before he could move toward her, she shifted forward first, kissing him with so much intensity that she felt as if she was stealing air from him.

As they entered his van, Lark only meant for them to mess around a little, but her hand somehow found the zipper of his pants, and he somehow lifted her skirt.

One thing led to another and they had done the deed.

Before any awkward conversation could ruin the moment, she straightened her skirt and left his van with a quick "thanks."

She'd assumed that was the end of it, but two weeks later,

it had happened again—that time it had felt more than being lust driven.

Her thoughts still lingered on Auden. If he showed at the party that night, Lark didn't know if it would be like the first time in his van or the second time, but she didn't want to think about it anymore. Maybe she didn't want any of it. No, that was a lie.

A knock at her bedroom door interrupted her thoughts. Paloma swung it open before Lark could say to come in. "Are you going with Imani, or do you want to ride with me and Cheryl?"

"I've got a bike," Lark said, not really in the mood to see Cheryl. But Shannon's place was far for a bike ride.

"I've got roller skates, but you don't see me using them," Paloma pointed out.

"That's because you don't know how."

Frustrated, Paloma ran a hand through her hair, exposing her lazy eye. She had enough eyeshadow caked on to where Lark could barely even tell. "Well?"

"Yeah, okay fine." She knew how much Paloma wanted her to go so her sister could impress Beth. It was most likely a tactic to keep Beth from returning to her old ways, a self-centered mother. "But if the party ends up being too shitty, I'm walking home."

Rolling her eyes, Paloma turned away and mumbled, "Okay, be ready when Cheryl honks the horn."

"Hey, Paloma!" she shouted.

Her sister ducked back into the room. "Yeah?"

Lark took a deep breath, trying to swallow the knot in her throat. "Do you... I mean, have you ever seen... you know, spirits? Weird, unexplainable things?" She wanted to test if they really didn't have any twin-dar.

"Um, no to ghosts. As for weird?" Paloma tapped her chin and smiled. "Only you." She walked away and left Lark with the realization that they were definitely nothing alike.

Stretching, Lark stood and wandered over to her small closet. She sifted through the clothes on hangers and on the floor. What was she going to wear? She tugged on a long black skirt and a neon blue sleeveless crop top that she never wore—ever. Immediately, she ripped the shirt off and tossed it to the floor.

Since when did she care so much about what she wore?

She picked the shirt back up and put it on, adding a pair of black jeans instead of the skirt, along with her black lace-up boots. Then she covered the ensemble with her jacket, zipping it all the way up.

A loud horn blared from the front of the trailer. Lark grabbed her backpack and Walkman, headed out of the room, and glanced out the front window. The headlights of Cheryl's car lit up the night.

Paloma, decked out in neon colors and lace, came into the living room. She wore about a gazillion bracelets on both her arms, and a long crucifix necklace dangled below her breasts.

"You know there's music at the party, right?" Paloma said, staring at Lark's backpack.

"I remember from last time. That's why I needed to come prepared." She rattled the backpack in front of her sister, tapes clacking together inside.

Paloma shook her head. "You're so weird."

"Yet you invited me," Lark sang.

"Technically, Mom asked if you were going."

"What?" Beth perked up as though hearing the word "Mom" fulfilled some sort of destiny.

"Just saying we'll see you later, Mom," Paloma answered with a wide smile.

"You two can stay out past town curfew, but don't get caught. I ain't paying nothin' if you do." With her hands laced behind her neck, Beth relaxed farther back in the recliner.

Lark wouldn't expect anything less from Beth. Her glassy eyes hinted she'd had more alcohol tonight than usual. Lark still didn't think she could ever bring herself to call that woman "Mom."

Outside the trailer, Cheryl's cherry-colored Chevy truck was already inching forward to meet them with the windows rolled down.

Paloma opened the door and hopped into the middle, followed by Lark. Cheryl's bleached-blonde head turned to Paloma. "I didn't know you were dragging your sister along."

"Beth wanted us to go together," Paloma muttered.

If Paloma wasn't Lark's sister, Cheryl would've made a huge ruckus about Lark being around. Lark didn't care because Cheryl was a twat who listened to shitty music and blended in with whatever was trendy.

As they passed trees and small shops on their way to Shannon's, Cheryl kept having Paloma rewind "Wake Me Up Before You Go-Go" to play on repeat. She kept rattling on about how sexy George Michael was in those short shorts. Before the third run of the overly peppy song, Lark unzipped her backpack and pulled out her headphones, intending to escape the mess with some New York Dolls.

The over-energetic buzz of Cheryl's music faded out, and in that moment, Lark didn't think about disappearing flute players or strangers in black, her sisters, Beth, or even Auden.

At least not until Cheryl slowed the truck to turn down the street leading to Shannon's house.

A dark shadow of a person slid into Lark's peripheral vision, standing in front of several tall oak trees and wearing a familiar hat. Lark sat up straighter in her seat, craning her neck for a better view.

The man with the rectangular object stood on the corner, watching as Cheryl's truck turned. The stranger shook his head at Lark before a silvery light spread and he blinked out.

What is happening?

Lark couldn't focus. She closed her eyes and chose to ignore it... for now. But how could she if this kept happening over and over and over again?

CHAPTER 6

Auden grabbed a soda from Shannon's kitchen and spotted her pouring a bag of chips into a large plastic bowl. Shannon's short bob of dark hair mostly lay hidden underneath a fashionable pink bowler hat, and her braces reflected the light as she chewed on several chips.

He'd arrived with Darrin only about five minutes ago, spending most of the earlier part of the day in his room listening to records and reading one of the books he kept beneath the bed on schizophrenia. He kept wondering if the strange music would stir again in his backyard. It hadn't. Then Darrin showed up out of the blue and dragged him to the park to watch him skateboard—he liked the comfort of that.

Since then, he'd been good. Felt good. Positively good. Only in the back of his mind, he wasn't good at all because he needed to uncover what was happening with him.

"So is Darrin not seeing Felisa anymore?" Shannon asked, crinkling up the chip bag into a ball before tossing it into the trash can.

"Hmm?" Auden almost spat out the soda he'd taken a swig of. Shannon was cool with Auden, but she always talked to Darrin like he was a piece of gum on the bottom of her shoe. Maybe it had to do with the fact that Darrin had screwed her and then started hanging out with Felisa.

"No, they're still doing their thing." He didn't know if he should say that Darrin would probably be more than willing to have Shannon on the side if she really wanted.

"Really? Because he's hitting on Paloma's sister right now." She bobbed her head in the direction behind him.

He whirled around as Paloma and Cheryl brushed past him to chat with Shannon. Ignoring their giggling laughter, Auden's gaze zeroed in on Lark and Darrin. Lark's back faced Auden, her left shoulder pressed up against the wall with her arms folded across her chest. She wore her black jacket, and her backpack was slung over one shoulder. Darrin's forearm was propped against the flower wall-papered walls, his eyes not so subtly flicking back and forth between Lark and Auden.

That little bastard. Auden knew what Darrin was trying to do, and it seemed to be working. Lark's head fell back, and deep laughter escaped her. Had he ever even heard her laugh? An unknown feeling brewed inside his chest. Jealousy? He didn't like it.

Auden sauntered across the room, watching Lark's arms fall daintily to her sides. He shot Darrin a hard glare and wanted to yank him by his red Mohawk across the living room.

Reaching forward, Auden tugged Lark's soft pinky finger. Her head twisted to the side and her smile fell. Without a single word, he let go and headed out of the house, but not before Darrin pulled him back and whispered, "Told ya."

Once outside, a light breeze swept across his body. He waited to see if Lark would follow him. Maybe she wouldn't after seeing the blasted hickey that was still on his neck, although it had faded somewhat.

If she did, would it be like the first time in his van or the second time? The first time was much easier to think about because the second time there had been a moment...

They both still had their clothing on like the first time they'd had sex. Her skirt was hiked up again and his pants had been shuffled down a bit.

Auden stared at Lark, her chest rising and falling just like his. He shifted closer and pressed his forehead against hers, whispering the first lyrics she'd ever written to him from "Running Up That Hill."

Lark blinked and replied with, "Thanks."

He couldn't help but feel like an idiot. Maybe he'd said something wrong.

Sucking on his lower lip, Auden scanned the area—no man with a hat, no hidden objects, and no strange flute music to make him contemplate his sanity.

Clunky steps sounded behind him, interrupting where his mind had veered off to.

"So you don't want to find the girl who gave you that hickey?" Lark suggested, stopping beside him.

Rolling his eyes and finding himself smirking, he studied Lark's haughty face. "Nah, I much prefer the one in front of me."

"I'll have to say, I don't much prefer the one in front of me." She was such a bad liar.

"So, Darrin then?" Auden tilted his head back in the direction of the house.

She crinkled her nose and shook her head. Her expression was rather cute.

"Do you want to come see Jenny?" Inside his van, his fingers wouldn't feel as fidgety and he wouldn't be searching again for something to show up... or disappear. Except Lark.

She looked hesitant at first. He didn't have to explain anything to her, but he felt he should anyway.

"Look, Drew cornered me in a room at a party the other night at Heather's." Auden held up his hand to stop Lark from saying anything. "But I thought she was you for a second."

"Why the hell would I be at Heather's party?" she whisper-shouted.

"I don't know? Why do you keep coming to Shannon's parties?"

"Do I really need to answer that?" She tried to hold a straight face, but failed as the sides of her lips quirked up.

Reaching forward, he ran a finger along the strap of her backpack before giving it a gentle tug. "I see you have your backpack on again. You want to go listen to *good* music?"

"Yes, please! I can't take the awful sounds in there anymore." She grinned. "Take me to Jenny."

"Let me lead the way."

They walked in comfortable silence down the path of the driveway until they reached his van in a shadowed area along the curb. He opened the door with a soft squeak, letting her hop in first, and trying to get a glimpse of her ass but that damn jacket was in the way. If only she was wearing the leotard.

She took a seat against the wall of the van and pulled the backpack in front of her, drawing out her Walkman.

"You have more boxes of records in here this time." Lark crawled forward and rifled through his vinyl collection. "I can't believe you have this in here." She yanked out a Tommy James & the Shondells album.

"Hell yes, I do." Auden snatched it from her and fished out the record, inhaling the scent that smelled of decades' past. He placed it on the record player, and the scratching sound of needle to record started right before "Crimson and Clover" filled the air with its relaxing melody.

Lark groaned. "No way. I can deal with the Joan Jett version—that's it."

He chuckled. "What? You're insane! Next thing I know, you're going to say you like 'Cherry Bomb.'"

"All right, maybe this is better than 'Cherry Bomb,' but I was never a Runaways fan."

Propping himself on the floor next to her, he let the music drift through the walls of the van with his shoulder almost touching hers, wanting to touch hers.

Auden couldn't stay relaxed for long. He felt frustrated with himself in that moment. Frustrated with wanting to listen to music with her, talk to her, kiss her, remove her jacket.

She must've heard his prayers because she leaned forward and tugged off her jacket. "Okay, I can't listen to this anymore. All I can envision is Beth dancing around the living room, sipping on her beer, in her *bra*."

"Who's Beth?" he asked, lifting the arm of the record player.

"My mom."

"You call her Beth?" He found it slightly odd that she called her mom by her first name, when he had no trouble calling his aunt "Mom."

"Yeah, she never won any Mom of the Year awards and now she's trying to."

A faraway expression appeared on her face, and he snatched her backpack away from her, hoping to snap her out of the funk she seemed to be in. "Let me see what I can find." Closing his eyes, he dipped a hand inside, blindly sorting through the cassettes. "We will listen to... this one!" He fished out a Phil Collins tape. "Ah, two names that can always lighten my mood."

Lark pulled the tape out of her Walkman and placed it in her bag, then took the one from his hand, her fingertips brushing against his during the exchange. Auden's heart sped up, whether from lust or something more—he didn't know. But he would pretend it was just lust as he stared intently at her. The shirt she wore revealed more of her skin than he'd ever seen before, since their clothing had never fully come off.

Lark pressed Play on the cassette player and placed the headphones between the two of them, then turned up the volume as high as it would go. Auden cradled the right side as she held onto the left—only a headphones' width between the two of them. As he shifted closer, a flowery scent, that must've been the shampoo she'd used, enveloped his senses. She always smelled good—even when he would lean forward in class to pass up his homework, it was there.

His gaze continued to shift from her red lipstick-stained lips to his red high-top sneakers. Auden couldn't decide whether he wanted to keep talking to her, have her on top of him again, or share lyrics with him. He was feeling *things* and he wasn't sure if he wanted to, because secretly, he was afraid of getting hurt or him doing the same to her.

Regardless, he shifted forward, and pressed his palm to her cheek, angling her face toward his. His lips were only a second from touching hers when he noticed someone peering in the window. All he could see was a shadowy outline of a person because it was dark outside.

He dropped his hand from Lark's cheek and scrambled to the door, flinging it open.

"Auden?" Lark asked from behind him, her voice hesitant.

Hopping from the van, he caught someone running in the distance behind one of the trees. Possibly in a dress? He couldn't see anything but the swish of fabric since the lights on this side of the street were mostly burnt out. "Someone was watching us and they just hauled ass to that tree." He pointed farther ahead.

Lark dropped down behind him, her boots making a soft crunch on the pavement. "Did you catch who it was? I didn't see or hear anything."

"Maybe a girl in a dress."

Her eyebrows waggled as she grinned mischievously. "Let's go embarrass the Peeping Tom then."

Auden was pissed because his lips had been so close to touching Lark's, but he wanted to see who it was. And he hoped to God it wasn't Drew because what would Lark even think about that...

The yard was huge and full of pine trees, their strong scent permeating the air. But even while straining his eyes, he could barely see. A squawk sounded from above him, loud and high-pitched, causing Auden to jerk.

Lark laughed. "It's only a bird."

Auden smiled, then two strong hands grasped his upper arms and flung him backward. Lark let out a small scream. His heart beat rapidly as he spun around with a grunt, ready to punch the person in the face. But instead his gaze connected with a red-Mohawked head.

"What the fuck are you doing?" Auden asked, and he could hear the bite in his words. Couldn't Darrin have just called his name?

"We gotta leave, man. Shannon's parents just came home early and they're kicking everyone out and threatening to call the police."

"Wouldn't that affect their daughter?" Auden asked as silhouettes of people rushed out of Shannon's house. Their feet pounded the ground to get to their cars.

"They don't care." Darrin shrugged.

"Do you want to keep on looking?" Lark asked.

"Lark!" a voice yelled.

Auden spun and saw Paloma standing across the street.

"Forget it," Auden said. "You need to get out of here. I'll see you tomorrow."

"Tomorrow?" Lark asked, arching a brow and ignoring Paloma.

"Yeah, I start working with you tomorrow at Bubble's."

"Come on, man!" Darrin shouted and hurried to tug Auden away.

"Lark, I swear to God!" Paloma ran across the street and marched toward her sister.

As he moved toward the van, Auden looked back one more time at Lark, but her sister was already hauling her off.

Struggling to find breath, he yanked the door of Jenny open on the driver side and peered out the passenger window toward the tree where he'd been going to investigate with Lark. In the distance, a tiny sliver of movement shifted forward and then the figure, mostly hidden in the darkness, disappeared with a flash of silver.

"What are you looking at?" Darrin asked as he scurried onto the passenger seat.

Auden took a deep swallow and rubbed his eyes. "Nothing." *Something you didn't see.*

"So what were you doing with Lark?" Darrin asked as Auden started the engine and took off. He needed to go home and figure this out with his mental health research books.

"Listening to music."

"You like her." Darrin grinned.

"Like is a strong word."

"Don't you mean love is?"

"No. I mean *like*. It's hard to like someone." Auden did like her which was the thing, and like could lead to stronger feelings. He didn't quite know how to feel about that, but if he had gotten to kiss her earlier, his heart would have grown closer to being hers.

"But you like me."

"Do I?" Auden chuckled.

"People can't help liking me," Darrin said, rolling down the window and lighting a cigarette.

"You didn't happen to see anyone watching us through the window earlier, did you?" Auden's voice came out soft, shaky.

Darrin scrunched up his face. "I may like watching porn but not *your* porn. But I didn't see anyone."

"Remember the other night when I said I saw something?"

"When you were drunk?"

Auden gripped the steering wheel, staring straight ahead at the road. "That's not the only time. I lied back there. I didn't see nothing—I saw something, a figure in some sort of dress, and then they disappeared with a silvery light. But I've been seeing and hearing other things too." He paused and shook his head while digging his finger into his bottom lip. "I know it sounds crazy."

"What you need is a good night's sleep. You need to stop stressing because you're starting to do the weird stuff with touching your lips. Stop that. Lack of sleep can mess with your head."

Auden nodded. His sleep had been off lately. It was possible. Maybe he hadn't seen the silvery light, but he knew he had conjured it up somehow. He continued to rub his lip.

During the drive to Darrin's, Auden thought about how he'd listened to music with Lark in the van. He and Lark could obviously talk to each other, not just through writing lyrics or screwing.

Auden pulled up to the apartment, and Darrin stepped out of the van. "You sure you don't want to hang out for a while? Maybe get some sleep here so you don't have to drive back home."

"No, I need to make sure I'm not late for work tomorrow. But thank you."

"Sure. Door's always open." Darrin seemed to hesitate a moment, but he finally walked away, giving a wave over his shoulder.

Auden would be seeing Lark tomorrow at work, and he wanted to start talking to her again, not only with words, but the best way he knew how. With a defeated sigh, he fished out his wallet from the back of his jeans. There were no pictures inside—the one he used to have of Drew ended up in the garbage months and months ago. But he tugged out the last small speech bubble Lark had written to him—lyrics from "Blue Monday."

Opening the glove compartment, Auden yanked out a new spiral pocket notepad and a pen. On the paper, he drew a quick sketch of himself with a speech bubble. Inside the speech bubble, he wrote different lyrics from the same song to give to Lark tomorrow. The lyrics helped him tell her how he felt, because sometimes he didn't know.

CHAPTER 7

To Lark:

Lyrics from "Limelight" — Rush

Lark woke to Lucy's furry tail flickering across her nose, and she let out a sneeze—probably from inhaling too much cat hair while sleeping. Yawning, she leaned forward, picked up Lucy, and sat the cat in her lap.

The night before flashed through her mind and Lark's body stilled. *Yeah, I start working with you tomorrow at Bubble's.* "Holy skeletons," she whispered. Auden was the new co-worker. Jimbo hadn't told her his name. She hadn't asked. The store had been so busy that day. She was totally unprepared to work with the boy from the music store next door.

Lark glanced at her alarm clock and realized she had just enough time to shower and eat before she had to head to work. She set Lucy down, threw off the blanket, and scrambled around her room, collecting the first clothing she found on the floor of her closet. Trembles coursed through her body —nervousness, excitement, even a little annoyance. Because she liked him—really liked him—and now instead of relying on clever lyrics, she'd have to think of what to say for an entire workday.

Springing from the room, she hurried across the hall to the bathroom to get ready. Beth was already at her cashier job at the grocery store, and Paloma had spent the night at Cheryl's, so it was just Lark. And she liked that. But then a slight chill crawled up her spine, like little handprints. She was alone. What if the cloaked woman decided to come inside? That one night she'd been right outside her home. Attempting to tame the rush of panic, Lark searched the trailer. No sign of the supernatural. One of the books Jimbo had given her mentioned that ghosts could have distinct smells. Lark took a whiff—no decay or pungent smells mixed with sickening sweetness. Her shoulders relaxed and she blew out a loud breath.

She finished getting ready and ate two slices of toast, all while her thoughts kept drifting to Auden and their almost-kiss—how they hadn't kissed but should've. Someone had ruined the moment.

Lark popped her headphones over her ears as she headed out the door, jumped on her bike, and blared Rush as she pedaled to work.

Skirting around cars in the store parking lot, she spotted a customer already standing outside of Bubble's. No, not a customer—an employee. Lark almost turned the bike around as her blasted heart pounded harder at the sight of him.

She slid off the seat, tugged down her headphones, and pushed the bike up the sidewalk. "Hey," she said casually, as though she met Auden every day like this.

"Hey," he echoed back, his hands in the pockets of his jeans.

She glanced at the laundromat, but the stranger in black wasn't there. Lark took the knife from her backpack and shoved it in her jacket pocket anyway. Considering the weirdness of the past few days, it might become a part of her new work uniform going forward.

Lark brushed past Auden, careful not to invade his personal bubble, even though she wanted to.

She unlocked the door with a loud click and stepped inside the store.

"So you're working two jobs now?" Lark asked, as he walked in beside her.

"No, I was fired for being late."

"Well, you weren't late today." She shrugged and produced two books from her backpack—a ghost hunting one and another V.C. Andrews novel—as she took a seat behind the counter.

"No, but you were." He tapped the cover of the ghost book as if he was declaring it had been late. His finger lingered against the cover of her book. "By like two minutes."

"Five, to be exact."

From the corner of her eye she watched as Auden sank down beside her on the other barstool, his dangling earring swaying. He pushed a small red notepad in front of her. Lark glanced at Auden, who stared in another direction as though he hadn't placed it there. She drew the notebook closer to her before opening it.

Inside was a picture drawn of Auden that wasn't very good, but he wore the same thing he'd had on last night. Dead Kennedys T-shirt, black jeans, and Converse. Written in the speech bubble were the same lyrics she'd sent to him all those months ago from "Blue Monday." Lark's breath caught. He wanted to begin again and so did she.

She grabbed a pen from the desk and drew a picture of herself in her jacket, long skirt, and boots that also wasn't very good. A song came to mind, one that would fit the situation in that moment perfectly. Within her speech bubble, she wrote Simple Minds' lyrics from the song "Don't You (Forget About Me)."

Trying to hide a smile, she slid the notepad to him. Without looking at it, Auden took the spiral-bound book and stuffed it in his back pocket. She wondered when he'd read it and what his lyric back to her would be as she grinned to herself.

"I suppose I should show you the oddity ropes, now," she said. Her nerves had slowed a bit, but they weren't gone.

Auden wet his bottom lip and nodded, distracting her. It was so easy to remember how those same lips had felt against her neck, and the skill he'd applied to their make-out sessions...

Lark blinked, snapping out of her daze.

"All right, you sign in and out here." She pointed to a yellow notepad with the days and dates of the next two months already written in a column. Waving her hand across the store, she continued, "You dust every day. Jimbo usually does the vacuuming. Water the plants when you feel like they need it. We do inventory once a month, and here's how you use the cash register." She showed him the basics, and he easily caught on. "Also, no purchasing from customers. Jimbo is the only one allowed to pick out stock and set prices. We're all equals here—there isn't really a manager or anything, so once you get your key to the store, that's about it."

"Easy enough." Auden's gaze slid to hers, and he gave her a one-sided grin.

As Auden signed in, she headed to the miracle remedy wall to rearrange things. The cowbell rang, signaling a new customer had come in. Lark peered around the aisle, noticing a guy with a Mohawk, carrying a skateboard—Darrin.

She started to walk back behind the counter when Darrin asked, "Where you running off to, lass?"

Before school let out, she'd had an art class with him, and he'd sat at her group table. Well, it was only the two of them in that group, but she'd found him funny.

"I'm preparing myself in case you need anything. I didn't realize you were... Scottish?"

"I can be whatever the ladies want me to be," Darrin said in an accent that sounded more Arabic than Scottish. "I just wanted to check and see how my boy was doing on his first day of work." He'd switched back to his normal voice this time.

"Aren't you supposed to be at work?" Auden asked, frowning.

"Grams has me on break at the moment. I already shampooed and brushed more dogs than I can count."

Auden shook his head. "Another four-hour break?"

"Always." Darrin turned to Lark. "What are you doing Saturday?"

"You mean tonight?" she asked, taking a seat on her barstool.

Darrin stopped in front of the counter. "No, next Saturday."

Auden was giving him a hard stare, and Lark didn't understand why.

"Uh, going to the midnight Rocky Horror show with Imani."

"Oh, Imani... is she still single?" She was not, but Lark couldn't out her friend. She'd promised to keep it secret.

"Aren't you with Felisa?" Auden asked.

Darrin waved him off and ran his hand across a skull on a nearby shelf, fiddling around with the empty sockets. "No."

"You're not Imani's type." Maybe if he had ta-tas and a vagina then Imani might be interested.

"We're going to a concert Saturday and wondered if you'd come with us, but maybe another time." Darrin cocked his head, just staring at her.

Who the hell were *we*? Because Auden was looking at Darrin as if he was out of his mind.

"See you later, Darrin," Auden said through gritted teeth.

"I can take a hint, man. See you after work." Turning around, Darrin headed out of the store and hopped on his skateboard as soon as he opened the door.

Auden slid on the stool next to Lark, and she was about to move when, once again, the cowbell rang. Beside her, Auden's spine visibly stiffened. She followed his stare, then froze. The new customer inched toward them—a figure she hadn't been expecting, or maybe she should've since he'd been appearing everywhere else. It was the guy swathed in black. The one who Lark believed was somehow connected to the cloaked woman playing the flute. Was she here, too? She cocked her head, listening for any sign of musical notes drifting into the store. There were only the sounds of his booted feet inching nearer and nearer.

Lark whipped out her knife and flicked it open as the new guest creeped closer, the large rectangular object in his grasp. It looked to be almost half the size of Lark.

"What do you want?" she asked through gritted teeth.

By her side, Auden's eyes widened when he caught sight of the knife under the counter.

Lark held her blade so tight the handle pressed roughly into her palm.

The creep placed the object on the floor and stood up

straight, tall with broad shoulders. Lark waited for him to disappear, for a silver light, or even flute music to play.

The guy's gaze—or what Lark thought was his gaze—fell to the thing he'd set in front of the counter, which were practically the same height. He pointed to it, then to Lark and Auden.

"We're not purchasing anything from you," Auden said, expression neutral.

In response, the stranger pinched the top of the crushed velvet fabric and tugged it away, revealing a top layer of something wooden. Lark remembered the glimpse he'd given her before. Again, he pointed at the now-unveiled object and then to Lark and Auden before pulling a sticky note from his pocket. Lark had seen him do this before, but this time, the words read, *Store bought.*

"Jimbo bought this from you?" Lark's eyebrows drew together as she inspected the wood.

The guy placed another note on top of the wood, then turned to exit. His movements—stiff, almost robotic—gave the impression that he was being led by something. Manipulated. Only this time, no music filled the air.

"He can't speak," Auden said, scratching the back of his neck.

"What?"

"He flashed me a note the other day that said he couldn't."

"Hmm, he showed me one that said he was sorry."

"Strange." Auden's eyes lingered on the object.

Through her trembling, a distinct part of Lark felt bad for the guy—another wished Jimbo hadn't gone out of town and that it was his shift in the store.

"Nice blade," Auden said, interrupting her thoughts.

"You never know." Closing the knife, she dropped it into her pocket.

"I have two fists." Auden was tall, but the other guy was big too.

Neither of them moved immediately, but Lark's curiosity had been piqued. Even if Jimbo hadn't really purchased it, she knew he would be interested in seeing it.

Auden was the first to move, and she followed around the other side of the counter—Lark from the left and Auden from the right—until they met in the center facing a... mirror. It appeared perfectly clean, not a single smudge in sight. In fact, it looked as if their images were overly sharpened.

A harmless mirror. She'd expected something else, something darker. The looking glass was large, and Lark could crawl through if it were possible. She studied the wooden trim with engraved zigzag markings. A heart-shaped piece of wood lay against the glass. It gave the illusion of movement. Almost as if it were bleeding down the surface toward the rectangular bottom. Mesmerizing.

Lark lifted another sticky note from on top and unfolded the yellow paper.

Sorry again.

"This has to do with me calling the cops the other day, but I don't trust him." She folded the note back up and pushed it into her pocket.

"So Jimbo bought this..." Auden rubbed his jaw, appearing calm except for the slight tremble of his hand.

"I'll call him in a bit and leave a message on his answering machine, but he won't listen to it until he gets back." As she inspected the mirror, she knew Jimbo would've purchased it if he'd seen it. But had he? She hadn't talked to him since the day before. Maybe he had ended up finding the stranger. "It does look rad, though."

"I hope he didn't pay too much for this piece of junk, if he did, because I'm sure Darrin could've made him one in wood-shop before school let out."

"You obviously have zero taste." She reached forward at the same time Auden did, both hands at opposite corners. A sharp shock ripped through her fingertips. She yanked her hand back and searched for a red mark. The zing was similar to the one she'd felt the first day she'd seen the stranger and he had struck her shoulder.

"The hell?" Auden hissed.

"You felt that, too?" There was still a slight tingling sensation in her fingers from the aftershock, but no mark on her skin.

"Well, my hand isn't touching the mirror anymore, is it?" She glared at him. "Don't be an ass."

Ignoring her, Auden reached forward again—because he hadn't learned his lesson the first time—and placed his hand against the "demonic" mirror. He looked at her and smiled smugly. *Okay, so the mirror isn't demonic, just a faulty occurrence of getting shocked. It's not as if I've never been shocked by something before.*

"Where do you want this thing?" he asked, struggling to lift it up. "It feels as if the damn thing is bolted to the floor."

"Is it that heavy?" Lark crinkled her nose and watched him take a deep breath as his face reddened from exertion.

"Hell yes, it's heavy."

"Well, the guy in *all* black came in carrying it just fine." The guy hadn't seemed to be struggling, but then again, his face was behind a ski mask. And who knows if he had some secret supernatural abilities hidden somewhere.

"I wouldn't be talking about his black clothing, Miss I-wear-black-pretty-much-all-the-time." He wasn't wrong there, but not completely accurate either.

Lifting a hand, Lark wiggled her red polished nails and pointed at her cherry-stained lips. "Not all black, maestro."

"What am I a maestro at?" He arched an eyebrow.

"Forget it!" She reached for the other side of the mirror to help him lift it, and she felt as if her spine was going to crack in half. "Okay, maybe this *is* heavy."

"No shit, Sherlock," Auden grunted through gritted teeth when they both finally lifted it together. "Where to?"

"How about next to the miracle remedy wall." She backed up as he pushed forward. Her hands shook as she held the bottom and side, figuring she would die in the store if the mirror fell on her. Then she imagined herself mummified and sold to a customer for Jimbo's profit. She didn't like that thought very much.

Auden maneuvered to the side until they were beside the remedies. Small beads of perspiration had formed on his temples. Slowly, he crouched to set his side down while holding onto the top, preventing Lark from crushing her hands as she gently brought her portion to the carpet.

"I'm never lifting that again," she said. "The customer who buys it will have to figure out how to get it out of the store themselves."

An off-time motion tugged at Lark's peripheral, and she quickly turned to glance at the mirror. But she only met her reflection in the glass. *My mind must be playing tricks on me*, she thought as she came face to face with herself. She grabbed the crushed velvet cloth from the floor and draped it over the mirror. As cool looking as it was, she didn't want to touch it again.

The cowbell rattled as another customer entered the store. Lark peered around the aisle, expecting the stranger who dropped off the mirror to be back. But it was just an older woman with short gray hair, heading toward the Samurai swords.

When they returned to the sales counter, Lark's eyes pushed the book she'd been reading in front of Auden.

"Do you believe in ghosts?" Lark asked as she studied the cover of the book and thought about all the strange things she'd seen.

Auden lifted the book and shook his head. "No, I think people can be delusional or crazy."

Well, that settles that matter. She'd keep her lips zipped on all supernatural activity.

After the customer left without buying anything, Auden headed out on break to get something to eat.

Lark picked up the phone to call Jimbo when a long, slow scratching sound came from behind her. Heart galloping, she turned around and peered at the radio. Above it, on the wall, rested the Kit-Cat Klock and the oval mirror with skeletal hands surrounding it that Jimbo had made himself. She blinked at her reflection, listening for the scratching sound, but nothing stirred. *Must be rats in the walls again.* That problem should've been solved a few months back. But something about the reflection of this mirror didn't feel right either —like the one the stranger brought in, her image seemed too sharp.

# CHAPTER 8

Auden walked away from Bubble's after Lark locked up. He'd tried not to watch her as she got on her bike and pedaled away, but it had been hard not to.

The first day had been interesting. He'd been close to Lark most of the time, and he'd wanted to say more than he had.

The stranger who'd dropped off the mirror wasn't by the laundromat. Maybe his ultimate goal in life was to find a buyer for that mirror. Auden hated to admit it, though, but he'd been scared shitless when the man had come in the store. Not scared of the person—because he knew the man was real —but of the suspected hallucinations his mind had most likely drawn up of him at the party and in other places. It was the only explanation and hopefully one that would now end.

Auden slipped in Jenny's front seat and pulled the notepad from his pocket. His fingers had been twitching in desperation to read Lark's words. But he wanted to wait until he was in this spot so he could focus on the first words she'd written to him since school let out. He opened the notebook to her page and read her lyrics.

Could he shout her name? Or just let her go?

Easier written than said, Lark, he thought.

Auden tossed the notepad onto the passenger seat, the lyrics circling inside his skull, as he headed to pick up food from Jack in the Box. Grabbing his backpack of essentials for the night, because he didn't want to go home, he jogged up the stairs and knocked on Darrin's door.

Darrin answered, wearing only his white underwear briefs and socks. U2 played in the background. A red-faced Felisa threw on a white tank top over a black bra. Auden darted his eyes back to Darrin. "Forget your pants?"

Unashamed, Darrin leaned against the doorframe. "I'm Tom Cruise in *Risky Business.*"

"Hmm, you're forgetting the sunglasses and shirt." Auden pushed one of the bags of food at Darrin's chest. "Here, stud, I brought you something. Sorry, Felisa, if I knew you were here, I could've brought you something too. Maybe you can share with Darrin—two straws in the soda and everything." He placed the drinks on the table and smirked.

"I was just leaving." Felisa fumbled with her purse and flicked her long locks over her shoulder before scurrying out of the apartment.

"Thought you said you two weren't together," Auden said as Darrin shut the door.

"We're not."

Auden didn't say anything else on the subject. Darrin didn't want to be tied down, but Auden knew Felisa sure as hell did.

He couldn't screw around the way Darrin did because he knew those girls would want more than he had to offer. Yet, he still had done it with Lark—twice. Almost three times.

"What's the plan for tonight?" Auden asked, popping a fry into his mouth.

"*Star Wars* trilogy. Maybe a little lightsaber action, if you know what I mean." Darrin waggled his eyebrows while tugging on his pants.

"Sorry, I don't swing that way."

"Man, you know what I mean!" Dropping to the floor, Darrin rolled out two plastic lightsabers and tossed one to Auden.

He barely caught it and looked the plastic over. "Did you actually buy these?"

"Yeah! Right after I left your work."

Auden rotated the black handle in his hand and stroked the long yellow part. "This is so choice." If he was ten right now, it would've been the best thing in his life. Hell, it was now.

"Quit jerking off the saber, and let's get down to business." Darrin leapt toward Auden like he was Darth Vader on a mission to destroy, and Auden's reflexes weren't that sharp. The saber fell to the floor with a clack. "Seriously, where's your game at?"

"I guess lightsabering isn't something I know how to do."

"Fine. We'll work on that later. Let me start the first movie." Darrin set his saber on the table and pushed the cabinet door underneath the TV to pop it open. He sifted through his VHS stash and pulled out all three movies, then fed the first one into the VCR.

Roughly six hours later, Auden had made it through all three, but Darrin had begun snoring away as soon as the opening scroll started on the second movie. He stood up and flipped the switch on the TV before heading into the bedroom to fall asleep.

Sleep was the one place Auden could fade. He didn't have to be anyone there, and he didn't have to think about anything —unless the nightmares about his dad started again. He hadn't had any of those in years. Mostly nights were full of darkness and dreams he couldn't remember—if he had indeed dreamt at all.

Tugging the heavy comforter over his shoulder, he closed his eyes and rolled onto his stomach to drift off. The ticking clock on the wall counted along with him as numbers floated their way through his mind—the only way he could properly fall asleep, for as long as he could remember.

He was almost there, or maybe he really was asleep, when he thought he heard light flute music. Something gently stroked his forehead and hair. His eyelids thrust open and he rolled to his side, pulling the blanket tighter. *Not here. Not now.*

Beside him, from the ground, a shadow rose, growing to a guy's height. "Darrin, you better cut that shit out right now." His voice came out in a rasp.

As the shadow leaned forward, even in the dark, Auden met the whites of the figure's eyes. It wasn't Darrin. Auden's body trembled and the shadow came closer toward him, to where he could see the outline of short hair.

Auden shot up, throwing off the blankets. "Darrin!" he shouted. "Darrin, get in here."

A hand from behind grabbed his hair and yanked it as he flipped on the lights.

Through the lighted bedroom, his eyes were bleary as they tried to focus and find the intruder. But there was no one. The only other person in the room was an image of himself, appearing sharper, in the mirror hanging on the wall. And the door to the room was still shut.

Auden flung open the door and turned on the light in the living room. Darrin was still deep in sleep, lightly snoring.

Approaching the sofa, he nudged Darrin's shoulder. "Hey, I tried calling for you." When his friend didn't stir, he shook his shoulders. "Darrin, wake up."

Groggily, Darrin opened his eyes and searched Auden's face. "Yeah?"

"There's something in your room." After the words left his mouth, he knew he sounded insane. There had been times he remembered when he'd wake up his mom and dad in the middle of the night, thinking his biological dad was there to off him, too, but he'd only told them he couldn't sleep.

Yawning, Darrin sat up. "Aren't we a little too old to be afraid of the dark?"

"Dude, screw off. Something was in there. It touched my face and messed with my hair twice." Auden held up two fingers.

Darrin's dark eyebrow quirked upward. "Are you sure it wasn't a sex dream? Because I'd kind of like to be in that right now. Not yours, my own."

Auden's nostrils flared.

"Fine, fine. Let me get something first." Reaching for the lightsaber beneath the couch, Darrin stood and headed toward the bedroom.

"The lightsaber?" Auden asked, incredulous.

"I need a weapon primed and ready."

As they walked back into the room, Auden only had his two fists. Apparently, he needed a knife, like Lark's.

Still empty.

Darrin yanked open the closet and swished his saber around. Auden knelt and peered beneath the bed. Nothing. He strode to the window and confirmed it was locked.

"Nothing here." Darrin lowered the lightsaber. "You were probably just in one of those in-between states. That happens to me all the time."

"Maybe." But he hadn't been.

When Darrin left the room, Auden unzipped his backpack

and drew out one of the books on schizophrenia. He cracked it open to the page he'd tagged, to the words he'd highlighted over and over.

Paranoia, hallucination, depression, hearing voices, fear, delusions.

Even though he knew the man in black was real, he kept wondering if he wasn't actually inserting him in places he really wasn't. As if the knowledge of the man allowed his brain to conjure images of him that weren't really real. Pushing him down a dark path. Just like his dad.

 # CHAPTER 9

To Lark:

Lyrics from "If You Want My Love" — Cheap Trick

It was only Wednesday, but it felt like it had been weeks. Lark hadn't worked the store by herself before and without Imani there, or even Auden's quiet self, two days had passed slower than a sloth trying to cross the parking lot.

What made it worse than being alone were the scratching noises. They kept coming and going, but no matter where Lark looked, nothing was out of place. She was absolutely sure it was rats, and it had become an annoyance. She'd left a message for Jimbo about that as well as the mirror, but she'd have to wait for him to get back to deal with both.

The sky was overcast as she headed next door to Music Revelations. With a quick glance, she peeked at the laundromat. The stranger with the pork pie hat had officially vanished after dropping off the mirror. She wasn't sure why he hadn't just done that from the beginning, instead of lurking around for days. But maybe the cloaked person with the flute must've had something to do with that.

Inside the music store, Jacee was working the counter. She probably hadn't hired anyone yet—the woman was prickly. Before working at Bubble's, Lark had applied there but hadn't even gotten a call.

Lark strolled to the cassette rack, scanning each case until she found Cheap Trick, which was in the incorrect place.

Plucking out the tape, she cradled it to her chest. After she paid for it and left, she immediately put it into her Walkman and pedaled to her next destination—the video store.

The video store was small and the selection decent, even if it always reeked of moldy carpet. An older man with white hair pulled into a low ponytail worked the counter and welcomed her to the store as she passed him.

She made her way straight to the horror movie section since Imani suggested a scary movie night. They had both seen *A Nightmare on Elm Street* about a billion times, but it was her choice and that five-finger knifed man lured her in. *Sweet nightmares, it shall be.* Two teenage guys from her school—they weren't important enough for her to recall their names—stood hogging the aisle. One was dressed in a pair of shorts and a jacket with his sleeves rolled up. The other's hair was cut into short spikes on top with long, stringy locks in the back. Stringy Hair grabbed the VHS she wanted.

Lark almost ripped it from his hand, but instead, she stood behind them, her foot tapping a rhythm into the faded carpet.

"Nah, that movie's bad, and not in a good way." Jacket snatched the movie from his friend's hand and placed it back behind the paper casing.

This was her moment. Lark pushed between them, plucked the VHS, and started to walk away.

"Hey, I was going to get that," Stringy Hair whined.

"No, don't mess with that one. She'll put all kinds of voodoo all up on your ass," Jacket whispered loud enough for Lark to hear.

Idiots. Just because she wore black didn't make her any sort of witch. Lark stopped and slowly pivoted, holding a fist up. She then opened it with flexed fingers. "Poof."

Stringy Hair swung his hands toward his boy parts with a

karate chop motion. "I don't mind a little poof down here."
He high-fived his friend while roaring with laughter.

"Sorry. If it's too small to see, it won't fit in my hand."
Feeling smug, she walked away and heard one of the guys say
"bitch"—like that would actually offend her.

After checking out the movie, she headed to Imani's place.
Her house was even nicer than Shannon's. A long driveway
led to the two-story home with a wide porch stretching across
the front. Tree after tree sprinkled the yard with blooming
marigolds around each one.

Imani was outside, sprawled across the porch swing as it
gingerly swayed.

"About time you arrived," she called, sitting up. "I
could've picked you up."

"I like to stop the rust from making the bike become
immobile." Lark propped the kickstand down in front of the
porch.

As soon as Imani had come back from the hair show with
her mom on Sunday night, Lark had called her that next
morning to tell her Jimbo had hired Auden. Imani had laughed
like it was the most hilarious thing in the world.

No matter how close Lark was with Imani, she had never
wanted to tell Imani how deep her story with Auden went. It
might not even be a story worth telling in the end. Their
shared lyrics proved Auden was a different person on the
inside, but she didn't know if she could break all his walls
down, even if they were only made of glass.

"Well, come on in. Dad made hamburgers earlier if you
want one." Imani patted her stomach.

Lark's intestines twitched as if they heard Imani mention
food. She was starving. There hadn't been time to take a break
at the store since it had only been her.

She glanced through the back window where Imani's parents were outside in the backyard, swimming in their figure eight pool that looked like a set of boobs. On the couch, Imani's sister, Sheena, lay on her side, snuggled up with a Rainbow Brite blanket and matching doll.

"Go to your room," Imani grunted to her younger sister.

"Nuh-uh. Mom says I don't have to." Sheena sat up, her barrettes at the end of her braids clacking together.

"You're not allowed to watch scary movies," Imani pointed out.

"Mom said I can."

As soon as she'd popped out of the womb, Lark had been able to watch any sort of movie, so she didn't see the big issue.

Imani crossed her arms. "Last time you had nightmares."

"No, I didn't."

"Then don't blame me if you have bad dreams." Imani took the VHS tape from Lark and turned the VCR on.

Not too far into the movie, Sheena left the room to go outside saying the movie was boring, when in reality she looked a little frightened. Recalling Imani's advice, Lark had to agree with her friend—maybe some kids shouldn't watch horror movies.

Lark wished for a moment she had a younger sister. Of course, Beth would've been the kid's mom, so maybe it was better to stick with her aloof older sister and a twin who was not her other half.

She focused back on the TV as a brown-haired guy came across the screen. "I don't know why people think Nancy's boyfriend looks so rad," Lark said.

"Johnny Depp?" Imani asked.

"Yeah." Lark waved her hand in the air dismissively. "But anyway, Robert Englund is choice all the way."

Imani rubbed her chin in contemplation. "Before the Freddy makeup or after?"

Lark pretended to think about it. "Now, now, that's a tough decision... but before the makeup."

"Either way is a no go for me."

"That's because you prefer Nancy."

"Shh!" Imani cupped a hand over Lark's mouth. "I don't want my parents to hear anything. Then they won't let Emilia come back for our senior year."

"You'll have to tell them one day, though." Imani shouldn't have to hide any parts of herself, especially something like this. It made her who she was, and she was perfect. Well, maybe perfect was a stretch, since she didn't find Robert Englund sexy.

"I'll wait as long as possible."

Lark drank the rest of her soda, then headed in the direction of the restroom upstairs. The lights softly flickered when she flushed the toilet. Lining the top of the mirror, the light bulbs flickered again.

She glanced at the light switch, and something silvery flashed in her periphery. She shifted her gaze to the mirror to find it... wobbling? Lark placed her hands along both sides of the mirror to steady it—something must be shaking the wall behind it. A clinking sound so soft that she almost barely heard it at all came from *inside* the mirror.

Lark pressed her ear to the glass, breathing deeply in and out, and listened to the barely audible notes coming from a flute. She jerked away and came face to face with only her familiar self. The red lipstick had practically worn off, and her brown hair looked a tangled mess from the bike ride. Taking a hard swallow, she ran her hands over her curls to tame them down a notch.

Somewhere in this room—in this house, following her around—was something unnatural.

Lark flew down the stairs in a rush, rounding the bottom of the steps, and entered the living room. "Imani! Can you come here for a second?"

"Huh?" Imani asked. Sheena lay snuggled up beside her sister. She must've come back inside to watch the rest of the horror film, just to prove she could. *A brave little girl, that one.*

"I mean, I need you to come here really quick." She didn't want to say anything in front of Sheena.

Imani wiggled out from her sister and met Lark beside the stairs. "What's going on?"

"I've been seeing and hearing things. Upstairs, just now, I heard 'Space Oddity' playing from a flute somewhere inside your mirror."

"Um, what?" Imani glanced up the stairs, mouth open, and started up them.

"I don't know exactly, but I think there's a ghost or something following me around. Jimbo said to leave it alone," Lark whispered as she followed Imani to the bathroom.

The bathroom light was still on, not flickering. Imani casually walked to the mirror and placed her ear against it. "I don't hear anything."

"That's because it stopped." Lark's heart still fluttered in her chest as she looked from the lights, to the mirror, to the walls.

Imani pulled back and focused on Lark. "Explain it to me."

Lark went into as much detail as she could about everything that had happened, from the creep in black, to the flute player in the cloak, the flashing lights, the *music*.

Biting her lip, Imani rested her shoulder on the door. "I'd say there's a possibility you may be haunted, but you could also be insane." Lark remembered Auden saying he didn't believe in ghosts, only people being delusional or crazy.

"Since you're my friend and you know I like the strange, I'm going to give you the benefit of the doubt." Imani wrapped her arm around Lark's shoulders. "But I'm not sure what to do about it. We'll have to get with Jimbo when he gets back since he knows more about the spiritual stuff. I'm sure the three of us can form some sort of circle and get rid of it."

Lark nodded, knowing if anyone would have her back, Imani always would.

On the way home, the pitch-black of the night already surrounded the town. A few dazzling stars lit the sky along with a thin sliver of a moon. The North Star guided her back to home-sweet-trailer park. If only the star could lead her elsewhere. Lark kept her eye out for anything out of the ordinary, but nothing out of the norm came.

She parked her bike around the back of the trailer, noticing the lights were still on as they illuminated the windows. Lark found Beth sprawled in her recliner—passed out. The ashtray sat full of cigarettes and three empty beer cans rested on the side table.

Doing her good deed for the day, Lark dumped the cigarette butts into the trash along with the beer cans.

"Thanks, baby doll," Beth slurred in her raspy voice.

"Not a problem. Goodnight." She was used to picking up

after Beth, and she was old enough now to not need her mom like she used to.

A mom who passed out drunk and missed her so-called boyfriend trying to rape her oldest daughter. If Paloma and Lark hadn't ganged up on him and called the police, things would've been very different for Robin. Beth would always be Beth, no matter how hard she tried—or Lark wished—to be different.

No wonder Robin didn't want anything to do with them anymore—everything was a reminder of a life that wasn't really one at all. But why couldn't she include her sisters who had helped her? She didn't want to start thinking about Robin not talking to her because that kind of pain was worse than anything.

The light shone from underneath Paloma's door, so Lark stopped and knocked.

"Yeah?" Paloma answered.

Lark opened the door. "You're not at Cheryl's again?"

"Does it look like I am?" Her sister answered with irritation.

Someone's not in a good mood. She left without another word. As soon as she walked into her own room, Lucy hopped off the bed and rubbed her small head against Lark's shin. Scooping her up, she held the cat in the air. "At least *someone's* happy to see me."

Setting Lucy on the floor, she tossed her backpack beside the mattress and got ready for bed, then pulled out a record from the sleeve and started it on the player. She tried not to think about what happened at Imani's house as she turned off the light and slipped beneath the covers. Lucy hopped on the mattress and curled up into a furball beside Lark's face as she drifted off.

A sharp prick on Lark's foot woke her. She rolled over. Then something feather-light brushed against her foot.

"Lucy, stop. I'm sleeping."

Something jabbed her foot this time, causing her to spring up in bed.

A shadowy form dashed across her room, but all she could see was curly hair bouncing. Her body shook as she stood and scrambled to the light switch.

Bright light lit up the room, as she frantically searched every crevice. Empty. She ran to the closet and pushed through her clothes. Nothing. Lucy still laid beside the pillow, just now lifting her head, waking from sleep.

It was late, but she hurried out of her room to Paloma's. Her sister's light was still on, and she could hear her talking to someone. Without knocking, Lark shoved open the door. "Paloma, did you hear or see anything… or anyone?"

"Geez, can you knock next time?" she barked.

"Did you see a person with curly hair?" Lark waved a hand with desperation through the air.

"No. I've been on the phone. What's wrong with you?"

"Nothing." Lark slinked back into the hallway, shutting the door behind her. Leaning against the wall, she took several breaths before padding back to her room. She found Lucy no longer resting on the pillow—the cat stood on all four haunches, hissing toward her dresser.

"Lucy!" Lark rushed to pick her up and calm her down. The cat went spastic when Lark's hands wrapped around her, hissing once again. A claw struck Lark's hand and she released her. Lucy ran to the other side of the room, sharp teeth bared.

Lark's hand throbbed, but it hadn't drawn any blood. "Why are you acting like this? It's just me. I know you don't prefer hanging out with Paloma or Beth, but if that's what you want."

The cat's gaze met hers, as if just now recognizing that it was Lark talking to her. She scampered back and Lark lifted her up. "It's okay. There's something strange going on around me, but it'll get fixed."

After setting Lucy down on the bed, Lark examined the bottom of her foot and the slight reddish tinge to it.

It was real. She was being haunted.

CHAPTER 10

To Auden:
Lyrics from "The Warrior" - Scandal, Patty Smyth

Over the entire week, just like at Darrin's, each night something tugged at Auden's hair. He hadn't caught sight of anyone when he'd tried to stay awake, but after he'd fallen asleep and felt them, they'd disappear before he could see anything. The lights always stayed on.

He wasn't sure where his logic was at currently, but he wasn't going to be his dad.

His finger stopped on a page of his book that highlighted ways to prevent schizophrenia symptoms.

Don't use drugs. He didn't.

Avoid abusive or traumatic situations.

Keep strong social ties. He had Darrin, and he would be more social with Lark.

Manage stress. Easier said than done.

He reclined his body against the wall and let the words Lark had once written from "The Warrior" repeat in his head.

Friday morning, Auden pried his eyes open, knowing that meant seeing Lark. As he went to sit up, his body tightened, and he couldn't move. He tried to pick up his arm but couldn't. His heart had to be pounding in his chest. Even though he couldn't *feel* it. With one hard jerk, his whole body leapt forward and plummeted to the carpet. His head struck the floor—hard. A harsh throb struck his temple.

During the night, there had been no secret touches to his face or stolen hair tugs. But now he'd woken up with his body in a frozen state?

Lifting his head, he shifted his eyes around his room until they stopped on things that shouldn't be there. Everything in him stilled. When his lungs finally decided to expand again, Auden shook his head to clear his vision. Things weren't the same as the night before. Records were sprawled across the floor, each vinyl pulled out of its case and set perfectly in the center on top of it. His closet door was wide open with clothes lined up on the floor, as though picked out and arranged for the week. His box of Lark's lyrics was now on his bedside table with the letters peeking out from inside.

Without blinking, he stared at the box for as long as humanly possible, which felt like ten minutes. Finally, he shut his eyelids, pretending everything was fine—as if he didn't need to see a counselor.

Auden got to his feet and threw on his clothes. Not ones from the floor. After tugging on his red sneakers, he palmed his keys and jetted out of the nightmare, stopping in the hallway outside his brothers' shared room. "Were you two in my room last night?" he asked, hands twitching at his sides as they tapped his jeans with nervousness.

"Why do you keep asking that lately?" Zach flipped to his side on the bottom bunk with a frown, his dark hair rumpled and sticking up everywhere.

"I just need to know, okay?" Auden tried to sound fine, but the words came out desperate.

"No," his brothers answered simultaneously.

Their mom rounded the corner at the sound of their voices. "You need to eat something before you leave."

"I'll pick something up on the way, Mom." The house was becoming claustrophobic, and he had to escape.

He headed outside and sped off in Jenny, his fingers tapping the steering wheel as he cranked the music all the way up. Something moved in his periphery, and Auden shifted his gaze to the rearview mirror but only the reflection of his tired hazel eyes stared back. It must've been a weird glare on the blue car behind him.

After almost passing the entrance to the parking lot of the strip mall, he slammed on his brakes and turned in, barely missing colliding with another car.

"I need to calm the fuck down," he mumbled in a jittery voice.

Maybe he should start smoking again or just leave town that night, but he knew whatever he was seeing or feeling would only follow him.

Glancing at his watch, Auden noticed he'd arrived at work an hour early. He considered driving next door to McDonald's, but instead he decided to walk. He bought four different breakfast sandwiches, two hash browns, and two orange juices—more than necessary.

He brought the food back to Bubble's and sat with his back propped against the glass. As he shakily took a bite of the greasy sausage biscuit, he stared at the laundromat. The ski mask guy wasn't there. Had the stranger been out there at all since he dropped off that mirror? He didn't know, but with him gone, everything had become worse.

"You're here early." A set of wheels rolled in front of him.

Auden's gaze trained on Lark's red lips. "Yeah. Don't want to get fired again." He glanced at his watch, feeling a little less unsettled now that she was here. "It's only 9:40, so it looks like you're early too."

Lark got off her bike and put the kickstand down. "Couldn't sleep." Her eyes looked as tired as he felt, but he didn't want to start talking about sleep situations. He wanted distractions, not reminders.

"Tell me about it." He handed her a bag of food. "I wasn't sure what you liked."

She opened the bag and sifted through. "So you bought three sandwiches?"

Standing, he crumpled the wrappers from the sandwich and hash brown. "Well, I'm going to eat one more."

"Is one a biscuit and sausage?"

"There was, but I ate it."

"That's fine. I like a good mystery." Sticking her hand into the bag, she dug out a sandwich and sat on the cement. "Come back down and sit at our breakfast table."

He took a seat beside her and grabbed another sandwich. Her hair was windblown, and he couldn't control the rapid beat of his heart when he looked at her.

After they finished eating, it was time to go inside. As he sat behind the counter, a rush of calm pushed away his feelings from the morning despite the animal heads everywhere with eyes that seemed to be watching him.

A glimpse of red caught his attention as Lark's delicate hand slid the notepad in front of him. He tried not to smile as he placed it into his back pocket. Lark had already pulled out another one of her books with a girl on the cover staring out of a window.

"Have you seen the man who dropped off the mirror again?" he asked.

"No," she said. "I'm just waiting for Jimbo to get back to ask him about the mirror."

Auden's palms beaded with sweat as his mind swirled once more—the wash of calm depleted—so he grabbed the dusting supplies.

"I was going to do that later." Lark looked up from her book. "You don't have to worry about it."

"I can't sit still today, I guess." All he kept going back to was how things were sprawled across his room. He must've somehow done it himself, possibly during sleep...

Her eyes narrowed at him, scanning his body up and down. "Are you on something?"

"No..."

"Bend down," Lark said as she stood in front of him.

He lowered his eyebrows in confusion but bent his knees, so his face was in front of hers. His breathing increased as his eyes stared into her brown ones. With her right hand, Lark reached forward and widened his left eyelid. Before he could move back, she stuck her tongue out and tapped his eyeball with it.

Jerking back, he covered his eye. "Why did you do that?" It felt like she had just tickled his eyeball with her tongue. "Also, I'm pretty sure it's completely unsanitary."

"Just giving you a distraction," she said and took her seat again as if she'd just gifted him a pony.

"That's so... weird isn't even the right word." He chuckled, finding her strangeness a bit intriguing.

The shop wasn't really dusty, but he cleaned it anyway, thinking that at least four hours had to have passed. In fact, it had only been thirty minutes.

Auden sat back down beside his lyric partner. "Talk to me,

Lark. Distract me some more." He held up a hand. "Without licking eyeballs."

She side-eyed him, slowly turning her head as if he'd lost his mind. Maybe he had.

"You want me to talk to you?" she asked, like it was the most ridiculous request in the world.

"Yes, pour your whole life story out to me right now. I don't care. Just keep talking to me." It sounded more like a declaration of love than a plea to keep him sane.

Closing her book, she scooted it aside. "All right. But only if you start."

"My father killed my mother when I was two," he blurted out.

Lark drew in a deep breath, her eyes wide. "Okay, I didn't mean we had to go that deep, but go on."

"That's it. That's my story."

"I think you can do better than that."

Auden didn't say anything. Everything in him wanted to continue, but he didn't. He was scared of letting Lark get too close, of knowing what she would think. He must've hesitated too long, because she nodded, as if she expected him not to continue. In that moment, he didn't want to hide himself from her. And he knew it would feel good to finally get things off his chest.

So he told her about how he lived with his aunt who he felt was really his mom, even though she wasn't. Lark didn't look at him as if she was sickened by what he'd said. It was so different from Drew, who hadn't even known about the situation with his parents.

Lark's lack of judgment—rather her soft expression of understanding—spiked something new through his veins.

"My dad died while drunk driving and killed another man

who was also driving drunk." She shifted uneasily on the stool. "But my dad was never around, so it's all okay."

Auden almost believed her about her feelings of being all right—almost. There wasn't a single note in her voice that hinted it was a lie. But by the way she blinked, he knew it was. Even if she didn't.

Her confession pulled at something in him, but he let her continue. "So I may have only been neglected with the mom I had growing up, but I've felt like an orphan for most of my life."

The sound of fingernails slowly sliding down the wall scratched behind him. He whirled around.

Not here. Not here. Not with her.

Lark grabbed his arm, preventing the collision. "It's just the rats."

"Rats?"

"Yeah, they've been making sounds all week from behind the mirror and clock."

His shoulders sagged in relief as he stared at his reflection in the mirror, but something didn't feel right—like the expression on his face wasn't the one he was currently wearing. It was all in his head—it had to be.

Lark must've noticed the change in him. Lifting her backpack from the floor, she set it between them. "Why don't you pick something to listen to? It'll be a good distraction."

For the remaining time, he listened to Lark's Walkman and waited on customers as a diversion. One such customer kept asking questions about the miracle remedy wall, forcing him to talk out of his ass with that one.

There were only about ten minutes left before closing when the cowbell rang. In walked Darrin wearing a fedora hat with his skateboard in hand. Electric green locks peeked out from the corners of his hat. He'd changed the color again.

"My girl!" Darrin shouted to Lark, brushing past Auden.

Lark looked at him with a warm smile. "Hey, you colored your hair, and I dig your hat."

"You can have it, if you want." Darrin pulled the hat from his head and rested it on top of Lark's curls. She pushed on the top to set it in place. Auden wanted to rip the hat off and throw it across the room, even though she looked killer wearing it.

Darrin's eyes darted to the side, and he took off in the direction of a table filled with unusual clocks. One clock was built upside down with the face at the bottom, another had skeletal feet attached all around it, and the last contained different animal furs for the outer layers, while eyeballs rested on the moving hands. But Darrin chose to stop in front of the small guillotine. "Does this really work?" He placed a finger where a neck would go if it was life-size.

"Don't pull it!" Lark shouted and hopped off her stool, charging forward to protect Darrin's finger. "You'll lose it, I swear. We've tested it on Barbie."

"Barbie?" Auden asked, a chuckle escaping his mouth.

"Yeah, Imani brought her sister's Barbie doll up here, and it cut clean through the neck." She did a karate chop gesture.

Darrin pulled his finger out and petted it. "I need these fingers, if you know what I mean."

Auden rolled his eyes and Lark wrinkled her nose.

The phone rang and Lark hurried to answer it.

"You want to invite Lark to the park to come watch us skate?" Darrin asked, elbowing Auden in the arm.

"You mean to watch *you* skate?" Auden actually wouldn't

mind if Lark came, and he knew the longer he was around her, the weaker for her he would become.

Lark hung up the phone and strolled in front of them.

"Lark, you going to come watch us skate?" Darrin asked, grinning.

Sometimes Auden wanted to strangle Darrin—and right then was one of those times. The thought crossed his mind that if he didn't do some damage control, Lark would probably fall for Darrin. She still had his damn hat on, for fuck's sake. But instead, Auden just kept quiet, staring at her with a blank expression.

"Um, where at?" she asked.

Darrin leaned on the counter, shifting closer to Lark. "The park."

"Yeah, I'll meet you there."

"You're going to pedal behind the van?" Auden asked. *Why didn't I just offer her a ride instead of saying that?*

"That's my means of transportation, so yep."

Before Auden could correct himself, Darrin butted in again, "We can give you a ride, just put your bike in the back of Jenny."

For confirmation she looked at Auden, and he shrugged. "Yeah, it'll be faster that way."

Lark removed Darrin's hat from her head and plopped it back down on top of his green combed-over Mohawk. Auden felt as if steam was brewing in his chest.

Darrin and Auden went to get Jenny then pulled the van to the front of the store for Lark to load her bike in.

"What the hell was that in there, man?" Darrin asked, messing with the wheels on his skateboard.

"I don't know what you're talking about." Auden didn't wait for a response as he stepped out of Jenny and opened the back door for Lark's bike. She started lifting it, but Auden took the bike from her and laid it down on its side.

"Oh, I forgot to tell you to go ahead and come in next week Tuesday through Saturday," Lark said. "I think you've done well enough."

"Really?" He quirked a brow.

"It doesn't take rocket science to work here, but you've succeeded."

"Cool, I'll be here."

Before they could say anything else, Darrin got out of the passenger side to sit on the floor of the van. Lark relaxed up front.

"You can pick something to listen to on the radio," Auden said when he sat down in the driver seat. "It doesn't take cassettes, or I'd let you pop in one of yours."

"Yeah, okay." She stopped for a second on Quiet Riot and started laughing. "No, I can't do that." She immediately changed the channel, and he could've kissed her for that. Their music made his ears bleed. Tom Petty drifted out through the speakers, and she leaned back in the seat, staring out the window as if she was absorbing the scenery, even though she'd probably seen it a million times.

They arrived at the park where a few other skaters were already doing tricks on the stairs. Other than that, it seemed deserted—only trees and empty swings. Darrin lit a cigarette then took off and did an ollie on his skateboard.

"Where's yours?" Lark stared at Auden's empty hands.

"My what?" It took him a second to realize what she was talking about. "Oh, I don't really skate anymore." When he thought about it, he didn't do a whole lot of anything these days, besides listening to music.

"Some of us aren't meant to skate." Lark smiled.

"Oh, he's good," Darrin said, riding back up. "Show her." He shoved the skateboard into Auden's hands.

Auden held up his finger. "One time." He took off toward the stairs, the wind striking his face, and brought the board up, letting it grind down the handrail, then he landed on the ground with a final kickflip. Picking up the skateboard, he ascended the stairs, breathing heavily, and handed it back to Darrin. A rush of nostalgia washed over him, but it wasn't important to him anymore.

Lark's jaw hung open. "I guess you *are* meant to skate."

"You want to try?" Auden asked.

"Maybe if I still had my pink roller skates from when I was nine."

"Pink, huh? I would've expected black." He grinned. Catching himself, he pursed his lips together, but he couldn't bury the smile.

"The options were minuscule for kids." She sat down on the ground and he scooted beside her, his knee almost brushing hers. He had been much closer to her before—much, much closer, but this felt more intimate.

Lark unzipped her backpack and swapped out tapes. "Here, try this." She set the headphones over his head, her fingernails skimming the tips of his ears. A large part of him wished her hands were touching him elsewhere.

Auden lay back against the grass, listening to the music while staring up at the sky. He tugged the back of her jacket and she slid down next to him with her ear pressed against his so they could listen together.

With the sky above, Lark beside him, and music in his ears, Auden forgot about everything else going on in his life. He let his two addictions—music and Lark—sweep him away from it all.

CHAPTER 11

Lark stared at herself in Imani's bathroom mirror. She'd found a maid costume at the thrift store and had teased her curls to make them even wilder. Earlier, Darrin had met Auden at Bubble's again and re-asked her if she wanted to go to the concert with him and Auden.

Over the past couple of days, she'd found that Auden got quieter and quieter each time Darrin was around. For the most part, his expression would stay neutral, but sometimes she could pick up flickers of irritation. There was a slip in Auden's expression, and he'd seemed slightly annoyed that Darrin had invited her. She wasn't sure if he legit didn't want her to go or if it was because Darrin had asked.

Leaning closer to the mirror, she reapplied her red lipstick, then added more black eyeliner than usual to get the look of Magenta's character from *The Rocky Horror Picture Show*.

The night before had been nice with Auden watching Darrin skate, and after today at work, maybe they were becoming actual friends beyond just sharing lyrics. She had to admit, though, she still loved their quiet, yet loud, written conversations, where she could debate her response to the song he'd chosen. As soon as she'd gotten to work, she had casually slid the red notebook to him—their new work tradition.

Staring at the mirror, Lark stirred the mascara wand, trying to gather as much as she could since the bottle was running on empty and appeared rather clumpy.

She focused on her eyelashes, gliding the mascara wand over them, when the eye before her—her reflection—blinked. How was that possible? A soft gasp escaped her mouth as the wand fell from her hand into the sink, black specks splattering over the porcelain. She backed into the door, never taking her eyes off the mirror.

Lark breathed in, then exhaled a nervous laugh. She needed to pull herself together. Since the evening the silhouette had poked her foot, she could've sworn whispering and feather-light caresses against her face had happened each night. She'd never been able to catch sight of a figure again, so she started sleeping with the closet light on. Being afraid of the dark shouldn't be a thing at seventeen but being haunted changed things.

The worst was when she'd awoken feeling paralyzed.

Lark opened her eyes, the hissing of Lucy emanating from the other side of the room. She told the cat to relax, but as she attempted to sit up, she couldn't move any part of her body. Inside her head, she screamed and screamed, as though it was the end of the world.

She was dead. That was it. Until finally her scream burst out and she rolled to the floor.

"What's going on?" Paloma shouted, throwing open the door.

Lark pushed up from the carpet and studied her sister's wide eyes and downturned lips. For the first time in a long time, Paloma appeared truly worried. And Lark didn't want her worrying about her.

"Nothing, just a stupid nightmare."

Lark wondered now if the supernatural could really enter one's body and use it as a vessel?

She pressed her ear to the mirror, straining to hear flute music or voices, but the only other sound in the room was her breath.

"Dammit," Lark grunted when she noticed streaks of black mascara under her right eye. Turning on the warm water, she rubbed the excess away and tossed the mascara into the trashcan.

A knock on the door made her jump.

"Are you ready yet?" Imani asked.

Releasing a sigh, she opened the door. "Yeah, I'm ready."

Imani practically radiated the character Columbia, with her gold sequined jacket and matching top hat, striped shorts, and red bowtie. She had spent a while taming her hair by slicking it back, and Lark missed the dandelion shape.

Imani's parents didn't mind them going to the theater so late at night, on the condition they come straight home after. Her mom knew how long the movie was, so they were granted fifteen minutes afterward to get home.

Leaning close to Lark's ear, Imani had whispered, "She'll be asleep way before then." A point proven when both her parents were already asleep before they even left.

But as Lark took a seat in the passenger side of Imani's car, she still couldn't shake the weird feeling from the bathroom. Her reflection had taken on a life of its own.

Imani started the engine and looked over at Lark. "What happened now?"

"In the bathroom I could've sworn something strange happened with my reflection." She paused and glanced at Imani. "Has that ever happened to you?"

"What do you mean?" Imani watched over her shoulder while backing out of the driveway.

"I mean, like seeing yourself wink." Lark had never felt her eyelid move.

"I get déjà vu a lot but never anything more than that."

"I feel like I'm drowning right now—more than drowning —and no one else could possibly understand." She sighed. "It sounds crazy saying it out loud, but I'd rather this be a ghost thing than me actually going insane."

"You're not insane. I'm not open to any sort of spiritual gateway, but Sheena claims two monsters live in her room." She placed a hand on Lark's shoulder, massaging it a bit.

"Sheena's eight," Lark reasoned. For all she knew, the monsters were imaginary friends. Paloma had all sorts of them when she was younger. And she preferred them all over Lark.

"So? Just because I can't see something, doesn't mean it isn't there. I believe you." Imani slid her hand down to Lark's wrist. "Just a few more days until Jimbo gets back. You know you can stay here whenever you like."

"Thanks." Lark needed Jimbo's expert advice because the books hadn't been helping very much. But one had said that ghosts could touch people who are susceptible, which maybe explained the nightly visits.

They pulled into the theater's full parking lot, then made way for the entrance. It was packed with people, most dressed up as characters while others sported lingerie-styled outfits for the occasion.

"Are you going to do the live performance of Rocky Horror one day?" Lark asked, smoothing out the skirt of her maid costume, attempting to brighten the mood.

"I've been thinking about it." Imani adjusted her hat, trying to get the perfect tilt to the side. "You?"

Lark fine-tuned the front of Imani's hat, tugging it down further, then positioning it slightly crooked. "Only if I can come in on an actual motorcycle like Eddie."

Imani sang a line from "Hot Patootie (Bless My Soul)," and Lark sang the next set of hyper lyrics right back.

After they bought their tickets and headed inside, Lark turned to Imani. "Can you save us seats? I need to hightail it to the restroom first."

"You got it!" Imani said, turning toward the theater door as Lark scampered toward the facilities.

No one was inside when she walked into the fairly clean restroom. Lark padded into one of the stalls, but immediately backed out when the toilet was filled with tissue. Thankfully, the next one wasn't worse.

As she grabbed several pieces of toilet paper, a heavy stomping of feet sounded across the tile floor. Clomp. Clomp. Clomp. Peeking below the door, she watched as two black boots matching hers ran past the stall.

As Lark flushed the toilet, a hard bang reverberated. She flinched. And then another, and another—the person slapped each stall door, then stopped in front of hers. Lark's breathing slowed during the brief pause. Through the slit of the door, an eye peered at her. Lark's heart caught in her throat. Someone was out of their damn mind, and it wasn't her.

Suddenly, a hard bang erupted against her door, followed by rapid pounding with alternating hands before the person ran away with a high-pitched giggle. The knife was already in Lark's pocket. Since it was late, she wanted it in there instead of her backpack.

She flicked the knife open but kept it hidden as she

decided to slip out. Slowly, she unlatched the lock and opened the door with a long creak. She took a few steps forward, hesitant. Defiant. Tonight, she wasn't going to deal with anyone's shit. A flute note, brief and low, sounded from behind her. Lark whirled around, only to find the tiled wall. Her breathing increased, up and up. The instrumental sound had been so soft, but it was gone now.

From the corner of the room, the door squeaked open and Lark clutched her knife tighter. She released it when a lady in tight jeans and seventies feathered hair like Farrah Fawcett strolled in wearing a pair of sandals—not boots. Lark let out a heavy sigh and closed the blade. People could get rowdy during the movie, and whoever had been in there was obviously overhyped and most likely on some kind of drug.

After rinsing her hands, Lark rounded the corner with an eye out for anything suspicious. Instead, Lark caught sight of someone familiar to her left. She did a double take, then slowly took two steps back when her eyes rested on chestnut hair slicked back and a blue jean vest over an AC/DC shirt.

Auden smiled a small close-lipped smile with the left corner curved up—his version of a real one, she supposed.

"What are you doing?" she asked, taking a step toward him.

"Waiting for Darrin." He tilted his head in the direction of the men's restroom.

"I thought you were supposed to be at a concert."

"We were." He ran his middle finger across his lower lip. "It ended already."

"So you came here?" Her heart sped up in her chest but then slowed down at his next words.

"Darrin's idea." Auden's gaze fell to her costume, and even though she'd worn black pantyhose, they were still sheer, and the skirt part was incredibly short for her. His eyes lingered on her legs before shifting back up.

When the shock of seeing Auden wore off and she remembered the restroom weirdo, Lark pointed back at the door. "Did you see some wild girl come out of there?" But she had a feeling that the girl was another thing that had to do with the haunting.

"No, I just got here a few seconds before you came out."

He stepped closer to her and reached for her backpack, his chest mere inches from hers. She felt a light vibration as he unzipped the pouch on the front side of her backpack. Pulling out the red notebook from his back pocket, he tucked it inside and zipped up the pouch.

Tilting her head up, she locked eyes with him. "Thanks."

"That's where you were going to put it anyway, right?" His minty breath gently hit her mouth.

"You know me so well."

"I think I may be starting to."

A heavy arm wrapped around Lark's shoulder. She wanted it to be Auden's. But it was Darrin with his other arm curved around Auden. "So, here we all are. Where's Imani?"

"She's saving seats," Lark said, wishing Darrin would've stayed indisposed for a while longer. "Well, seats for me and her."

"Perfect." Darrin's green hair was twisted and bent into a messy Mohawk. Instead of all the pieces being straight up, locks of hair pointed in different directions.

They started toward the theater room and Lark's stomach fluttered as she walked next to Auden. She wanted to fling those butterflies against the wall because that meant she was feeling too much, and she liked it and loathed it all at the same time. Truthfully, she *really* liked it.

Imani sat toward the middle of the theater, and Darrin hopped over the seat, landing perfectly beside her. "My girl."

"Sorry, I'm taken." Imani smiled. "Also, green hair isn't my thing."

"You wound me so." He gripped his chest with mock sadness.

Lark was starting to believe that Darrin considered every girl to be his girl. Well, Imani would never be his. Besides, he had plenty of other directions to veer off in.

As the movie started, Lark and Auden took the two empty seats directly behind them. She hoped this would be the perfect opportunity to take her away from the paranormal. Lark, Imani, and Darrin were super into it. When "The Time Warp" came on, Lark elbowed Auden who was standing beside her stiffer than a board. "Do the dance!"

He elbowed her back. "I'll just watch you."

"Do it!" she yelled over the music and elbowed him again.

Auden rolled his eyes. "Fine." He followed the directions on the movie screen, appearing a little looser than before.

After the song ended, Lark caught a glimpse of teeth. "Is that a smile I see?"

His smile spread. "Could be."

"Mm-hmm. 'The Time Warp' can make anyone feel good." She was practically beaming, creating her own type of light.

For the rest of the movie, they watched, sang along with the songs—or she and Imani did. Auden didn't choose to join in with the singing parts or maybe he didn't know the words. But toward the end, Auden tugged her jacket sleeve, stood, and tilted his head toward the exit.

Furrowing her eyebrows, Lark got up and followed him until they turned the corner. Without hesitation, he backed her up against the wall, and his lips pressed against hers. She kissed him back, desperation bubbling between them. She'd missed his lips, missed the way he could crowd her with his body while still allowing room to breathe. Missed his hands on her hips… All the water in the ocean couldn't quench her thirst, but salt water wouldn't help anyone. Melted glaciers couldn't even satisfy her needs, either, at least not in the way Auden did in that moment.

Lark tugged him closer, but it wasn't close enough. She kissed along his jaw, making her way to his ear. "Why did you come tonight?"

"Darrin wanted to," Auden murmured.

"That's the only reason?" She nibbled the tender spot right below his ear, and a deep shiver coursed through him.

"Yeah."

Lark tasted his lie, unaware one little fib could taste so good. Heavy footfalls, thumping to the music of the rolling credits, drew near, and she shifted away from him. He brushed a thumb across her hand as she scooted closer to the carpeted wall.

"There's my girl *and* my man." Darrin shot both Lark and Auden a grin when he spotted them.

"Just waiting for you two slowpokes," Lark said, leading the way out the theater room and into the parking lot, while sneaking glances at Auden.

People were so multi-faceted, and Lark found that her personality always seemed to reflect the company she was keeping—chipper with Imani, sarcastic around Paloma, bitchy around Beth. But with Auden, she couldn't put together the right words. Different as they were, those facets were all a small bit of her—just as there were different versions of Auden. She wanted to accept all of them—no one was perfect.

Emotions were a tumultuous thing. No one could ever know Lark better than Lark herself, but if she truly let Auden in, he might get pretty damn close.

Yet she couldn't bring herself to tell him what was going on with her, because she didn't want him to see her differently. She thought again about how he'd told her he didn't believe in ghosts, only crazy people. What if it affected their growing bond?

"I guess I'll see you at work Tuesday," Lark said to Auden.

"I guess so." Auden gave her his tilted-lip smile and left.

"So what was that about?" Imani asked when they got inside her car and Lark popped the Ramones into the tape player.

"What? Darrin hitting on you?" She knew what Imani was asking, but she didn't know the answer herself.

Imani waved her off. "No. Auden."

"I don't exactly know." She smiled and unzipped her backpack to pull out the notebook. Lyrics from "Back In Black" were scrawled down the page in dark ink. When she finally stopped smiling to herself, she angled her gaze to the car door mirror, but in the lampposts' glare, she could've sworn her reflection was still smiling.

CHAPTER 12

A soft tap on the window woke Auden from his slumber, followed by a click-click sound. Then came a harder knock on the glass. He rolled away from the wall and shuffled across the carpet, hitting his hipbone against the corner of his desk.

Rubbing at the sore spot, Auden moved the curtains to tell Darrin to go home because he had to go to work. The morning light shone against Auden's eyes, and he blinked a few times as his vision focused—no one was there. Only his empty backyard. He unlocked the window and pushed it up, poking his head out and twisting it side to side. Nothing more than grass in need of mowing and two banana trees. His pulse thrummed in his neck as his blood swam faster and faster through his veins. No one was there.

Auden shut the window and lay back on the bed, trying to pretend it hadn't happened, but when another tap, tap, tap came, he jumped out of bed and stumbled across the room to the window. A black cloaked figure stood by the fence. The face was hidden, but he could tell it was a woman by the shape of her body. He stilled, his throat dry, as she raised a flute inside her hood and played it between gloved fingers. One note. Two notes. Then a slowed down version of "Space Oddity" spun through the air. Before he could react, a flash of silver light crackled, and she vanished.

"Wait!" he yelled. This had to be the person he'd seen at the party, spying as he'd almost kissed Lark. The cloak swished in the exact same way.

At the window, she reappeared in front of him and cocked her head. Inside the cloak, he saw nothing. No face. Empty. Invisible. He couldn't breathe, not at all. Auden reached his hand forward, his flesh moving through her, feeling nothing. A flash of light flickered once more, and she disappeared.

Another tapping emanated from somewhere over his right shoulder, and he stumbled back, head whipping to the mirror above his dresser. His lips parted as he stared at the reflection and slowly approached it as if his own image might attack.

Auden's duplicate stared back at him—rumpled hair, tired eyes, and lips now tightly pursed together. From somewhere inside the mirror, voices sprang to life, whispers increasing. He backpedaled into the wall, and everything fell silent.

The past week had been surprisingly quiet, no unexplainable occurrences since he'd discovered all of his belongings rearranged in his room. Things seemed almost back to normal and even his sleep had improved.

I have to make this stop.

He spun around, reaching for his research book and stopped cold as his delusions became concrete in front of him. On the opposite side of the room, his box of memorabilia lay open, the notes between him and Lark spread across the floor. They were arranged in order by the dates he'd written on them. Auden's eyes fell right on "Let's Go Crazy." Next to the notes, laid all of his saved movie ticket stubs, also arranged by date, along with a picture of his real mom.

Auden's hands clenched. He hurried to pick up his things and placed them back inside the box, then shoved it beneath his bed. Grabbing his research book, he flipped it open, and ran his finger down the page to where he'd underlined *no cure* over and over.

He threw the book and sprinted out of his bedroom, straight into his brothers' shared space.

Auden nudged Zach's shoulder. "Were you in my room? Did you... hear anything?"

"No." Zach released a loud yawn, struggling to open his eyes.

Climbing the ladder to the top bunk, Auden shook Nick's shoulder. "If Zach wasn't in my room, did you move any of my stuff?"

"For the last time, no one wants to go into your room, Auden," Nick grumbled, scrunching up his face.

"I believe you." Dejection pumped its way through his veins because, of course, it was only him seeing and hearing these things.

Auden chewed on his lip as he headed to the kitchen. Grappling with his emotions, he poured himself a large glass of orange juice and forced it down before pouring another. He placed two slices of bread into the toaster. The cloaked woman had been so close, the voices so loud. Yet if it were real, someone in the house would've heard something. His parents were still asleep, and he didn't want to bother asking his mom if she'd been in his room to sprawl things across the floor for no reason. She'd probably take him to see the counselor, and he wasn't going to talk to anyone about this.

As he took a bite of toast, it seemed to turn to cement in his throat as he swallowed. He couldn't sit here and eat like everything was all right. In an effort to distract himself, he thought about Lark and their past week working side by side at Bubbles. They hadn't kissed since Saturday night, but they had created their own noise together in the comfortable silence between them. Inventory and their infinite discussions of music had kept them busy. Nothing too deep to people on the outside, but to him, it was as deep as it could get.

Sliding back his chair, Auden grabbed his keys from the counter. It was still early, but he had to get out of the house. He had to get to Bubbles where he actually felt safe—with Lark.

Auden sat in the back of his van, parked in the lot outside the store, until it got closer to ten o'clock. Jitters still clung to him, though he'd relaxed a bit. He pulled out the Kate Bush record and placed it on the player, listening to the track that contained the first song lyrics Lark had written to him. The familiar melody turned his thoughts inward, to how it had all begun.

Drew had ended things months prior to when the lyric writing started, and even though they would still do their thing at parties, he'd discovered that he didn't really care as much as he thought he had.

Auden had walked into math class, the same as always, never realizing that day would be different. He took a seat behind Lark—he had always noticed her but not truly, until that day.

After grading homework, without turning her head, Lark passed his paper back to him—her bright red nail polish stood out against the white sheet. He'd lowered his brows when he noticed the red speech bubble and lyrics written inside from "Running Up That Hill." To the side she'd written, *Kate Bush*, and in that moment, he'd wanted to know how she felt about things, what she had to say.

He bought the album after that.

Each following day, he wanted to twirl her wild curls around his pencil or take her to the back of his van. The lust consumed him—that was all it would ever be.

But now, as he sat alone in the back of his van listening to Kate Bush, he wasn't sure what to call the feeling. Maybe it was still lust, only a different form of it.

A tapping sound, similar to the one he'd heard in his room, cut through the lyrics, and he shoved off the arm of the record player to stop the music, accidentally scraping the record.

His throat tightened as he searched out each window, his gaze finally landing on the rearview mirror. Nothing. He ran his middle finger across his bottom lip as he stared at his own reflection. Shaking his head, he took out his Walkman and got out of the van, pulling the headphones over his ears.

Auden sank down onto the walkway in front of Bubbles, hugging his knees to his chest, hoping the music would squelch the hallucinations. For a brief moment, he'd hoped they'd gone away. Now he knew the truth—they wouldn't. They would only become worse, the same way his father's had.

# CHAPTER 13

To Lark:

Lyrics from "Take On Me" — a-ha

The eerie sound of a flute, the music slowly building, caused Lark to bolt upright in bed. Her eyes searched the sunlit room. A whole week had passed without any random weirdness. One week of what she considered normal. One week of her heart not pounding against her ribs when she saw something... strange. And now this again.

The cassette tapes that were in her backpack now lay scattered across the floor, alphabetized by musician. *Maybe the ghost had a liking to music and order*, she thought, tilting her head to the side. She didn't scream, didn't cry, only sat in stunned silence.

Lark looked toward her closet where a mini skirt and crop-top lay on the floor, a long crucifix necklace resting on top. It was something she'd never wear—only Paloma would choose something like that.

Swallowing hard, she scooped up the cassettes and placed them back into her backpack. Nothing else in her room had been moved.

Lark grabbed her sister's clothing, padded across the hall, and opened Paloma's door, throwing the outfit and necklace on the bed beside her sister. "Hey, did you touch my cassette tapes and put your clothing in my room?"

147

"Hold on, Cheryl." Paloma covered the mouthpiece of the phone. "What?"

"I said, did you take my cassettes out of my backpack?"

"Why would I do that? You have terrible taste in music." Paloma turned around and started talking to her friend again. "So, Cheryl, what did he say?" She could hear the smile in Paloma's voice.

Lark shut the door and found Beth in the kitchen eating a burnt biscuit. "Hey, baby doll. You hungry?" She motioned to a pan lined in aluminum foil with five blackened biscuits remaining on top.

"Did you go through my tapes?" Lark already knew what the answer would be, but she had to be sure.

"Tapes? I only like my records." Beth appeared confused with her face scrunched up.

Lark trudged to the stove, put two blackened biscuits on a plate, and sat at the table across from Beth. Beth poured them both a glass of juice.

"What's going on, baby doll? You look like you've seen a ghost." Beth reached across the table to grasp her hand, but Lark slid it back and tucked it underneath the table.

"I have," she said with a dry tone.

"No one's died in the trailer, so this is a ghost-free zone." *Apparently, Beth is now the holy expert on ghosts and all things paranormal.*

She knew from Jimbo's books that not all ghosts stayed where they'd died. How dumb would that be? If she'd died in a chair somewhere, for example, she wouldn't spend all eternity sitting there. She would be traveling the world. And she would never waste time haunting people.

"I've got a surprise for you." Beth clasped her hands

together. Lark's head jerked up as Beth collected a plastic Kmart bag from the counter and handed it to Lark.

"What is it?" There was enough going on inside her head without having to worry about surprises from Beth. She'd never given Lark anything before—in fact, Beth had forgotten almost all of their birthdays.

"Open it."

The bag crinkled as Lark stuck her hand inside and pulled out a pair of pajamas. It was a white shirt with the roadrunner from *Looney Tunes* plastered on the front. The pants were just as hideous with the coyote chasing the roadrunner with TNT. She didn't even like the show when she was five. Why would she like it now?

"Um, all right." Lark closed the bag and set it on the table.

Beth's smile fell. "You could be a little more grateful."

"Thanks." Lark attempted to smile, but knew it probably appeared like a grimace.

Beth's face beamed. "I got your sister the same pair, so the two of you can match."

Lark palmed her forehead and shook her head. "That's fabulous," she said with as much false enthusiasm as she could muster. Again, Beth should've known that even when Paloma and Lark were younger, they never wore matching clothes— not once, unless there was some little-known evidence some- where in the non-existent photographs from their infancy. But then again, Beth would never really know since there were no photographs of them anywhere. It stung when she was younger, but now that hollow spot was filled with music.

After putting her plate and glass in the sink, Lark stopped at Paloma's room and tossed the plastic bag on her bed. Her sister, now off the phone, painted her nails a vibrant hot pink.

"I hear you got one of these gracious gifts from Beth too."

Placing the polish brush back into the container, Paloma narrowed her eyes at Lark. "Don't even start. She's been nice lately."

"Like I said before, you can't erase seventeen years of shit and say it's good." *Apparently, Paloma can.*

"Same as I said before. She's trying." Paloma lightly blew on her nails, moving them back and forth in front of her lips.

"Beth never actually apologized for how she's acted over the years to us," Lark whisper-shouted. "She's pretending she never cared more about drugs, sex with strange men, and being gone for long periods of time. She still went back to her old ways, even after Robin could've been raped!"

"Robin didn't have to pretend like we didn't exist once she moved out, either." Paloma sighed. Lark shoved away the pain from those words.

"Okay, fine. For you, Paloma, I'll try and keep my bitchy thoughts about Beth to myself—unless she royally screws up again."

"She's lasted longer than I expected." Paloma shrugged.

Lark picked up the plastic Kmart bag from the bed. "Tonight, we can be real twins."

"God, I hated that cartoon." Paloma rolled her eyes.

"At least we have that in common."

Lark showered, threw on a pair of clothes, and left for Bubble's under a clear sky. Yet the more and more she traveled, the clouds grew darker, threatening to release their fury. She pedaled faster, hoping to make it to the store before a downpour.

The one downfall of having a bike—rain. Lark should've packed an extra pair of clothing just in case, but the weather hadn't looked bad when she'd left the trailer. Finally, the parking lot slid into view, and she quickened her pace until she made it onto the sidewalk. Someone was already there—Auden—sitting beneath the overhang. The moment Lark pulled up beside him, the rain began to pour in earnest, filling the air with its earthy smell.

"You're lucky you missed getting wet," he said, lowering his headphones.

"I know." Lark let out a heavy breath, pressed the kickstand down, and lifted her headphones right as the chorus of "Take On Me" drifted into her ears. At least she was having good luck with the music in her life.

"I can give you a ride if you ever need one." His voice was soft and assured, the usual nervous wavering absent.

"You probably don't want to come to my side of town." She was sure no one did except Paloma's friend Cheryl or Imani.

"Why's that?" he asked, one dark eyebrow rising.

Lark hesitated, but the words tumbled out anyway. "I live in a trailer park."

"And?"

"And... I don't know." She let out a nervous laugh that didn't sound like her at all. Why should she care what anyone thought of where she lived? She didn't care about what anyone thought of her bike, the way she dressed, or anything else for that matter. *Yet, I do care enough to not tell him about my supernatural problem.* She needed the Ghostbusters to come out already.

Auden's fingers thumped and padded the sides of his jeans, his face pale. He didn't seem a hundred percent okay anymore—he had the same look as the previous week. Like how she'd felt this morning.

"Are you all right, Auden?" She stepped closer to him, biting the inside of her cheek.

"Yeah, why wouldn't I be?" The speed of his answer told her more than his words, as did the flexing of his hands.

Lark reached for his fingers and gently squeezed them, his hand relaxing in hers. She didn't know if he was thinking about his family like he'd confessed to her in the store before, but she left it alone and unlocked the door to Bubble's. When she flipped on the light, her body froze in place as her eyes surveyed the topsy-turvy store. The plants were on the left instead of the right. The artsy crafts made with doll pieces were at the small table instead of the larger one. The seed rack was relocated to the middle of the room. Shrunken heads dangled from the center rack when they should've been on the far-left one. *Everything* had been switched around.

Auden, speechless, followed her to the miracle remedy wall where the bottles were now alphabetized instead of color-coded.

"Did you do this?" Auden asked. "You're seeing this, right? I'm not crazy."

"No, I didn't do this," she finally said, voice surprisingly firm. Auden's presence helped quiet her nerves, but it didn't stop her brain from going into overdrive, connecting the dots. "And I'm guessing you didn't either since Jimbo hasn't given you a key yet." That was when she remembered Jimbo was supposed to return sometime that day. "Maybe Jimbo came in early and rearranged the store. He was supposed to come back today, remember?" It was a flimsy attempt at trying to reassure herself. Jimbo had never rearranged the store once since she'd worked there. He'd put things out, and they stayed there until they sold.

"Oh, okay. That slipped my mind."

"Let me try calling him, though." And God help Jimbo if he said he hadn't been in. She'd put in a formal request for an exorcism if so, because secretly, she knew that it most likely wasn't her boss's doing.

"I'll check around the store and make sure no one else is here. Just in case."

"Just in case," Lark repeated. While Auden wandered to the back, she walked down each aisle, peering behind all the plants.

As she approached the now-uncovered mirror, something didn't feel right. Like it was watching her. Like *her reflection* was watching her.

Or was she just watching herself?

She backed away, still staring at the mirror and turned around, crashing into Auden's chest. He grabbed her elbows to steady her.

"Coast is clear. Did you call Jimbo?" he asked.

She shook her head and pulled herself back together. "No, I'll do it now."

Picking up the phone, she dialed the number and waited through each ring until the machine picked up. It was full with other messages already, so she was unable to leave one. She hung the phone up and turned to Auden. "He's not home, and his machine was full."

"Maybe he had other things to do." Auden pinched his lower lip between his fingers. "It had to have been him though."

"Yeah." Lark wasn't sure why she didn't tell him about the store never being rearranged before. Maybe she didn't want him to worry. Maybe that was why she didn't want to tell him she thought a ghost might be following her ass around. She scoffed. Who was she kidding? She wouldn't have told Auden because then he would've looked at her differently. No, she didn't want that.

Maybe if she talked to the ghost face to face, the guessing games could be eliminated.

Placing her backpack on the counter, Lark unzipped the pocket and pulled out the red notebook. She slid it across the table as if the store hadn't just been hit by the paranormal.

And maybe it hadn't.

Maybe it really was Jimbo.

Auden grasped the notebook and stuck it in his back pocket. It looked like it had been in use for longer than two weeks because of the ratty edges, what with all their shuffling it back and forth.

"I guess on Monday we can come up here in the morning and meet with Jimbo about our work schedule," she finally said, breaking the heavy silence.

"Do you want me to pick you up?"

"It probably won't be raining."

He rolled his eyes. "Just give me your address, Lark."

A couple silent moments passed, and they just stared at each other before she finally rattled off her address to him. Auden had almost taken her home that night after watching Darrin skateboard, but she'd insisted on riding her bike home since it was close to the trailer park.

"That wasn't so bad, was it?" The side of his mouth tilted up, and she wanted to rub her thumb against it.

The cowbell rang, and an older couple walked into the store and started browsing. Saturdays stayed consistently busy, and it kept Lark's mind occupied until it was time to leave. Bubble's usually felt like a safe place to Lark, but without answers to what was going on, it reminded her more of a prison.

Auden finished dusting, and Lark shouldered her backpack before heading out.

After locking up, Lark and Auden studied each other before he finally spoke. "So maybe after we get our schedule on Monday, if neither one of us has to work, we can go to some of the music stores downtown. I know you like to buy your albums on Wednesdays, though." He smiled, showcasing his perfectly imperfect, slightly-crooked bottom teeth.

"I don't know, Auden. Wednesdays are my jam." She pretended to think about it, taking an exaggerated long time to give an answer. "But, I could possibly... go a few days early." Lark was never one to cheer with joy, but in that moment, she could've done maybe two jumps in place.

"I do like that, you know?" he murmured, angling his head forward.

"What?"

"When you call me Auden."

"It is your name, isn't it?" Her big smile overrode the sarcastic tone.

"So, why did you come into the music store that day all dressed up?"

Lark shut her eyes, trying to block out the memory of that day. "Don't remind me. And I think you know the reason, *Auden.*"

"Yeah, maybe I do." His body inched closer to hers.

"Hey, man, sorry I'm late." Darrin hopped his skateboard over the curb onto the store walkway and pulled to a stop in front of them.

"You didn't say you were coming," Auden muttered, stepping away from Lark.

"Where else would I be?" Darrin glanced at Auden as if his question was pointless.

Lark assumed he could've been at Felisa's or a number of other girls' places. "I have to leave anyway. Beth, a.k.a. my mom, is making dinner tonight for me and my sister. Burritos —another way to keep my Spanish heritage alive." She fist pumped the air and hopped on her bike.

"I'll be there around nine thirty on Monday," Auden called while walking away with Darrin.

As she stood there watching Auden, she closed her eyes and told herself to stop being such a coward. On Monday when they talked to Jimbo, she would let Auden in on it. Allow him to hear everything. She promised herself, because she believed he might actually want to help her too.

CHAPTER 14

To Lark:
Lyrics from "I Think We're Alone Now" — Tommy James & the Shondells

A zing ricocheted through Lark's arm, sending her jolting upright. Too tired to worry about anything, she closed her eyes, drifting back off to a place with no supernatural.

Lark rolled over in bed, not wanting to wake up just yet. It was Sunday after all, and those days were her lazy ones. But the aroma of burnt bacon, eggs, and toast wafted underneath her door from the kitchen.

She stretched her arms to the ceiling and smiled to herself. Her room was as it should be—the records stacked neatly in the corner, clothing not set out in a line. As she got up, she yawned and headed to the kitchen in search of the blackened goodness.

Paloma was already seated at the table, twirling a lock of dark hair around her finger and flipping through an old *Rolling Stone* magazine with Billy Idol plastered on the cover.

"Can't get enough of ridiculous idols, can you?" Lark laughed, slumping down in the already-pulled-out lawn chair. "Pun intended there because idol and *Idol*. Billy Idol has to be the male version of Madonna. Hanging crucifixes from..." She leaned forward and inspected the cover more closely.

"What is that exactly? Underwear made of belts? Real hard, Billy."

Paloma ignored her, didn't even bat an eyelash. Lark furrowed her eyebrows, anticipating her sister's comeback that never came.

Lark glanced at Beth, who was loading two plates with darkened bacon. Beth placed one plate of food in front of Paloma and the other at her own spot. She then went back and filled two glasses with orange juice and set them in front of herself and Paloma again.

Lark's lips parted, wondering if she'd done something to offend anyone—more than usual. "What about me?" she asked, acutely aware of how much she sounded like a toddler desperately seeking attention. But she was sitting *right* there. If Beth didn't want to make her breakfast, that was fine. Lark could cook her own.

Still, no one answered.

"Hello?" Lark waved her hands in front of them, but neither moved an inch, not even a roll of the eyes. *Okay, they can't be that good at putting up a front.*

Lark ripped Paloma's magazine out of her grip, accidentally knocking over her sister's cup of orange juice. The cup shattered into fragile pieces as orange juice slicked the beaten floor tiles.

"Sorry, I didn't mean to do that. Let me clean it up," Lark said, handing the magazine back to Paloma, when she stopped cold. Her sister was already holding a new magazine. No, not a new one—the Billy Idol one.

Confused, Lark flipped over the magazine she had tightened in her hand—it was a duplicate. "You have two of the same magazines at the table?" Her voice came out strained as her eyes fell to the still-full cup of orange juice resting perfectly in front of Paloma. Lark's stare shifted immediately to the spilled broken glass scattered on the floor.

Inside her chest, Lark's lungs couldn't keep up with her hard breaths as she examined the scene before her, more than confused by all of it. Her head spun too fast to think.

"You might want to go and wake your sister before the food gets cold," Beth said, bringing a charcoal slice of bacon to her mouth.

"But I'm right here," Lark whispered. Then she slapped her hands against the table and screamed with everything in her, "I'm right here!"

"Lark!" Paloma shouted from the kitchen table.

Lark left the *Twilight Zone* of an episode, and she sprinted down the hall to her room as Beth yelled her name from the kitchen again.

Rounding the doorway to her room, Lark stopped mid-step.

On her mattress, just now opening her brown eyes, was a girl with curly chestnut-colored hair. A girl who looked like Lark—*was* Lark.

But that *couldn't* be possible.

The impersonator in her bed smiled. Who the hell was she smiling at?

Stretching in a sensual way that Lark would never do, the girl twisted to a seated position. She wore the same *Looney Tunes* pajamas Lark had on. "I don't know if you're still here, but if you are, enjoy your new life in the mirror. I'm going to relish mine after being locked away." The girl turned her head in the direction of the mirror, but there was no reflection—not of the fake Lark or the real one.

Was she insinuating that she was from the mirror and Lark would be her reflection? Anger and confusion stormed its way through her veins like a deadly tornado. Lark lunged for the girl, ready to choke her until she was dead, not caring if she'd be sent to jail for... for what?

But Lark, as if nothing more than vapor, passed through the imposter and hit the mattress with a soft thump. She tried it again, this time with her fists, then her hands constricted into claws, and finally with open-handed slaps. Nothing connected with flesh.

"Hey, Lucy," the girl purred toward Lark's cat, which had been resting on the other pillow still asleep.

The cat's eyelids opened, and her tired blue eyes focused on the imposter. Lucy pounced back and hissed at the girl, all her teeth on display.

"Bite her," Lark snapped. But the cat didn't listen.

"Now, now, Lucy. It's just me—Lark." The imposter reached for the cat, and Lucy sprung across the room to the corner, still hissing. "Fine, have it your way."

Was this like some kind of doppelgänger? Lark sure as hell wasn't going to refer to her as Lark Part Two.

The girl started for the door, and Lark followed close behind her as she took a seat in the lawn chair where Lark had just been.

"Good morning, baby doll," Beth said. "You want me to make you a plate?"

"No, I got this, Mom," the doppelgänger replied in a sickly-sweet voice that made Lark want to vomit. Before preparing her plate, the doppel gave Beth a hug. "I know how I've treated you lately, even though you've been trying, and I wanted to attempt to be different, too." Beth blinked a few times before smiling like it was the greatest gift in the world. The room around Lark seemed as if it were swaying and shrinking in on her.

Paloma leaned closely to the girl's ear while Beth prepared her a plate of food. "You decided to call her mom now? After complaining to me about doing it?"

The girl slowly nodded. "It took me some time, but I figured you were right. Why not give her one more chance?" The doppel's gaze fell to the magazine in Paloma's hand. "I absolutely love Billy Idol."

"Oh my God. He really is an idol! And how gnarly does he look here?" Paloma flipped the pages to a picture of Billy and shoved it in the imposter's face.

"Stop it! Stop it! Stop it!" Lark shouted, slamming her fist against the wood-paneled wall and having enough of this shit show. "Both of you should know that isn't how I act at all!"

Lark scrambled to her room, leaving everyone else in the dust, and grabbed her backpack from the worn carpet. It worked. But then she noticed it hadn't. Not really. There sat a double of the backpack still on the floor beside the mattress. Not caring about changing clothes, she tugged on her boots— duplicates again.

Lucy's hissing had ceased, and she rested curled up in the corner. Lark tried to lift the cat, but it didn't work. Only non-living objects, apparently. "I'm sorry, girl." Fishing out the knife from her backpack, Lark flicked it open. *Maybe an object can kill the beast.* She ran out of the room and down the hallway until she stood in front of the doppel, who was delicately eating the eggs while Lark would've been wolfing them down.

With a hard thrust, Lark plunged the blade into the side of the girl's throat, waiting for blood to blossom to the surface— but it just passed through her. Lark studied the blade in her hand, biting her lip. *Maybe if it's not connected to me, it'll work.* She held the weapon by the blade, then threw it as she would a dart toward the doppel's leg. To her dismay, it still passed through the girl.

"Screw this." She needed to talk to Imani.

As she pedaled with frenzy, Lark thought she should've tried to take Beth's car, but she still had never learned to drive. Lark kept putting it off since she wouldn't have been able to afford a car anyway.

She thought about the past two weeks as the sun blazed down on her. Things shifting around, strange pokes at night, movements in the mirrors, the flute music: it all added up. Then she wondered about how she couldn't touch anyone, and how Beth or Paloma couldn't see or hear her.

The realization hit her. "I'm dead, aren't I? A ghost stuck in the in-between. I wasn't that bad, was I?"

She shook her head as she barreled through a red traffic light. There was no reason for her to bother to stop since she was most likely deceased.

After pedaling for what seemed like days, Imani's long driveway slipped into her line of sight and she flew up the slope. Knocking the kickstand down, she tugged off her backpack and placed it on the ground. For the first time, she hadn't been concerned with music as she'd ridden.

Lark banged on the door and rang the bell at least ten times. No one seemed to hear it, yet everyone's cars were parked in the driveway.

She rattled the locked doorknob—it wouldn't budge. Every passing second felt like life slipping through her fingers. Impatient, Lark ran to the back of the house. Once through the gate, she shook the backdoor, finding it also locked. Couldn't they have forgotten to lock it this one time?

Craning her neck, she focused on the window to Imani's room and decided that was her only option. Her gaze shifted to the side of the house. Pressed against the brick was a trellis crawling with bright green vines and small purple flowers. Lark wasn't sure if the structure would hold her weight, but luckily, it did.

Hands shaking and sweating, she reached across the wall to slide open Imani's window. To her relief, it was unlocked as she pushed open the window and then swung her leg up, managing to plop it over the edge. Her entire body ached. In that moment, she realized she was stuck—if she didn't jump the rest of the way, she'd collide with the ground. *I might be dead, but what if there's a chance I'm not?* Drawing in a sharp breath, Lark threw herself the remainder of the way in and dropped to the floor, panting.

Lark peered over at Imani's tidy bed. Blondie, Joan Jett, Pat Benatar, and Stevie Nicks posters covered her walls.

Imani lay on her back with the phone pressed to her ear. "I know, I can't wait until you come back, too. I've missed you a lot, maybe too much."

"Imani!" Lark shouted, not meaning to, but she couldn't control it. "Remember the haunting stuff that's been going on with me?"

Imani glanced toward her door. "Oh yeah? What do you want to do when you come back?"

Lark let out a few silent curses. She didn't have time to sit around and listen to phone sex between Imani and Emilia—or at least Imani's one-sided version of it.

Padding to the side of the bed, she tried to shake Imani's shoulders, but it was the same thing all over again. Her hands passed right through her friend as it had with the doppel, neither colliding with coldness or warmth.

She slammed her hand against the things on top of Imani's side table, causing the doll-parts lamp, alarm clock, and a few notebooks to crash on the floor. But Imani's attention remained focused on the phone conversation. And Lark knew why. Because despite her actions, a duplicate of everything she'd knocked to the floor still rested on the side table.

Completely unaffected.

Lark wanted to scream and break everything in sight. She'd do anything to get someone to hear one word she was saying. When Imani's hand started to drift to the button of her jeans, Lark knew it was time to leave.

She would try and come back later.

Instead of scaling down the side of the house, she leaped out the window just to see if she would wake up. All it did was hurt like the dickens, but nothing was broken. Rolling onto her back, she stared at the angry globe of yellow burning fury in the sky.

"That's how I feel right now, Sun." Lark picked herself up from the ground and dusted off the dirt from her pajama pants.

Where else? Where else could she go now? *Jimbo.*

He lived in an older neighborhood not far from Imani. She got on her bike and stormed down Imani's driveway, pumping her legs until she felt they might explode.

Lark reached a street with mostly one-story houses, all on pier and beam. Jimbo's was the corner lot with a lime-green painted house and dreamcatchers dangling from the ceiling of the porch. She found him there, sitting in his rocking chair, smoking his pipe.

"Jimbo!" she shouted as she pressed the kickstand down and jogged toward him. He didn't glance up as the acrid smell of the smoke from his tobacco enveloped her. "Come on! You said you've seen ghosts. You say you have ghosts here!"

She pressed her hand to his wrist, not able to feel flesh—or anything else—as her hand pushed through.

"No. No. No." Lark dragged her hands down the sides of her face. Who else?

Auden. He'd seen the things rearranged in the store. He'd even seen the creep in black. Maybe there would be a slim chance he could hear her now.

She knew where he lived—the address had been on his new hire paperwork when she'd looked over it his first working day in the store. 3032 Orchid Street. Lark calculated the route in her head, configuring the quickest way to get there. On bike, it would probably take her thirty minutes.

The ghosts, the doppelgänger, the weirdness—her life was spiraling, and her brain felt shattered, broken into thousands of pieces all trying to make sense of it. She pulled her headphones over her head, took breath after breath, and pushed off from the curb.

The Clash pulsed through her ears during the entire bike ride. Lark turned down a street, one she'd never been down before with each house perfectly constructed on well-maintained yards. Holding her breath, she read the addresses.

3228. 3030. 3032—bingo. Large, evenly-spaced pine trees surrounded Auden's house. She braked to a stop in front of the orangish-brown house. The lyrics playing in her ears matched her thoughts—stay or go?

She had to try.

As she hurried up the rock path leading to the door, her eyes connected with something that made her freeze—a duplicate of her bike parked next to a bush. She cursed under her breath, wondering how and why the other girl would be here.

Her nerves kicked up as she banged on the door, then fiddled with the locked knob.

Heart hammering, Lark darted around to the side of the house, not knowing which window or room would even be Auden's. Floral curtains covered all the windows. She peered through the slit inside one, seeing their living room with a large striped sofa and a recliner chair in front of a TV. A man and a woman were seated on the furniture, and two young boys on the floor, but no Auden.

There was another window on this side of the house, farther down, but the curtains were drawn too tight. She rounded the back of the house. Inside the first window she found there was a small room cluttered with hundreds of action figures on a tall shelf. If this was Auden's room, he needed severe help with his toy hoarding.

Where is he?

When Lark reached the next window, she pressed herself forward and paused. Low, muffled sounds trickled out and a sight she didn't want to see left her both stunned and extremely confused. Because the other *she* was in Auden's room. Her doppel was on top of Auden, wearing only a bra and underwear, kissing him fiercely. "I Think We're Alone Now," sang its way through the window and she wanted to break the vinyl in half.

"Stop it, you dick!" Lark shouted at Auden in a panic. But he didn't hear her voice or the sound of her hand almost cracking the glass. She was livid—and possibly murderous in that moment.

"Good to know the real you is out here," a male voice whispered from behind Lark.

CHAPTER 15

A knock on the door sounded, and Auden rushed to see who it was because a shit storm was brewing inside his bedroom. He had seen a replica of himself with Lark, but had he really? His parents hadn't heard him. His brothers hadn't either. This was something new entirely. Every item he'd lifted left one of the same behind—making a duplicate for him to use.

After he threw open the door, his gaze connected with two of Lark's bikes, and he knew then that she had the same problem he had. Darting around the side of the house, through the neatly-trimmed grass, he caught sight of Lark staring into his bedroom window at the unfortunate events.

"Good to know the real you is out here." He sighed, relief rushing over him that the real Lark wasn't stripping down inside his room and sleeping with a stranger. Then his body froze. "I'm seeing you, right? Really seeing you?"

Lark whirled around to face him, her hand over her mouth. She was still wearing her pajamas and her curls were mussed. "Yes, I'm real!" she shouted. "How?"

"I could ask you the same thing. I thought—" His gaze shifted from the tilt of her chin back to her clothing. "Also, you still have on your pajamas."

"Sorry, I wasn't as concerned about getting dressed after I

found out no one can *see me*." She waved a trembling hand up and down in front of her body.

"I can." He wanted to get down on his knees and kiss the ground because she could see him too.

"You're the only one!" Her eyes fell to his clothing. "I see you at least found time to get properly dressed."

"I got dressed before discovering there was another me in there. Then I didn't know if I was conjuring up what I was seeing." He tried not to hide anything from her—he should've told her the truth before.

"You're definitely not imagining this. Did he say anything?" Lark paused, craning her neck at the window. "Let's get away from this side of the house. I can't listen to this anymore while trying to think."

He thought... he thought he had been going out of his mind, like his dad. But what if he still was? Quivering, he reached out and brushed the sleeve of her shirt, needing desperately to know that he could. "Real," he whispered.

"What?"

"I just wanted to make sure you were real," he murmured as they walked to the front of the house.

"I am and so are you."

Auden spun around to face her, feeling quite the epiphany of his life, when he realized he hadn't imagined what the fake Auden had told him. "So, that guy in there couldn't see me, but he spoke to me in case I was there. He told me he'd swapped places with me, and I'll be getting a new home in the mirror soon." Auden paused. "I tried to get my parents and brothers to see me, but they couldn't. Shortly after that, you— or who I thought was you—rang the doorbell, and when the girl answered, she said 'Ridley' in a low voice and he whispered 'Leni' before they started kissing and he dragged her to my room. I didn't understand the name exchange then, but I do now."

"Leni." She tapped her chin, her eyes growing wider. "So that's my doppel's real name."

"Doppel?"

Lark relayed her story of what had happened at her house in the morning, then asked, "Have you had anything weird happen to you during the past two weeks? Besides the store shuffling incident."

The time had finally come for Auden to really talk to someone. "Yes, I have," he admitted. He confided in her about the nightly interruptions, the mirror incidents, the flute playing woman with no face, the thoughts about how he believed he was becoming schizophrenic like his father.

Lark didn't look at him differently—not one bit—as she then relayed all her stories to him. Auden wished he'd been upfront with her before, had asked more questions, had pushed the subject once he'd seen the store switched around. He hadn't, though, because he thought she would've reacted the same way Darrin had when Auden mentioned seeing something in the dark. He never wanted her to think he was crazy.

"So, we both had secret touches and general weirdness start two weeks ago," Lark said. "And before that, we both heard music and saw the man in black and the cloaked woman." She stopped talking for a moment, gripping her curls. "What happened between then?"

"I started working at your cursed work." Auden managed a smile, despite it all, because more than anything he was relieved. "You're the cause of all this, aren't you?" He teased.

She didn't smile back. "If anything, it's all your fault for working at my store and bringing in bad karma."

Her words jogged a memory. "What about when the guy brought in the mirror?"

"Yes!" She looked at him and paused. "Mirrors…"

He waited for her to finish her sentence. When she didn't, he echoed, "Mirrors…"

Her eyes widened, and she licked her lips. "In the bathroom at the movie theater, I saw boots matching mine beneath the stall when the girl in there went crazy. In my room, there was another incident where I caught a glimpse of curls that I now know match mine."

"Oh!" He snapped his fingers. "There was a night where there was a shadow, but I noticed hair that, now that I think about it, was similar to mine."

"Leni had said to enjoy my life in the mirror and there was no reflection of me or her." Her breaths came out ragged. "Auden, what if they were our reflections? And what if they mean for us to be theirs? Then we have the man who brought in that mirror, which shocked our fingers, and he'd shocked us both once before—I almost forgot about those tiny *gifts* of pain. But then I felt the shock last night, too—so what if it all connects somehow?"

He remembered a shock the night before too. "What does? The store was gifted a mirror, and in return it felt the need to gift us twin demons?"

"Something like that." Lark bobbed her head side to side. "But I still don't know about the 'Space Oddity' music…"

"You know what I think?" He hadn't had time to see if Ridley had a reflection, but when Lark told him about her and Leni not having one, it could be possible.

"What?"

"If it is that mirror in the store that started all this, let me grab my baseball bat and we'll find out. The Rolling Stones would say to paint it black, but I say, we break it."

"Do you have two?" Her eyes brightened and a smile spread across her face.

"I have three." They were his and his brothers', all resting in the garage for years without being touched. Now was the perfect opportunity to pull them out.

Lark clasped onto his wrist. "Auden, you're not your father, and I'm not my parents. And if you ever feel you're really slipping, then talk to me, okay?"

He pressed his lips together and nodded. "All right." Despite everything, he felt more himself than he had in a long time after confiding in her.

Out of the corner of his eye, he glanced at Lark. The rising sun lit up her profile, and she looked more fresh and real than the girl in his bedroom could ever be. He couldn't put into words what exactly they had between them, but the thought of losing it frightened him most of all.

CHAPTER 16

To Lark:

Lyrics from "Burnin' For You" — Blue Öyster Cult

Lark hadn't been sure if taking the van would work the same way as her bike, but it had. They'd had to venture back into Auden's house to get Jenny's keys. Auden's family had been in the living room, far from the action between the doppels, but it'd still been weird. Auden had slipped into the room and quickly came out with what he needed.

All Lark heard was her doppel's voice saying, "Our lips are sealed until this is over."

Bitch, you better say something, Lark had thought.

Auden loaded Lark's bike in the back of his van. She had tried snatching the doppel's bike, but her hand passed straight through it. Lark realized then that objects only duplicated once—she could take one thing from an original source, but not anymore after that.

As Auden backed the van out of the driveway, it felt as if they were coming out of a mother's womb, being pushed out from the original, all while "Burnin' For You" played through the speakers.

Outside the front of Bubble's, Lark fumbled with the store keys. "Are you doing all right, Auden? You still look shaky."

Auden leaned on his baseball bat, as if it was a cane, and studied the ground. "I still can't help thinking I'm envisioning all of this, but I know I'm not."

"Trust me, I wish this was all a nightmare," she said. "I thought I was being haunted and that there were ghosts."

"I don't believe in ghosts, but now maybe I should." He shrugged and smiled a fraction. "Is that why you asked me if I believed in ghosts?"

"Yeah. And since you didn't, I kept quiet, but I had actually decided on telling you when I saw you next." Lark stepped into the store and flicked on the light—she had an idea. "Wait, let me try something."

She scurried down the aisle to the phone and picked it up, dialing Jimbo. He hadn't heard her before, but maybe this could be a way. It rang and rang and rang as she tapped the top of the baseball bat against the floor. Not even his answering machine clicked on. Hanging up, she tried Beth and let it ring for several minutes—no answer.

Lark slumped her shoulders and turned around to face Auden. "What's Darrin's phone number?" She pressed the numbers he gave her, and the same thing occurred. "They can't all not be home. Beth has the day off."

"Let me see it." Gently, he pulled the phone from her hands and dialed 9-1-1. "Someone has to pick up the phone there."

She watched in hope as she held up her crossed fingers.

"And... we're fucked," he said and hung up the phone. "If we try and call someone, they aren't going to hear it."

They strolled over to the edge of the counter. Auden lifted his baseball bat with what looked like determination and focus. He walked to the mirror like it was any other normal day and slammed the bat into the wooden portion of the mirror. *Crack!*

Auden's muscles tensed, and the veins in his hands bulged. The mirror didn't even move an inch—the glass and wood were still intact. The bat, however, had a large split running up the side.

Lark lifted her bat and swung it over her head, striking the mirror at the top with a hard whack. Her body rattled and her arm muscles ached with the contact. Still, the object stood as pristine as before, except for the fact that her bat now had a long fissure etched in it too.

She geared up for a second swing straight into the glass, where she should've struck the first time. "I think we're on the right track, and whatever's happening to us does have something to do with the mirror."

"No shit, Sherlock," Auden muttered.

"That's the second time you've called me that, and I'm glad we've established I'll be leading this investigation, Watson." Lark took another swing, steadying herself for the force of the connection. The mirror rippled without a sound and Lark pitched forward, almost falling into it as the bat passed straight through. Adrenaline flooded her as she pulled back—barely escaping her plunge into the unknown cavern behind the glass.

Auden's eyes widened and Lark dropped the bat on the floor beside her. She fell to her knees and punched a fist through the glass. The surrounding reflective surface rippled like a wave around her arm, sending tingles up and down her skin.

"Holy shit!" Auden whisper-shouted.

Stunned for a moment, Lark took her hand out and stared at it before thrusting it into her unzipped bag. She fumbled until she pulled out the knife and flicked it open. "I have an idea."

"How often do you drag that thing out?" Auden asked, indicating her knife.

"More often than you'd like to know. Just hold my feet, and if it's okay, I'll wave you in." Lark was almost a hundred percent sure she wouldn't die—at least not at the moment. Or maybe she was dead already. If so, she was willing to take chances in this alternate reality.

"I'm not letting go of you." Auden's warm hands wrapped tightly around Lark's ankles as she scooted forward. As she slowly inched forward, she extended the knife, hoping Auden didn't notice the slight tremor in her hand. Whatever was behind that mirror would meet her blade first. The mirror rippled across, and she pressed her head through. A rush of frigid air ruffled her hair. Her lungs seized, refusing to fill with oxygen. Her heart pounded in her chest. Her eyes rounded, a sting forming from her refusal to blink for the entire trip into the unknown.

It was as if she'd passed through a curtain that lifted while her body tingled. Dark purple walls, almost black, formed a triangular-shaped room, smelling of pine. A thick silver chain hung from the ceiling, holding a large metal bowl that burned with fire to light the room. In the middle of the space sat a circular table and—

Two strong arms pulled her from the mirror.

"How long did you plan on staying in that position?" Auden asked, frowning.

"I was barely in there a second." She needed to see more of it. "I think it's fine to go in."

"You think?"

"Sure." There hadn't been time to really explore the area, but it seemed fine enough. At least it was lit, so they could see. If it had been in total darkness, that would've been a different story.

"Okay, it's my turn to try something," Auden said, his body fidgeting.

Lark moved out of the way and watched as Auden crawled through the mirror and then disappeared. A few seconds later, his head popped back out. "This proves we can go back and forth," he said, sticking out his palm for her to clasp.

Placing her hand in his, she soaked in his warmth as he pulled her into the glass while she still clenched the knife in her other palm. *It's kind of like Alice in* Through the Looking-Glass, she thought.

A faint sound, resembling a bee flying by one's ear, buzzed in the room before it faded to silence.

On the circular black table from before, she now noticed a small golden box covered in silvery glass jewels resting on top. To her left, a large rectangular mirror, with the name "Auden" written above it in a fancy cursive script on a wooden plaque, hung on the wall. Behind her was the mirror leading back to the inside of Bubble's, and at her right was another rectangular mirror with the name "Lark" penned in the same cursive above it. None of them showed her or Auden's reflection.

In front of her, a hallway opened at the juncture of the two walls, and as she carefully peered down it, Lark could see mirrors of various shapes and sizes plastered its purple surfaces. Too many to count. She turned back to the jeweled box on the table that Auden had already opened.

Inside, the box was lined with purple velvet. He dipped his hand in and withdrew a yellowed paper scroll, then unrolled it.

"What does it say?" Lark asked, trying to catch a glimpse around his bicep.

"I don't know yet." He pulled his bottom lip in between his teeth as he scanned over the words. "It says we have fourteen days."

"Let me see that." She tugged the scroll, so it was between the both of them, and immediately recognized the hard-to-read handwriting.

Lark & Auden,

You will not understand what is happening to you, nor can you escape it. From the day you awoke to find yourselves fading from the real world, you entered Phase Three. You have fourteen days to rid yourselves of the curse, and make no mistake, for it is a curse. Your innocent selves were chosen for this path. If you do not break the curse in a fortnight, you will become a mirror image. It's what keeps my world existing in order to keep yours alive. But if you manage to break it, the curse will move on.

Do not waste time searching the halls past this room. They contain more questions than answers, and you will only waste time. The Realm of Mirrors is just that—an in-between place that connects your Earth Dimension to my Mirror Dimension. Whether you heed my warning or not, that is your choice.

I cannot undo what has been started, which leaves your fates where they ultimately should be—entirely in your hands.

Deepest Apologies,

The Mirror Keeper

"Piece of shit," Auden growled, ripping the scroll from her hand and attempting to shred it into pieces. But it wouldn't even tear.

"I was right! We *will* end up reflections!" Lark shouted. "That thing didn't even say how to break the curse! Just some shit about keeping dimensions alive!"

Auden inhaled and exhaled roughly, fists shaking, yet his voice came out even. "We have fourteen days, right? We'll make a list of all the ways we know how to break curses and test them out."

"Considering I know *all* the ways to break curses, I'm going to say my ideas are zero." Why couldn't stabbing the doppel have been the way to break the curse? Then Lark would've ended this whole charade earlier. "And what is this Phase Three business?"

Auden scratched the side of his cheek and shut his eyes. "Shock one—"

"From the Mirror Keeper. And shock two from the mirror after we touched it, I'm guessing," she finished the sentence for him. "Then the third would be from last night."

"That has to be it." He walked to the edge of the hallway where Lark had been earlier, studying each aspect of the walls. "Do you notice all the mirrors have written names above them and reflections of people inside?"

Furrowing her eyebrows, she crept closer until she stood beside him and inspected a few of them. She hadn't gotten close enough earlier to notice.

"A realm of mirrors like the *hint* in the scroll says, yet I have no intention of visiting, anyway." Lark turned to leave and stopped, noticing a mirror with Paloma, then another with Beth, Robin, and then Imani, and so on. "The scroll stated that two dimensions connect from this room. What if somehow our reflections are created somewhere else? Like in this Mirror Dimension..." Lark bit her lip, shaking her head. "Maybe that's a stupid idea."

Auden ticked his finger in the air. "I wouldn't have believed that before, but with these mirrors, and that scroll and our curse. I... I think you might be right."

She covered her mouth and moved down the hallway, away from the mirrors. "I'll meet up with you later. I need to go home, change, and grab some supplies because, Auden, we're going to break this curse."

"I think the *Looney Tunes* pajamas are working just fine." Auden grinned.

"Shut up," she said, before crawling out of the mirror and back onto the carpeted floor of Bubble's. Auden followed.

Lark attempted to shake the mirror, but it didn't budge. She glanced around the store, knowing it would be quiet. "Since Bubble's is closed today, how about we meet back here in a few hours?"

"I think we could meet in a concert of people at the moment and still have complete privacy."

Lark held up a finger. "You..."

"Yes?" He quirked an eyebrow.

"I don't know, but I'll be back later." She had to give herself time to think, to form a plan. Why couldn't breaking the mirror have just worked?

"Wait," Auden whispered. "We need code words or something since we both have look-alikes running around. I know they can't see us, but with all the strangeness that has happened, it would be good, just in case."

Lark imagined Leni pretending she was her, kissing Auden the way she had with Ridley earlier, and she shuddered to herself at the thought. His idea was smart. "Lyrics," she said.

"Curses," he replied. She couldn't have thought of two better words for the situation.

In a rush, Lark left the store unlocked for Auden to be able to get inside if he made it back before her. He unloaded her bike from the van, and she put on her headphones, finding the hardest heavy metal cassette to bleed out her thoughts. Trapped in a mirror, following some twat around all day? Lark wasn't having that.

And she had thought waking up invisible was a tragedy. But being alone, held hostage in a mirror, would be even more horrific. She was frightened. Angry. Annoyed. But most of all, she was determined. This curse was going to be *so* over.

When she made it back to the trailer, Lark pulled her headphones down, her music giving way to a melody, coming from behind her, slow and fierce. A flute—playing "Space Oddity." She turned around, and only a few feet from her, the woman in the black-hooded cloak stood waiting. She wore dark satin gloves. Her black pants and heeled boots peeked out from the sliver of the cloak opening. Lark didn't move and the woman didn't either—they remained frozen, silently watching each other. The silver flute rested in the woman's hands.

Lark's breaths increased as she strained to see beneath the hood of the cloak, but only darkness came from within. Over the woman's heart, Lark's gaze locked onto a small object—a dark pendant that almost blended in with the cloak. A butterfly. Trembling, Lark reached forward to touch it, but before she could make contact, a quick silvery light flashed and the woman vanished, leaving Lark with more questions than answers.

That woman obviously had something to do with the curse, not just the Mirror Keeper. She had already known that the two were connected, but she could never have imagined any of this. The Mirror Keeper hadn't left them empty-handed, though. There was the scroll and the sticky notes. Was it possible she could find him near Bubble's again?

After stepping into the trailer, Lark found Beth relaxed in the recliner watching an old black-and-white movie and smoking a cigarette. From the looks of it, she was already on her third can of beer. Lucy lay curled up on the couch, safely away from "the doppel's" room.

Thankfully, the doppelgänger, Leni, was not inside Lark's room. She threw on a pair of black jeans and a black sweater, then tossed a spiral notebook along with a couple pens into her backpack. Lark needed a shower, but decided not to worry about it too much since she didn't exactly feel like she was part of the real world. Cleaning up wasn't a high priority with so many missing pieces to the puzzle. What she knew was that the Mirror Keeper and the flute player were from a place known as the Mirror Dimension and that was about it. She wouldn't know direct answers without first finding the Mirror Keeper, and that left her frustrated.

Paloma's voice radiated from the other room, sounding as though she was talking to someone on the phone. Reining back in her thoughts, Lark crossed the hall into Paloma's room and found her sister sitting on the floor against the side of her bed.

"Shannon's party is this Friday? Will Craig be there?" Paloma smiled to herself with a lovelorn expression, and the thought made Lark sick. Craig was a total jerk.

"Yeah, I can go, but I'll have to drag Lark with me. Yeah, yeah, not my choice, though. Beth's new rules."

Screw this curse, and screw Paloma.

A door shut from the front of the trailer, and Lark hurried to see who it was. It wasn't one of Beth's men. No, it was the demon who'd returned, making her grand entrance and giving

Beth a kiss on the cheek. Lucy slunk to the very end of the couch.

"Do you want to come watch TV with me, baby doll?" Beth asked, putting out her cigarette.

"Sure. Let me put up my things first." Leni smiled to herself as she walked down the hall to Lark's room. Instead of lightly putting the backpack down, the doppel threw it like a sack of garbage. Lark was pretty sure she heard the sound of some of the cassettes cracking. Her blood boiled at the thought.

"You don't have to be such a twat." But of course Leni didn't hear her. "And don't think for a moment that carrying around my bag of cassettes will keep people in the dark." Lark seethed.

"Lark!" Paloma called from across the hall.

"Yeah?" Lark and Leni said in unison, and Lark cursed to herself as she followed Leni into Paloma's room.

"Shannon's having a party this Friday and her parents definitely won't be coming home early this time. Will you go?" *Say no. Say no. Say no!*

"Totally!" Leni exclaimed.

"Really?" Paloma lowered her brows. Lark hoped the genuine enthusiasm in Leni's voice would be enough to make Paloma realize this couldn't be the real Lark.

"Yeah, I mean, I started dating Auden. And being around him has made me want to try new things." Leni stared in the direction of Paloma's closet. "I'm sure you know what it's like when you're head over heels for a boy. Maybe I could borrow some of your clothes?"

A high-pitched laugh escaped the real Lark. "No way Paloma's buying this load of baloney!" Her sister had to spot the imposter. But rather than the dramatic reveal she hoped for, Paloma put the phone back to her ear.

"Cheryl? Yeah, we can go. Let me call you back. I have a new mission." She hung up the phone and looked up at Leni. "I knew there had to be a reason for your change. And I knew there was something going on with you and Auden after these last few parties! So, you want to keep a boy impressed? Well, I've got you covered. How about we also go through my makeup and jewelry?" Paloma smiled, bouncing on her bed with excitement.

"Thanks. We just connected through music, and since I've explored more with sounds, why not do the same with clothes." Leni shrugged just like Lark.

For Lark, the world as she knew it was officially falling apart.

# CHAPTER 17

To Auden:

Lyrics from "Edge of Seventeen" – Stevie Nicks

Auden pulled into the driveway to his house, "Edge Of Seventeen" on the speakers, reminding him of one of Lark's lyric notes she'd given him during class. He found his parents' cars still parked in the driveway. Leni's bike was gone, so she wasn't there anymore. He hadn't wanted to walk in on Leni and Ridley again, even though in reality, he wouldn't have minded looking at Leni because she did resemble Lark.

But Leni wasn't Lark.

Inside his house, Nick and Zach sat on the floor in front of the TV, his dad relaxed on the couch, and Ridley stood in the kitchen, wearing one of Auden's Sex Pistols shirts, a pair of black jeans, and a flowered oven mitt on his right hand. Auden's mom closed the oven door and straightened.

They're baking together?

Ridley let out a loud laugh that sounded nothing like Auden. *Fuck. This!*

"I've missed us baking together," his mom said with a smile. It had been years since he'd last helped her in the kitchen. A sharp pang of guilt nudged his chest. Maybe he should do more for his parents. Show them how much they meant to him.

"I remembered what you said, about needing to be better because of my younger brothers." Ridley looked in the direction of the boys. "So I thought helping you around the house would be a good start."

Auden shook his head and went straight to his room. He grabbed his box from under the bed, a few changes of clothes, and a notebook.

He wasn't going to stick around a moment longer and play imaginary friends. Taking off again, he drove Jenny the short distance to Darrin's place and pounded up the steps. The door was locked, and when he tried knocking, Darrin either didn't hear him or wasn't home. *Figures.*

Auden sat outside the door and propped his back up against the gate surrounding the porch, letting the hot metal warm the cold ache he felt inside. He truly didn't know what to do. Feeling lost was something he was used to, but this was a whole different ballgame.

After an hour or two—Auden hadn't even glanced down at his watch to see what time he'd gotten there—Darrin opened the door barefoot, wearing only a pair of jeans. He slid a cigarette from behind his ear and stuck it between his lips, then pulled the lighter from his back pocket and lit it.

"I guess you can't see me, even though I'm sitting right beside you," Auden muttered.

He stood and moved in front of Darrin. The smoke came out of his friend's mouth and the strong scent hit Auden in the face, filling his nostrils. "Can you hear me?" he shouted, growing more irritated by the second. "You claim the Force is always with you. Let it be with you now. Come. On. Dammit!"

Darrin shifted forward and let his hands dangle over the rail, a grin spreading across his cheeks. "You're skating today? Not just watching?" Darrin yelled down to the ground below.

Auden's head jerked over the rail to see his doppelgänger hanging out at the bottom of the stairs.

"Yeah, it's been too long." Ridley smiled up with Auden's old skateboard in his hand.

"So, more than one trick?" Darrin pressed his cigarette against the rail, snuffing it out.

"Yeah." Ridley cocked his head and motioned for Darrin to come down.

What is this guy trying to prove? Be Man of the Year or some shit? Darrin went back inside, grabbed his skateboard, and followed Ridley to somewhere over the rainbow.

Auden headed back to the oddity store to meet up with Lark. He hoped to God Ridley wouldn't show up there because everywhere Auden had chosen to go so far, there his ass was.

The door was unlocked just as Lark had left it, so he went inside the already lit store. No Lark in sight. He placed his spiral notebook on the counter, tapping his fingers on the cover as he continuously shifted his eyes between it and the mirror.

"Screw it," he said with a sigh.

Approaching the glass, he lowered himself to the carpeted floor and swiftly crawled through the portal. The mirror rippled, sending tingles across his skin. Once inside, the triangular room looked the same as earlier—purple walls, dark floor, and a mysterious flame lighting the area. The scroll still sat unraveled on the table beside the opened jeweled box.

Tugging out the knife from his back pocket, he flicked it open—a trick he'd learned from Lark.

He inhaled a deep pull of the woodsy-scented atmosphere, even though no trees or grassy areas were in sight.

Auden followed the wide hallway of mirrors, illuminated

by the bowls of fire suspended from the ceiling. The mirrors were different sizes and shapes—tall and thin, oval, circular, short and wide—with names written in cursive above. His chest tightened as he read the familiar names he'd seen earlier —his mom, dad, brothers, Darrin—but stopped when his real dad's name and face came into focus. Gary Ellis. His birth father appeared the same as he had in the older pictures his mom had shown him, except for the deeper lines etched into his forehead and surrounding his eyes. Strands of gray laced through his brown hair. Was this really his birth father or was it just another imposter, like how Ridley was his?

Unsure if he would find his real father on the other side, Auden reached forward. But his hand only encountered ice cold glass. While pressing onto the mirror he exhaled, and steam poured out through his mouth as if he'd been standing outside in the freezing cold.

He touched his hands to the others—his mom's, his dad's, his brothers', strangers'—all solid and cold. Gnawing at his bottom lip, he grabbed the frame of one and tugged, then pulled harder. It wouldn't budge. He tried another and another, unable to pry any—it was as though they were stuck in place with hundreds of nails.

Behind him, he found Paloma and Imani's names and faces alongside others he didn't know.

At the end of the hall, the next room broke into a large square space filled with stairs, halls, and more mirrors with names and faces. Two sets of stairs against the far wall went straight to the next level. And in the middle of the room, one spiral staircase also led upward, while an open area in the floor held another set, leading down.

If these mirrors are connected to all the people in the world, it really would take forever to walk this never-ending

*labyrinth, and at the end of that journey, I'd find myself
trapped in a mirror.* The thought slightly intrigued him. Get
away from this town? Maybe. But not in the way he'd hoped.

"Auden," a low female voice called—unmistakably
Lark's. "Auden!"

"I'm here!" he called back, closing his knife and shoving
it into his back pocket. Turning around, he spotted Lark at the
end of the hallway fully dressed in black jeans and a black
top, already striding toward him.

"Lyrics," she said, stopping in front of him.

"Curses."

"What are you doing in here again?" she asked. A note of
worry sounded in her voice.

"Just getting away for a little bit, trying to uncover *something.*" Being here had been better than seeing Ridley with his
mom and Darrin.

"Mmm." She lifted an eyebrow. "Well, did you find
anything?"

"Not really. The mirrors don't come off the wall, and
they're cold to the touch." Auden walked down the hall
toward the table and scroll with Lark following closely.

"The scroll said it would be wasting time exploring down
here, and I think it's true. We should do curse research now.
Maybe there's a possibility the Mirror Keeper will show up
again." She paused, glancing at the walls. "I know it should
feel weird to be in here, but it really doesn't."

"I think you're right, but I'm not sure if he'll show up. We
haven't seen him since he dropped the mirror off."

"While I was gone, I *did* see the woman with the flute, so
maybe there's a chance."

Auden ran his hand over the jeweled box. He lifted it and
examined the gold outer layer, searching for a clue. He flipped

it over and his fingers stopped moving when he noticed words etched on the bottom.

For Butterfly

"What is that? That would be an odd name," Lark said, wrinkling her nose. Then, her brows shot up. "The woman with the flute. When I saw her earlier, she was wearing a butterfly pendant. Do you think that's her name? It could be a coincidence, though…"

"I don't know," he replied. "Maybe."

"We'll add someone named butterfly to the list and put a question mark next to the flute player."

"Sounds good." He glanced at the mirror with his name. "It's weird not seeing a reflection."

"It is." She shrugged. "But if we run out of time, I'm sure it will be us there. Let's go."

Auden nodded and Lark crawled out to Bubble's. He wasn't far behind.

"Did you encounter anything else besides the lady when you were gone?" he asked, standing.

"No, only her. And she vanished." Lark took a notebook from her backpack and crossed off *break the mirror* since they'd tried that earlier with no success. "Let's see what else we can do."

Auden grabbed one of the old-fashioned lighters from a shelf in the corner and went back to the mirror. He pressed the flame to the woodgrain in an attempt to catch it on fire.

Nothing.

"Should we try that new occult shop next to the antique store across the street?" Lark asked. "Maybe they have something."

"Good idea."

They left the oddity store and jogged across the not-so-busy street and opened the door to Norma's Occult Shop. Two small white pentagrams were painted above and below the shop name. Inside, the place reeked of coconut incense. The store was cramped with only one room—two walls were painted dark blue and the others, black. Several wooden shelves and glass curio cabinets filled with figurines lined the walls. Neither of them had ever been inside the shop before.

Lark skimmed her hands across several cream candles. Her fingers flipped through a deck of astrology cards and then a set of tarot cards. She turned over the top card and shuddered. *Death.* "I don't think these will help us."

Auden walked to the other side of the store, where a woman wearing a flowy red skirt and a peasant top stood. She dusted the glass counter in front of her. He peered down at mostly necklaces, rings, and bracelets with the pentagram emblem. On top of the glass rested a box of various crystals.

To his left, a shelf lined with books was nailed to the wall. His fingers brushed over the titles. Mostly summoning books, and he had no intention of trying to call on demons to make matters worse.

A loud squeal echoed in the store. Auden covered his ears and whirled around to find Lark messing around with a record player on the other side of the store.

"What?" she said when her eyes met his. "There was an Ozzy album sitting around and he did bite the head off a bat and all. Maybe there could be a secret message here on how to break a curse."

"Come on, Lark, nothing would be that easy." He smiled. "Besides, if there were a secret message, it would probably be about how to initiate a curse. You probably should've tried Culture Club or something. I can get it out of my van if you really want it while, you know, I continue searching."

"I can't believe you have that," she said as she stepped away from the record player and sifted through what looked to be bundles of herbs.

"Can't deny it's catchy."

She clasped one of the bundles and swung her hand up. "Got it! Let's try burning the sage. It's supposed to help with bad karma."

After grabbing a few white candles and sage, they left the shop and darted across the street. Lark came to a stop on the sidewalk and didn't move. She let out a real laugh that was low and throaty and beautiful all at once. "Sorry... I shouldn't be laughing at this, but it's so screwed up." Her chuckles turned into sobs, and before long, tears slid down her cheeks.

Auden froze, not knowing what the hell to do. Should he pat her back? Stroke her cheek? Carry her off somewhere? Or just stand there and keep on staring at her? He went with the fourth option, too chicken to do anything else.

Finally, he spoke, "How about we light these things, then go listen to music in the van and get something to eat. We'll figure out something else to try later. I think you need a break —you look tired."

"Okay." She sniffed, wiping the tears from her face. "Pretend you didn't see the waterworks. I haven't done that since I was a kid."

He shrugged. "I don't know what you're talking about. I didn't see anything."

Auden thought about the last time he'd cried—it'd been because of Drew and her duplicitous nature, which was stupid. Before that, when he was younger, he used to cry about his real mother because he couldn't remember her. He only had what remained in old photographs. He didn't know the way her voice sounded, the way she smelled, or if she ever even truly loved him, yet he missed her.

Once they were back in Bubble's, Lark burned the sage while Auden lit the candles and set them on the floor in front of the mirror, watching them flicker and burn. They then took a break to go and get food.

Afterward, Auden opened the back of Jenny and helped Lark inside. His hand lingered on hers for a second longer than necessary before he joined her on the van's floor and pulled out his music.

For the little bit of daylight Auden and Lark had left, they listened to records in his van and worked on notes for the next day.

"Are you going home?" Lark asked when night started to fall.

"No, are you?" Why go home and lie in bed next to his mirror twin and pretend like the situation wasn't screwed up? He'd rather spend the next two weeks in the parking lot, sleeping in the back of his van.

"No." Lark looked around the van for a moment. "I guess I'll go inside the store and sleep."

As she started to rise, Auden tugged her back down. "There's plenty of room in here." He tossed Lark one of the sleeping bags and a pillow he'd brought.

Unrolling his own bag, he slid inside while Lark watched. Her parted lips made her look as if she didn't believe he'd meant the offer, but then she removed the elastic from the material and spread the bag beside him.

"Thanks, Auden," she murmured.

"Yeah." It wasn't a big deal, and if he didn't want to sleep at home, he knew it was better for her not to, either. And sleeping in the store would just be dumb when he had his van.

Lark closed her eyes, and he listened as her breathing became steady, wishing he could fall asleep that quickly. But it would be a while.

Auden placed his headphones over his head and let David Bowie sing "Heroes" to him, hoping the words were true.

Slipping out of the sleeping bag, he peered through the front window, and looked toward the laundromat. He wondered if the Mirror Keeper would show up before their time ran out.

# CHAPTER 18

To Lark:

Lyrics from "Light My Fire" — The Doors

A trickle of bright morning light stirred Lark from sleep, draped in something snug and warm. She opened her eyes to look down at the thick sleeping bag she'd fallen asleep in.

Auden was nowhere to be seen, but a flash of red caught her attention. Dragging herself out of her cozy position, Lark plucked up the spiral notebook and flipped it open to the new entry written in Auden's steady handwriting. Lyrics from "Heroes."

Smiling to herself, she tucked the notebook into her backpack, then wiggled herself completely out of the sleeping bag to peer out the front window and look toward the laundromat. No Mirror Keeper. The driver-side door opened and she startled, but it was only Auden. He tossed in several full plastic bags.

"What is all that?" she asked, inching forward to have a peek.

"Finally awake?" he said, not answering her question but pushing a bag closer to her.

It was heavy and filled with all kinds of bottled drinks. Then he gave her another bag brimming with muffins, peanut butter, and bagels.

"Where did you get all this?" It felt as if she'd just struck gold.

Auden shrugged. "The convenience store."

Yesterday, they had gone to McDonald's, so this would be better than eating fast food again. And it wasn't technically stealing if the original source was still there, but even if it wasn't, Lark would've gone ahead and jacked it. This was a crisis. They were hungry, so all would have to be forgiven. She opened the wrapper and took a bite of the banana-nut muffin.

"Jimbo just got into work, too," Auden said, twisting the cap off his soda.

"He's here already?" she asked, maneuvering her way to the passenger seat and opening the door to get out.

"Yeah. I saw him unlocking the door right when I got to the van."

Jimbo might not have heard her yesterday, but she needed to try again. It was a new day.

As Lark headed across the parking lot, she finished half of the muffin, then handed the rest to Auden. He quickly stuffed it into his mouth.

From her left, something dark and flowing caught her attention—a flash of a black cloak before flickering to silver. Lark snatched Auden's arm. "You saw that, right?"

He'd stopped chewing, his mouth still full. Taking a deep swallow, he nodded. "Yes. She seems to be the only person who can see us."

Lark wanted others to see her, but not that kind of person —or thing.

Inside the store, Jimbo sat behind the front counter with his hair in two braids, writing something down on paper. His glasses hung low on the edge of his nose, and his brow rested furrowed in concentration.

"Jimbo!" Lark ran to him and this time yelled near his ear

as loud as she could. She tried to tap his shoulder, but her hand passed through him and landed on the counter. "Come on, come on, come on! Open your otherworldly powers up to me and Auden!"

Auden waved his large hand back and forth in front of Jimbo's face, but he didn't even glance up. "You say he can see spirits and ghosts, so maybe we're something else, and that's why this isn't working."

That had to be it. She knew they weren't spirits—they were in some sort of in-between before becoming Leni and Ridley's mirror reflections.

The cowbell rang and Lark turned around and froze when her gaze met the couple of doppelgänger clowns. But she wasn't laughing.

"I suppose I didn't forget to pick you up this morning," Auden said with sarcasm. She'd forgotten all about their arrangement for Auden to pick her up before work. And she was sort of relieved she didn't have to go through the awkwardness of her leaving the trailer to step into his van. Her nerves would have been screaming at her to dart back inside her home.

Jimbo glanced up at the intruders. "Hey, I was just working on your schedules for the week. I was a little confused at first when I came into the store with everything moved around."

"Yeah, we did it the other day," Leni said with a smile. "Figured it would be nice to organize things for you."

Lark narrowed her eyes at Leni. Her doppel was wearing a short, lime-green skirt and a bright pink top, paired with the yellow heels Lark had worn to try and impress Auden weeks ago. Ridley was dressed the way Auden always did, *so good for him.*

"What the hell is she wearing?" Lark seethed.

"Yeah," Auden replied, but didn't take his eyes off Leni.

Lark smacked his arm and immediately wanted to do it again.

"What the hell was that for?" Then he smiled. "Jealous?"

"Um no," she lied.

He wrapped his arm around her shoulders. "Good, because there's only one Lark, and she's standing right here."

Jimbo curled a finger at Leni. "Can I speak to you alone for a moment?"

"Sure," Leni said and came around the counter while Ridley went down another aisle, scanning a few of the stuffed bats with long pointy fangs.

Lark didn't want to leave the comfort of Auden's warm arm, but she moved closer so she could make sure to catch every word.

"I finally got a chance to listen to my messages this morning, and you mentioned rats, which I already called an exterminator for, but also something about the man you've been seeing dropping off a mirror." He scratched his head. "But there's no new mirror here."

Lark and Auden both exchanged a surprised look.

"He can't see it," Auden said with a sharp inhale.

Lark tried to think if anyone had come in and checked it out. Imani was going to come with Lark once Jimbo returned, so she hadn't been there. Neither Lark nor Auden had pointed it out to Darrin, and no other customers had asked about it.

She felt so stupid.

"Yeah, sorry. Right after I called, the guy came back in and took it. I tried ringing you again, but your messages were full." She paused, looking a little nervous. "But the weird thing is, I haven't seen them again. Do you know why?"

Way to play it, Lark thought, rolling her eyes.

"Sometimes that happens." Jimbo shrugged a shoulder. "Maybe they moved on. Are you all right? You look different today."

"I've been getting into fashion lately... to match the music I listen to."

"Oh, right. To be a teen again." Jimbo adjusted his glasses, then called Ridley over, and rambled to the doppels about the store being open longer since sales had been up.

"I think we should go to the library to research curses and mirrors," Lark said. After the occult shop, and their lack of findings yesterday—besides the name Butterfly—they needed clues.

Too bad one of the books at the occult shop didn't have a spell on how to be visible.

"It's not my usual idea of entertainment, but there could be something."

The library was at the end of the street, so they walked there. They had a little less than thirteen days to break this thing.

Lark and Auden both had on their headphones when they entered the library—two peas in a messed-up pod. "Light My Fire" pulsed through her speakers and it gave her the determination she needed. Auden took the left side of the library while Lark went right, deciding they'd both meet up in the center where all the studying tables were.

When she was younger, she used to come to the library all the time until Beth forgot to return a couple of library books. Now there was a huge late fee.

She drew in the scent of old decaying pages with her nose. Because paper did die, like people, just on a slower scale. The odor of this particular kind of death smelled good, nonetheless.

Lark shifted her backpack as she strode past a small counter. Behind it, a lady wearing thick orange glasses with her hair pulled into a tight black bun organized books on a metal rolling cart.

Squeezing behind the counter, Lark took the cart's duplicate from the original. She unloaded the books and piled them on top of the library counter, big stacks at a time. The wheels squeaked as she rolled the cart through a high archway to the nonfiction side.

Travel guides lined several rows. Ireland, Greece, Spain, Japan, Iceland—places she'd never go, yet wished for with everything in her. Since they weren't given many details to help in their search, Lark grabbed as many books as she could find that might hold a key. At least she hoped they did. On a whim, she picked up a few books on the Salem Witch trials. They couldn't hurt, and who knows, she might have hit the jackpot with them. Next, she found some things on Charles Manson, and his little group of what Lark considered pretend witches, so she put his book back.

Down another aisle, she discovered a few books with curses or hexes in the titles, and she added those with the others. Even if they were made-up stories, the ideas had to have come from somewhere. The only book she found on mirrors was the construction of antique ones, so even if it wouldn't be much help, she snatched it up too.

By the time the cart was almost too hard to push, she felt it was time to head back to the middle of the library. In the inner circle of tables sat a group of three college-aged students studying. Auden was already seated at the table in the far back. While flipping through a book, his hand clenched the front of his hair.

With what he'd found and what she'd found, there had to be something.

The squeaking of the cart's wheels echoed throughout the entire library, reminding her of the sounds the Wheelers made in *Return to Oz.* She'd seen it with Imani, and it was dark and killer, even though it was *supposedly* meant for kids.

"Could you be any louder?" Auden smiled and cocked his head as he set his book in the chair beside him, staring at the wheels on the cart.

"I don't know! Could I?" Lark yelled. "Could I?" she screamed louder, scanning the area. No one looked up from their work, and it felt good to yell as loud as she could in a place that was supposed to be quiet at all costs. And she needed the scream, had been feeling it building up in her for weeks, and finally, she could release it. She pulled out a chair across from Auden, used it as a stepping-stone to stand on the table, and cupped her hands around her mouth. "Hello, fellow readers!"

Lark peered down at Auden. "You going to join in or just sit there?"

A grin spread across his face, and he leaned back with his arms folded over his chest. "I don't know, Lark! Should I?" he shouted across the library, slapping his hands down on the table.

Shaking his head, he climbed up on the table beside her. "Welcome one and all to watch as two people from the real world will vanish without a trace. Abracadabra." Auden waved a fake wand in the air. "I did it."

"Oh yeah, now make us come back!" Lark shouted to all

the non-listeners. Nothing in her life had ever felt this good, and they were the only two people to witness it.

"I don't know those words. So we'll repeat the same word again. Abracadabra."

"Tada!" She waved jazz hands in the air at the invisible crowd. "Hmm, I guess it didn't work."

"Now, on the count of three, scream," she continued. "Just let out how you've been feeling."

And they did. Lark yelled with so much emotion, she didn't know if she could ever compete with that much passion in one single sound from herself ever again.

Auden hopped from the table and stuck out his hand for Lark to grab. She could've leaped off without his help, but she liked the feel of his hand cradling hers. Once she jumped down, Lark kept her hand folded in his for a couple seconds longer than necessary, gathering encouragement.

"What did you find?" he finally asked.

Lark tore her gaze from his and let go of him, so she could point to her discoveries. Tugging out a book on the Salem witch trials, she held it up for him to see.

Smirking, he took the book from her hand and examined the description on the back. "These weren't real witches."

"Are you sure? I mean are you *sure*-sure?" she asked in a way that would make him think that maybe there was a possibility since the Mirror Keeper's scroll hadn't stated otherwise.

"You know," he began, "over two-hundred people were accused of 'the devil's magic' so it's highly doubtful."

"But couldn't at least one of those people have been a real witch?" She believed there could always be a chance.

"No." His answer came out so fast, there wasn't even time for him to really think about her question.

"Show me what you found, then." Lark angled herself so

she could watch Auden grab from his stack of books in the chair beside his. It wasn't much of a stack. More like a couple books. "That's it?" Her voice squeaked.

"Yeah, you gave me the sections with a lot of animal picture books." He handed the two findings to Lark: *Sleeping Beauty* and *Snow White*.

"What? Neither one of us is asleep." Cursed apple and cursed spindle—both had princes awaken a princess with a kiss. Lark was no princess and Auden definitely wasn't a prince.

"Hey, Snow White has a mirror," he pointed out.

She thought again about magical kisses from princes and an evil queen with a mirror. "I guess we'll have to kiss in front of the mirror and find out if it works. Maybe we can try talking to the mirror, too?"

"I think I like the first idea the best. But I didn't think about talking to it."

Enough talking about kissing, because I like the idea too.

"Okay, let's go through these other books and find a few more ideas just in case."

They discovered a lot of different things actually—immersing themselves in natural sources of water, prayer, burning a bay leaf at sunset, bathing in a bunch of herb crap. There were also a few other noteworthy items, mostly on casting spells. No remedy to make Lark visible, though. The informational mirror book didn't have much beyond the history of when they were created, and she didn't know if that was accurate anymore, given her new-found knowledge of the Mirror Dimension.

The easiest curse-breakers to start with would be the bay leaf, prayer, and kiss. So they left the library and took Jenny to the grocery store to find bay leaves.

"Do you think this will work?" she asked. "Why would it need to be a bay leaf and not some other type?"

"Well, they do give food flavor." He picked up one of the leaves and licked it down the center.

Maybe they should get as many leaves as they could find and burn them all together.

When they got back to Bubble's, she picked leaves from different bushes and trees, but that only gave her a total of five varieties.

Lark placed the new additions beside the bay leaves inside Jenny to save and use at sunset. Then she headed into Bubble's and found Auden flipping through a deck of oddity cards. The King was the strong man, the bearded lady the queen, and the wolf boy the jack. And the back of each card contained a different entertainer.

"You going to play a game of Solitaire with those?" she asked.

Clucking his tongue, he placed the cards in his back pocket. "I just might."

"Let's start this prayer."

"Do we need to kneel in front of the mirror?" he asked. She wasn't sure if he was being serious or sarcastic.

"Uh, okay." Lark crouched to her knees and put her hands together in prayer position. It was weird because there were customers along with Jimbo inside the store, but no one noticed them.

Lark elbowed Auden. "You say something."

Sighing, he closed his eyes and murmured the prayer intro lyrics from "Let's Go Crazy."

Lark elbowed him again. "Not Prince."

Auden huffed and began a prayer about letting them return

to their bodies so Lark didn't have to worry about being seen in non-black clothes like Leni had been wearing.

She laughed and said a small prayer of her own—something she wasn't sure actually constituted a prayer but was one she'd always said when Beth dropped her off at the church when she was younger. It was the best she could do.

"We still seem to be ghost-like," Auden said.

"Let's try talking to the mirror." Lark closed her eyes and pressed her palm to the top where the wood was. "Why are we like this?" No answer. "Mirror, Mirror on the wall, can you make us visible and break the curse and all?" she grumbled.

"Mirror seems to not have an answer." Auden placed his hand to the wood, and said, "Please, help us and give us our lives back."

Lark waited about a minute and dropped her hand from the wood. "You want to try the kiss now?" Her heart beat faster from just asking. She shouldn't be feeling anxiety over a kiss with Auden when they'd already done it several times. But talking aloud about it was odd, especially in front of Jimbo, who was there, but not really.

"Yeah, okay." He licked the center of his lower lip and inched forward, clasping the back of her neck as he pressed his lips softly against hers and pulled back.

That's it? A little more would've been nice, but maybe it worked.

"That didn't seem to work either," Auden said as he waved at a customer passing him.

After the disappointment from the failed prayer, the mirror talk, and the kiss, they again attempted to break the cursed thing. Unsuccessfully. Lark left and went home to check on Beth and Paloma to see if anything had changed, but it had only gotten worse. Ridley was there with Leni at the kitchen table. Beth had pulled in another lawn chair from somewhere, most likely off the side of the road.

The daily check-in finished, Lark pedaled back to the store. Auden hadn't returned yet, so she decided to go to the laundromat and see if the Mirror Keeper was there.

He wasn't.

The guy sure liked to show up when no one wanted him, but the moment she needed to talk to him, poof! Vanished. He must've been off playing some new deceptive game.

There were a few customers inside the laundromat when she peered into the window. A low noise—one that sounded like fingers snapping—trickled into her left ear. A hand grabbed hers and pressed something against her palm, wrapping her fingers around it. Flute notes came from the distance, growing closer, and then whatever was next to her blinked a bright silver and vanished.

Then the sound of the flute came even nearer. Lark tightened her grip around whatever was in her hand and placed it behind her back.

"Are you Butterfly?" Lark shouted to the parking lot. As she turned to the side, the cloaked woman stood before her, almost frozen, then her hand holding the flute dropped to her side. "You are, aren't you?"

Before Lark could ask anything else, the cloaked woman blinked out with silvery light and disappeared.

Lark unwrapped her hand and peered down at a butterfly that looked as if it was created by mirrors. The way the world around her reflected its images onto it appeared overly sharp. He'd given her this—she knew it. The Mirror Keeper had been there beside her, and the lady had done something to him again.

Keeping the object close, she walked in front of Bubble's,

and sat down on the cement, not wanting to feel confined inside the shop. The sound of Auden's engine blasted through the air, and Lark tugged down her headphones.

"Lyrics," she said scrambling to her feet as he came toward her.

"Curses," he replied.

"While you were gone," Lark rushed out, "I saw them... or I *think* I saw the Mirror Keeper's silver light. But I did see the woman, and she is definitely Butterfly. Something about the way she stopped when I said the name." She opened her palm and showed him the delicate mirror butterfly. "He gave me this."

Auden passed her the leaves in his hand and took the butterfly from her. He rolled it in between his fingers. "So he's hinting at her name being Butterfly, but what can we do with a name?"

"I wish I knew, but we'll find out." At least, she hoped so.

"Nothing of interest on my end. Ridley was gone, and I went to the park and watched Darrin skate for a few minutes."

"Ridley was gone because he was at *my* house eating dinner with Leni, Paloma, and Beth." All becoming one big, happy, fake family. It grated on her nerves more than she wanted. She shouldn't care if Beth and Paloma were the biggest fans of Lark's imposter, but it bothered her because as short of a time the doppel had been around them, she'd already surpassed Lark in daughter and sister popularity. A small part of her had always craved that loving attention from them.

"Of course he was..." Auden produced a lighter and exchanged the butterfly for the bay leaf, then squatted down beside her. "Hopefully, this works."

He struck the lighter and let the flame eat away at the bay

leaf while Lark lit the other ones. They watched together as each leaf thoroughly burned, and a heavy scent filled the air.

A young woman with her hair pulled into a side ponytail exited the laundromat carrying a full basket of folded clothing, tipping to the side.

"Hey!" Auden shouted.

The woman didn't even flinch as she adjusted the plastic clothes basket in her arms. Lark supposed the bay leaf hadn't worked either.

"I guess I'll just keep wearing my sunglasses at night." Auden pretended to slip on a pair of sunglasses. She got his reference instantly—sunglasses hid things and no one could still see them. Despite his face being filled with laughter, Lark noticed his dull eyes and the stiffness of his upper back.

She leaned her head against his shoulder, letting him know that she was with him every step of the way.

CHAPTER 19

To Auden:

Lyrics from "Happy House" - Siouxsie and the Banshees

Auden leisurely counted to ten, letting the water sway around him as he held his breath below the surface. Slowly, he lifted his head and leaned against the back of the tub. Last night, the leaf thing hadn't worked—neither had the praying. He'd already guessed it wouldn't have helped—none of his prayers when he'd been younger were ever answered.

Then there was the kiss with Lark. In that moment, he'd wanted to *really* kiss her, like he had in the movie theater, but that would've just been screwed up with everything else going on. He wet his chapped lips just thinking about it.

His fingers and toes were deeply wrinkled from sitting in the water for so long, the smell of herbs overwhelming. He didn't even know all the names of what he'd thrown into the tub.

Earlier, he and Lark had stopped by a health food store, snatching as many things as possible. Then they'd parted ways to try out the bath thing. For obvious reasons, they couldn't try it together.

There I go again. Auden shook his head, trying to push away thoughts of seeing Lark naked. With his toes, he pulled out the plug from the drain and allowed the water to dissipate around him, until it was just him sitting there. A lingering scent of peppermint remained.

They'd attempted scavenging holy water from the Catholic Church and tossing it onto the mirror—that didn't work. Scattering the tea with herbs around the home didn't work either—Lark had told Auden she'd attempted that while Paloma was in the shower.

Standing, Auden turned the shower on and rinsed away the herbal smell with his shampoo and Ivory soap bar.

A few splashes of water remained on the back of his neck, and he wiped them away as he entered the living room. His mom was seated on the couch with pink hair rollers all over her head.

He sank down beside her on the couch. "Mom?"

Her focus stayed on the TV, never once swaying to him. She was watching an episode of *One Life to Live*, one of the several soap operas she tuned in each day to watch. Auden thought they were garbage.

Leaning his wet head against the back of the couch, he tried to pull the words together. Even though he knew she couldn't hear, his hands trembled as he voiced his feelings. "I wanted to tell you I'm sorry for being bratty in my younger years, jerky in my junior high years, and distant the last few years. You're my mom. But more than anything, I'm afraid of losing you, and that's why I never wanted to be close. Because maybe you wouldn't like the real Auden if you knew him. I don't know if I like the real me—I'm not even exactly sure who I am. I know I'm not my biological father and he's not me, but there's always a part of me that's terrified I could end up like him." Pausing for a moment to swallow, he faced her again and attempted to hold back his tears. "He killed your sister, and you still loved me anyway."

Auden stayed beside his mom as she leaned on the couch arm with her hand pressed against her cheek, thoroughly entranced in her TV show and completely oblivious of what was going on. He lingered, finishing the soap opera with her —the same one he'd always refused to watch. She would never know how much he truly cared if they couldn't break the curse. And even if they did, the fear of losing her would probably still imprison the words in his throat.

He needed to figure out more about the Mirror Keeper and Butterfly. He didn't know who they were—or what they were —exactly, and from the clues gathered all he could think about were demons. But something, told him that wasn't what they were. Then there was Lark's mirrored butterfly. Where had it come from?

After returning to Bubble's parking lot, Auden found Lark already outside the oddity store window—their new hanging spot—with her eyes shut as she listened to music. He guessed she'd also found out the bathing-in-herbal-shit didn't work.

The sight of her relaxed his stiff shoulders. Quietly, he approached her and brushed the tip of his finger against Lark's wrist. She flinched as if she'd just been tickled, and her eyelids flew open.

When her eyes focused on him, she smiled. "Lyrics."

"Curses." He sat down beside her, resting his back against the wall. "Sorry, didn't mean to startle you."

"No, there are worse things that can happen."

There were, but if Lark hadn't been here in this curse predicament, he would've probably just taken off somewhere and waited for the fourteen days to end because his optimism wasn't on par with hers.

"You know I was thinking that we know the Mirror

Keeper and this 'Butterfly' lady, who I like to now think of as the Pied Piper—"

"She doesn't lure around rats," Lark interrupted

"No, but from what you told me, and from how I've seen, her music affects the Mirror Keeper at times..." He thought about the Mirror Keeper's movements whenever the melody would play.

"That's true, but what about Ridley and Leni? She doesn't seem to be controlling them."

"Maybe not now, but we don't really know that either." Auden shrugged. "The room inside the mirror is filled with still images. It could be possible the reflections are controlled from their side and that Ridley and Leni had once been, too."

"Speaking of the duo of doppels, they're inside, in case you're wondering," she said dryly.

"I have no doubt of that." When he hadn't found Ridley at the house, he could've guessed Bubble's was one of the places he'd gone to.

"I take it the bathing didn't work?"

"No." Lingering lavender caressed his nostrils. Snagging a wild curl from Lark's bob, he twisted it around his finger. "Your hair's still wet." That was the best thing he could come up with when there was so much more he wanted to say.

"Paloma was in the shower when I got there. I thought that would be weird for us to be in the bathtub at the same time and her not knowing I was there. So I waited in my room, which has gotten a makeover in the last couple of days." She gave a shudder.

"Mine still looks the same." All his posters were gone off the wall from when he'd ripped them down, but no new fashion wardrobe or music had appeared.

"That's because you have immaculate taste," she said in a proper British accent.

"I do, don't I?"

She nudged his arm with her elbow. "You could've said 'as do you.'"

Squinting his left eye, he looked toward the ball of sun in the blue sky. "You'll catch up one day."

And she nudged him again, causing him to let out a low chuckle.

He leaned forward and grabbed her hand, pulling her up. "Ready?

"Where are we going?" she asked.

"Something about that butterfly is telling me we should go into the Realm of Mirrors again."

Lark quirked a brow but followed Auden. Inside the store, Leni was chatting with a customer and smiling broadly, not acting like Lark at all. She was cute like Lark, but he preferred the original, not the imitation.

His Lark.

He froze in the middle of the store.

"What?" Lark asked.

Auden shook his head, because she wasn't his. Was she? "Nothing."

Ignoring his idiotic self, Auden crawled through the rippling mirror and cleared his head as he entered the triangular room. Lark popped in right after him.

"I'd say it appears the same," she said, surveying the walls and the leafy-textured ceiling.

Auden stared at the mirror with his name written above it —he hadn't touched his before. Curious, he approached the glass and pressed his hand against it. Instead of the coolness, a warmth, like a toasty fire, caressed his palm. Without warning, the temperature soared, almost scalding his hand, and he jerked his palm away.

A clinking sound came from the other side of the room. Auden turned to find Lark pounding at hers with her closed pocketknife.

"I think it's safe to say they don't break," he said, walking over to hers.

Taking a step back, she shoved the blade into her jacket pocket.

Auden placed his palm against her mirror and the same heat struck him. "All the others are cold. Not ours."

She cocked her head, giving the mirror a hard stare. "Probably has to do with no one being in them at the moment."

He didn't even really care about why—he just hoped there was a way to at least get Lark's evil twin back to where she belonged. "Come on."

Inside the hallway, Lark pressed her hand against Imani's mirror, feeling the coldness like he had the other day with the ones he'd touched. The visible breath escaped her lips as if she'd just stood outside in a blanket of snow.

"I do suppose ours will be cold if we end up inside the mirrors, though."

Auden shrugged. But it was safe to say she was right, and his life would be to follow that asshole, Ridley, around.

They approached the square room with the stairs and cluttered mirrors. "Up or down?" he asked.

"Down seems a bit creepier… so let's go down." Lark's voice was filled with more excitement than it should've been.

He slid his eyes to her and smiled. "Let's do this."

She brushed past him with her knife flicked open. The stairs were wide enough for them to walk beside each other, and the metal groaned beneath their feet as they went in a spiral downward to the next level. Auden swept his gaze everywhere, trying to see any loose objects scattered about. Nothing. Not even a speck of dust.

Lark stepped off the last stair to a stone floor. "Well, this is a mirror carnival straight from hell." She pulled out the butterfly from her jacket pocket and flicked her eyes from it toward the mirrors.

There were walls of mirrors, all different sizes and shapes. Auden edged closer. At the top of each one rested a wooden plaque engraved with names. Names and faces he didn't know but assumed were people out in the world at that moment. He pressed his fingers against the glass, and the cold rushed through him, just like the ones in the hall above.

Lark held up the butterfly.

"What is it?" he asked. "You notice the over sharpness of everything it reflects, too?"

"Yes, but that's not the only thing." She squinted at the wall. "All these mirrors have the same silvery sheen as this butterfly. Not like a normal mirror coloring, slightly darker."

"Like the cursed mirror in Bubble's." His eyes widened at the same time Lark's did when he came to another realization.

"Like the silvery flicker of light from the Mirror Keeper and Butterfly," Lark answered for him.

"So it's safe to say that the glass butterfly has to be from the Mirror Dimension since there seems to only be mirrors here," he said, digging into his lip with his finger. "But what conclusion can we draw about the silvery light?"

"I wish I knew." She sighed.

They headed back up the steps and attempted three more flights of stairs, first the spiral one that went up and then the other two in the corners of the room. All of them led to mirror mazes, labyrinths of sorts.

But the mirrors never reflected Auden and Lark when they stood directly in front of them, only the people's faces who matched the name.

The quiet of the place should've terrified him, but it only relaxed him.

"Do you think we're really going to find a way to break the curse?" he asked. The hint in the scroll from the Mirror Keeper seemed accurate—there was nothing useful down the mirror halls.

"If I'm being honest," Lark started, "I don't know, but we're going to fight until the end."

He liked how Lark said things the way she thought them —without endless amounts of false hope, but with just enough good sense. There was no sugarcoating anything. He wouldn't either.

Auden followed her out of the mirror and back into the oddity store. To Auden's surprise, Darrin was standing at the counter talking to Ridley.

Darrin ran a hand over his green Mohawk, rotating the skateboard in his other hand. "Are you ready?"

"For?" Ridley asked.

"Alfred Hitchcock night, remember?"

"I can do one movie. Then I'm going to sneak into Lark's bedroom, if you know what I mean." Ridley waggled his brows.

"Seriously?" Lark groaned. "I'm going to burn my sheets."

Darrin turned around to observe Leni dusting. "My girl has been looking different lately."

Ridley narrowed his eyes at Darrin. "I like it."

"I kind of prefer the old Lark."

"My boy," Lark cheered, smiling.

"I'm going to go with them and observe," Auden said. "Do you want to come?" He couldn't just do nothing, even though being around his look-alike aggravated the hell out of him.

"No, you go ahead. I'm going to go check on Imani." Lark shot him a glance that said "see you soon" before she left.

Auden waited in his van to follow Darrin and Ridley. Darrin strolled out on his skateboard and lit a cigarette. Auden noticed the way Ridley watched Darrin as if he wanted to push him off the skateboard. But instead, he hid behind a false smile.

Something was off. Auden needed to start paying attention to his instincts.

Ridley drove slower than Auden. Like he wasn't quite used to it, and maybe he wasn't, since he'd been trapped in a mirror. But then again, the mirror had reflected Auden driving. *So shouldn't that mean this dumbass should know how to drive, too?* Either way, Auden's frayed nerves couldn't take it, so he sped past the slower vehicle and then stood for about five minutes at Darrin's apartment, waiting for them to show.

When they finally arrived, he followed them up the stairs, bolting inside as Darrin unlocked the door. It'd do him no good being locked outside. He'd figured out from Lark that if they unlock the doors from inside their duplicate world, it would stay that way, unless they locked up themselves.

Auden never talked as much as Darrin by a longshot, but Ridley was even quieter. Darrin must not have noticed because he rambled on and on, never questioning Ridley's silence.

Auden, however, noticed the difference.

Darrin held up three VHS tapes. *"Rear Window, Psycho,* or *The Birds?"*

"Rear Window," Auden answered at the same time Ridley chose *Psycho.*

"Come on, *come on,* Darrin. You know I don't like *Psycho!* It's overhyped."

"You've finally crossed over to the light and know what's good," Darrin said enthusiastically, slipping out the VHS tape from its case.

"You're pissing me off, Darrin!" Auden shouted. But no one cared about Auden's yelling. No one noticed.

Mid-movie, Auden considered leaving because nothing was happening but decided to stay the night like old times. Once Ridley decided to finally leave, Auden would then go and pick up Lark to bring her back to Darrin's.

Ridley fidgeted with a piece of string hanging from his shirt instead of just pulling the son of a bitch out. When the credits finally started to roll, Ridley stood to leave, and Auden headed to the door and unlocked it so it would stay that way for when he returned.

"So it seems you've been feeling better?" Darrin asked. "No bags under your eyes. Better sleep?"

"Much better," Ridley said, rubbing the back of his neck.

Darrin opened the door and glanced to the side where a large oval mirror hung on the wall. He did a double take between the mirror and Ridley, his lips slowly parting.

Auden knew Darrin had caught onto something. "Thank Darth Vader." He slapped the side of his thigh. "I knew you weren't a total idiot, my friend." Now if only Darrin could put two and two together, but Auden doubted he would be able to come up with the crazy shit that had happened.

"Uh"—Darrin scratched the shaved part on the side of his head—"I think something's wrong with my mirror."

"What?" Ridley asked, confused. He glanced at the mirror, then at Darrin. His expression darkened to something sinister. Darrin took a step forward so he was standing in front of the glass. "Wait, no, I'm right here. But you're..." His Adam's apple bobbed and he blinked a few times as he inched backward. "I should've noticed before—there's something wrong with you—"

Auden didn't have time to do anything, not that he could have anyway. Ridley snatched Darrin by the wrist and yanked him forward. One second Darrin was in front of Auden, and the next he rocketed through him. The thumping sounds of Darrin's body rolling down the stairs ended with a loud snap below. As the blood roared inside his ears and through his veins, Auden tried to convince himself that Darrin was all right. His best friend couldn't be dead—he was like a brother.

People have said time slows when encountering death. This wasn't even Auden's death, but everything played in slow-motion. His heart thudded against his ribs, as if screaming and screaming while trying to break free. Loosening himself from the sluggish trance, he flew down the stairs to Darrin, skidding to his friend's side, desperate to make sure Darrin was okay.

He wasn't.

Darrin's body lay at an odd angle. If he couldn't get to Darrin, if his hand passed right through the body, did it mean that maybe this wasn't real at all? But no matter how much he hoped for it, Auden knew Darrin was gone. Just... gone.

Auden still tried to shake Darrin to life, pleaded with his only friend to come back, but his hands never connected with the body. Though Auden had people at school who would constantly talk to him, Darrin was one of the few he hadn't wanted to slam the door on.

It all felt surreal. He couldn't cry. His hands passed through Darrin every damn time he tried to pick him up. That must've been the reason tears wouldn't fall. Because it didn't feel real. He couldn't even help his best friend—the friend he'd had since sixth grade when they had bonded over movies. Darrin had been there to help when Auden was too drunk and when Drew had broken up with him—he had always been there.

Auden looked up the stairs and noticed Ridley had vanished. Immediately, he took the steps as fast as his legs would carry him and found the bastard in the living room on the phone.

"He fell down the stairs. I don't know what to do. Please hurry—I think he's dead," Ridley cried, almost as great as any Academy Award winner for best performance.

Jaw clenched, Auden lunged forward to strangle Ridley, but his hands passed through his neck. The frustration was palpable.

He hurried back out and down the stairs, not wanting to leave Darrin's body alone, even though he was already gone. It wasn't Auden's fault, and he wasn't going to blame himself for some bastard bringing a tainted mirror into the store, but he still loathed himself for not being able to do anything.

"You should've just told me to go to Lark's instead," Ridley said in a hushed voice from the bottom of the stairs, causing Auden to whirl around.

Ridley didn't look thrilled about what had just happened, nor did he appear unhappy. The whole incident seemed more like a rock in his shoe, easily tossed to the side.

The ambulance sirens wailed their high-pitch squeal,

turning into the parking lot. As the paramedics rushed to Darrin, Auden couldn't stick around any longer to listen to the bullshit Ridley was spewing about how Darrin went outside to smoke a cigarette, then somehow slipped and fell.

In the distance, Auden spotted the Mirror Keeper, gloved hand covering his mouth. Anger boiled in Auden's veins but before he could bolt toward him, the man vanished with a blink of silvery light.

Auden pressed his eyes closed for a moment before heading to the van. He banged the door to Jenny and drove back to Bubble's, letting the speedometer go up, up, up as fast as she could go. Why did it matter anyway?

Why did anything matter?

He swerved into the parking lot and hopped out of the van, needing to desperately talk to Lark but she wasn't back yet.

God he needed her.

And he hated that so damn much.

That need, that addiction—*filling him.* He shouldn't have to talk to anyone.

The "Happy House" lyrics Lark had written flashed through his mind, but now the path to that place seemed to be further away than ever before.

A roar of anger and sadness escaped him, echoing across the parking lot and drifting up into the sky. He yelled—what felt like a thousand times in a row—as loud as he could. He continued shouting his rage at the indifferent world until his throat felt dry and his voice raspy. Hot, fiery tears of fury slid down his cheeks, blurring his vision, and he didn't try to stop them.

CHAPTER 20

To Lark:

Lyrics from "Please, Please, Please, Let Me Get What I Want" — The Smiths

The waves of the bay pushed against Lark, and she let them. She snaked through the water until she came up and met with air, breathing deeply through her mouth. A brackish taste lingered on her tongue, despite spitting out the liquid that had seeped inside.

Treading water for a few minutes, Lark stared out at a crackling campfire where a group of people were roasting marshmallows and blaring "Sweet Home Alabama" on their boombox.

The sky had already faded to a darkened slate accompanied by a few stars and the moon. Imani hadn't been home when Lark had stopped by. She'd forgotten the beauty salon where Imani and her mom worked was open late on Tuesday nights.

On impulse, Lark decided to pedal her way to the beach and immerse herself in a natural source of water in an attempt to break the curse, which was how she now found herself swaying in the murky water. She had no problem with the human body per se or the fact that no one could see her, but there were children still running around near the water while their parents partied and listened to the boombox. So the clothes had remained on.

It was her first time being in the bay, even though Sylvan

Beach was so close. She wasn't even sure if she liked being in the water—didn't really know what was swimming beneath her feet. Another thing she didn't understand was why they called Sylvan a beach when it wasn't one at all—it was just a bay with no sand.

"I think I've been in here long enough," Lark muttered. She looked up to the almost full moon in the sky, hoping this would break the curse.

"Help! A shark!" she yelled, knowing she was crying wolf and not caring.

Because no one heard her. The people partying around kept doing their own thing.

Defeated, she stroked her way to the shore. Imani was the one who actually taught Lark how to swim in her backyard pool when she'd moved to town. Survival skills were yet another thing Beth hadn't taught the girls.

As her feet hit land, the pebbles embedded in between her toes, and she wiped away as much as she could before rolling her socks back on.

She slipped on a boot and hopped while struggling to put the other one on, almost crashing onto the loose pebbles. With a sigh, she unzipped the small pocket on her backpack and pulled out the mirror glass butterfly, wishing it would somehow call the Mirror Keeper to this spot. It didn't.

"Tell me what to do, little butterfly," she murmured. Of course there was no answer, just as there wasn't from the Mirror Keeper. She wrapped it and placed the object back in the pocket of her backpack.

Lark's hair clung to her neck, and her clothes rained drops of water down her arms and legs as she rode her bike to Bubble's. It didn't take her long to make it there through the dark. To her surprise, Auden's black van was already parked there.

Lark braked in front of Jenny and peered toward the laundromat, studying it for a whole minute. Nothing. She opened the back door to fish out clothing from her bag and stopped. In the corner, Auden lay nestled on his side, facing away from her. She wasn't sure if he was asleep and didn't want to disturb him.

Slowly, she reached for her bag, and he turned around. "Sorry," she whispered. "I didn't mean to wake you."

"I'm not sleeping." His voice sounded sad, defeated, nothing like Auden. She couldn't see his face clearly in the dark to catch his expression.

Lark turned on the dome light at the front of the van, and it illuminated just enough to see that the whites of his eyes were bloodshot. "Lyrics."

"Curses." Before she could reply, he asked, "Why are you wet?"

Giving a tug to her clingy shirt, she knelt in front of him, concerned. "I was basking in the bay, attempting to break the curse with the natural source of water. Is something wrong?"

A few tears slipped from the corners of his eyes. "Darrin's dead." His voice cracked on the words, and he released a soft sob.

Lark stilled—her back connected with the wall of the van, finding it hard to breathe and to speak. "What?" Auden had to be mistaken—Darrin was just at the store hours ago.

Auden harshly swiped the side of his face with the palm of his hand. "Ridley pushed him down the stairs when Darrin didn't see the psychopath's reflection in the mirror."

"Oh no." *Could I have said anything stupider at the moment?*

Lark wasn't good with death. She wasn't good with her own father's death—she hadn't even shed a single teardrop. Death was a disease that didn't seem real, an insidious thing that picked people off one by one. Lark knew she needed to make an attempt at comforting Auden, even though he might pull away.

Kneeling and reaching forward, she tenderly stroked his arm. "Come on."

"I just want to sleep," he said without looking at her.

"I know. Come on." She tugged his arm in the direction of the open back door.

He crawled from the van, his feet plopping down to the graveled parking lot with a heavy thump.

"Hold this for a moment." She handed him one of the sleeping bags. With the other blue roll, she unzipped it and laid it across the floor of the van, resting the two pillows beside each other at the top.

Lark took the other sleeping bag from his hand, unzipping it all the way and spreading it on top of the first one. Grabbing the top corner, she folded it back so they could slip inside.

"Just turn around for a second," she said.

Keeping quiet, Auden moved to face the other direction. Lark pulled off her partially wet top, followed by her boots and pants.

Chest heaving, she slipped beneath the sleeping bag in only her bra and panties. "Okay, come back in." He turned around and scanned her with a confused expression. "I'm not going to take advantage of you tonight if that's what you think, but take off your shirt... and maybe your pants."

Silently, Auden climbed back in the van and did what she said, leaving on his boxers. Her heart pounded, like a ticking clock, counting each second as she watched him. Lark held up the blanket for him to lie beside her. Switching off the light, he slid in and rolled to face her.

"I'm not going to pretend I know what to say or do," Lark started. "But when my dad died... Even though we weren't close, I wish there had been someone that would've held me. I know how close you and Darrin were, even though you probably wouldn't have admitted it before. But I know he would have."

A single tear crawled down Auden's cheek, and she rubbed it away with her index finger. She inched closer, folding her arms around him, and his warm skin pressed against hers. His arms circled her, holding her tight. She didn't have the perfect words, but she wanted him to feel that she was there for him. Softly, she kissed his shoulder once, gently running her hands through his hair, and writing lyrics on his back with her finger to try and soothe him until his breathing slowed.

Lark had woken up several times throughout the night, finding Auden and herself still clinging to each other. Now, there was only the absence of his heat as she rolled over to face him. But he wasn't there. Instead, a torn-out sheet of notebook paper laid beside her face.

Picking it up, she read the lyrics from "Please, Please, Please, Let Me Get What I Want," which were scrawled across the page in blue ink. He'd written different lyrics from this same Smiths song to her in the past. Pressing her lips together, she folded the note and stuck it into her backpack.

She must've slept hard because she never heard him stir or shut the door. The scent of salt lingered on her skin from the previous night as she took out a new set of clothes from her bag and got dressed before going inside Bubble's.

The cowbell rang as Lark entered the store and found Jimbo seated in front of the counter next to Leni. The clock showed it was already ten thirty.

"Auden called me this morning and won't be in to work until next week," Jimbo said. "It's a shame about what happened to his friend. I know he went to your school, so if you need to take off the rest of the week, you go right ahead." The reminder of Darrin really being gone made her insides hurt.

Leni appeared sullen, but Lark knew what a good actress the doppel was. "No, I'd rather be at work to take my mind off of everything that's going on."

Before Lark's temper could get out of control, because she couldn't rip the girl's hair out, she crawled through the mirror to see if Auden was hiding in there. She picked up the scroll, still resting on top of the table, and quickly read it again to see if maybe new miracle answers had appeared.

They hadn't.

"Auden," she called.

Lark started down the narrow mirror-filled hall, inhaling the piney scent as she continued to shout out Auden's name to no avail. She turned to the left where Darrin's mirror had been —it was no longer there. It was as if all the mirrors had shifted down to cover up the empty space. She gently rubbed the spot in between two mirrors where his should've been.

Lark was just guessing, but she supposed since Darrin had died, he no longer needed a mirror image. Her chest sank at the thought, then filled back up to the point where she felt she needed air and wasn't getting enough of it. Even though her lungs were working perfectly fine. Every single part of her had to get out of there and back outside. She didn't want to stand any longer in a hall that was now empty of Darrin too.

Leaving the store, Lark pressed her hands to her knees and gasped for breath. She stood and looked to the right, not seeing a sign of Auden. He could've gone anywhere. She knew he probably needed time to himself, and maybe he didn't want to see her. Should she have left him alone the night before? Auden hadn't seemed bothered by it.

Breathing raggedly, she glanced toward the laundromat, and her eyes widened. "The Mirror Keeper," she whispered. He stood in front of the window with his boot propped up against the glass—his usual stance.

He turned his head and faced her, and she wanted to say that their gazes were locking, but she could never tell with that stupid black mask over his face.

"Hey!" she yelled. He didn't move the slightest inch. Could he not see her now either? It had to have been him who handed her the butterfly.

Taking off at a fast pace, she shouted every name in the book she could hurl at the Mirror Keeper. When she was an inch from his chest, she shoved at it, connecting with muscled hardness beneath her hand. His back struck the window, but it didn't break the glass. Lark stared in shock at her palms. It was one thing to guess he'd be different, that she could touch him since he'd started the whole curse, but it was quite another to feel real muscle under her hands. Fury filled her, overwhelming and dismissing any rational thought.

Scowling, she had to crane her neck all the way back to look up at him. She grabbed the collar of his black trench coat, wishing she could rip it off. Angry about Darrin, worried about Auden. "You can still see me, can't you?" she said through gritted teeth. "And you gave me the figurine, right?"

Slowly, he nodded.

With a hard thrust, she released the jacket like it was burning her hand and leaving pink scars behind. Plucking the hat from his head, she tossed it on the ground and stomped on it until it was flatter than a pancake—as if that would bring Darrin back.

"Because of you," she screamed with outrage, "Auden's best friend is dead! Because of you, that bitch in there is ruining my life!" She pointed to the oddity store, then reached forward, snatching the black ski mask covering his head and pulled it off. A loud gasp escaped her lips, and she dropped the mask to the cement and jerked both hands up to cover her mouth.

He had neither face nor head. She could've dealt with a monstrous deformed beast, a scaly lizard man, or possibly something straight from a monster film. But this...

Or maybe he was from the monster films. She guessed he was closer to the Invisible Man, who did so happen to be insane and was popular during the classic monster movie era. There was no expression for her to read, and that alone made everything a hundred times worse.

Reaching down to the cement, she handed him back his mask since he was making no move to get it. It felt weird to have to stare at what appeared to be a decapitated man.

Taking it with a gloved hand, the Mirror Keeper slid the mask back over his invisible head. Neither of them made a move to pick up the hat.

"Can you not speak?" she asked. "Auden told me you showed him a note where you said you couldn't."

A low snarling groan came, like a struggling zombie, possibly worse. Squaring his shoulders, he shook his head slowly.

A light bulb of an idea went off in her head. "But you can write, correct?" He'd shown her notes and also written in the scroll.

He cocked his head, then gingerly nodded.

Holding both hands up, Lark motioned at him. "Stay here and don't leave."

She took off on a sprint for Jenny and sifted through her backpack, pulling out the mirrored butterfly, a spiral notebook, and a pen.

While she was gone, she worried he might vanish. After all, stripping down would leave him invisible, but when she came back, he still stood there, in all his black-cloaked form.

Lark sat down on the ground, gesturing for him to do the same. He stared at her. With her right hand, she tugged the edge of his trench coat, and finally, he snaked down and sat beside her.

Handing him the notebook and pen, she asked, "Did you really write Auden and me that message on the scroll we found on the other side of the mirror?"

The Mirror Keeper nodded.

She needed to know if he was being controlled. "Was it your choice to do this curse?"

He shook his head. Paused. Then he shrugged, as though he was confused.

"What do you mean?"

His hand vibrated and it took him ages to write the words, *Must do it.* If it took the Mirror Keeper this long to write that, then how long did it take him to write the letter?

"Fuck, would it be faster if I get a Ouija board?" There were four for sale beside the goat skulls in the oddity store, and she could go and grab one.

With a tilt of the head, he shrugged again. She took off and ran inside Bubble's, scooping the one that was already out of the box for display along with the triangular planchette piece. In actuality, he could just use the pen to point at letters on the board. She also realized she could've just written the letters of the alphabet on a sheet of paper in the spiral notebook. But she already had the Ouija in her hand, and she was going to put it to good use.

"Is there really a way to break the curse?" she asked, handing him the objects.

He probably could've just nodded, but he pushed the pointer to the word that read *YES*. This was much faster than the shaky writing.

"How?"

Hands shaking, he used the letters across the board to spell out *FORBIDDEN TO SAY*.

Of course... Why couldn't any of this be clear and easy?

She held up the mirrored butterfly. "You gave me this. There was also the name Butterfly written on the bottom of the box in the mirror. Is this the name of the flute player? It is, right?"

Using the planchette, he moved to different letters. *I CALLED HER.*

Lark's eyebrows lowered. Called her where? Her back straightened. "It's your nickname to her?"

He nodded.

"Is she controlling you?"

The triangular piece pointed to *YES*. But then it slid to *NO*.

"There's someone else?"

He nodded.

"Who?"

The Mirror Keeper's hand stalled, then became jerky, dropping the planchette.

"Please, you have to tell me!"

A noise penetrated the air—slow melodic sounds of the flute. *No. Not again.* Lark whirled around to the familiar "Space Oddity." There, only a few feet away, stood the cloaked woman—Butterfly—with the flute raised.

"Just, wait!" Lark screamed, her heart galloping. "Just explain to me what's going on."

The woman crept closer and stopped playing, watching Lark, then she shook her head. She pressed back the hood, revealing only emptiness, like the Mirror Keeper. The notes poured again out of the flute.

With a trembling hand, the Mirror Keeper reached forward to the planchette to spell something out, but the piece wouldn't budge. His body stiffened and his chin lifted to hers, unmoving. Before her very eyes, he and the woman vanished into thin air like a genie disappearing, minus the bottle. A silver glow lingered and then snuffed out. The pen and notebook in the Mirror Keeper's lap had disappeared along with him.

If Auden had been there, he probably would've stabbed the guy. In fact, maybe Lark should've tried stabbing the woman, but she felt it would've done nothing except cause her to maybe bleed invisible blood.

The butterfly figure still remained, and Lark brought it up to her face. "With your wings, tell me where to fly to and break this curse, little butterfly."

CHAPTER 21

To Auden:

Lyrics from "Sweet Dreams" – Eurythmics

Auden stood in front of the place where Darrin's mirror should've been, and it wasn't there. All the mirrors had shifted down as if Darrin's had never been there at all, as if his wasn't as important as the living. If this place was an in between sort of thing, then he wondered what the actual Mirror Dimension was like. Most likely a shithole.

It was Friday evening, and Auden had been gone for two days. He hadn't wanted to go, though. Selfishly, he'd wanted to stay wrapped up in Lark's arms, but it felt wrong to feel something in his chest brewing, an elated emotion, when his best friend was now being prepared for a funeral.

Auden had spent Wednesday and Thursday drowning himself in alcohol at the beach. He'd been surprised he hadn't needed to get his stomach pumped at the hospital. After that last bit, he knew he needed to stop medicating with alcohol. It was that need again—that crutch trying to prop him up—when sometimes all a person needed was to fall apart to get better.

The thing that bothered him most of all about Darrin dying was that Ridley had the same face as Auden. To Darrin it had looked like Auden pushing him down the stairs. Darrin had known something was wrong with Ridley, but did he even guess that it wasn't really Auden? That was the image Darrin carried with him to the grave, and it hurt more than anything. An alcohol binge was the only way to make the pain stop.

Auden knew Darrin wouldn't want him to sit around acting pitiful, especially if there was a girl involved. He smiled to himself, imagining Darrin's reaction. *Auden, are you going to leave my girl hanging?*

He quietly sang lyrics from "Sweet Dreams" slowly and softly to any of the faces remaining in the room before leaving.

As he crawled back out of the mirror to the inside of Bubble's, Jimbo was the only one working, and he had the Everly Brothers cranked up. Auden almost chuckled to himself as Jimbo danced while unwinding the cord of the vacuum cleaner.

Outside the store, Lark's bike still wasn't there. Disappointment filled his chest once again as it had earlier when he came back to find her gone. What had he expected? For her to sit around and wait for him? Maybe he *had* been wanting that —selfish as it was. But she had a curse she needed to try and break, and so did he.

Auden opened the back door to Jenny, giving her a soft pet —an apology for distancing himself from her too. It had felt good, though, to be able to walk away for as long as he'd wanted.

A flash of red caught his attention, and he hitched forward to grab the notebook and a sheet of lined paper, folded in half, beneath it. He flipped open the notebook first, eager to see if she'd decided to leave it blank or not.

The page wasn't empty—she had written lyrics from "Don't You Want Me."

Quickly, he shut the book and placed it in his back pocket.

He unfolded the note, heart thundering in his chest as he scanned it over.

Auden,

I don't know if you'll be back or not to read this, but I'm going to Shannon's party to watch over Paloma since she'll be with Leni. It could be possible that I may overhear something too. Maybe I'll see you there.

Lark

With a defeated sigh, Auden refolded the note. He should've been around, contemplating how to fix the curse for Lark. Instead, he'd been too busy dwelling over his friend, who he couldn't even help anymore. Lark was still there, and he may not have cared that much about what happened to himself, but he didn't want her to end up stuck in a mirror.

Lark would hate having to dress like Leni, and if the circumstances weren't as dire as they were, he might've teased her about it.

Maneuvering himself to the front seat, he started Jenny's engine and listened to her purr. Auden was going to head to the party, but he wasn't going to drink, just as he hadn't at the last party. Instead, he said the words aloud that Darrin used so frequently, "I'm going to find my girl."

🎧 CHAPTER 22

To Lark:

Lyrics from "Safety Dance" — Men Without Hats

Lark parked her bike beside the wooden steps of her trailer, worrying about the curse and thinking about her interaction with the Mirror Keeper. Since Auden had been gone, she'd waited for long amounts of time outside the laundromat, hoping for the Mirror Keeper to return. He hadn't.

Lark arrived as Cheryl's truck flew through the trailer park, her brakes screeching as she slammed on them. Then she punched the horn.

With hurried motions, Lark lifted her bike into the bed of the truck and hopped inside before Leni and Paloma came out.

Cheryl honked the horn again. Paloma and Leni finally came strolling out, wearing matching red miniskirts with leggings. The only difference between them was that Paloma had on a shorter and tighter tank top.

Lark wished she was blind, so she wouldn't have to see the display of her body like that. She cringed to herself because Leni even walked differently than she did, more flirtatiously, a little sway with the hips. Like the way Lark had attempted to do in the music store to impress Auden…

Cheryl's driving felt vomit inducing most of the time. But it was a thousand times worse from the bed of the truck, where every single bump jolted Lark. She lay on her back and watched the sky move above her, before realizing it only made things worse. The truck's brakes slammed, and Lark lurched upward, striking her head against the metal. Rubbing the sore spot at the top of her skull, Lark struggled out of the hell machine. She took out her bike and placed it beside a tall and thin pine tree in front of Shannon's house.

Once inside the two-story home, Lark leaned against the wall, arms crossed, and observed everyone. Her classmates were smiling, laughing, and drinking, not the least bit bothered by the fact that Darrin, someone they all knew, had died.

Even Shannon seemed okay, and she'd had a thing with Darrin. It all felt abnormal—and *wrong*. One second Darrin had been alive, the life of the party, and the next he was forgotten—yesterday's news. She supposed people just wanted to pretend like it didn't happen and escape for a while. Felisa wasn't anywhere to be seen, though, and Lark was sure *she* cared.

Thoughts of Darrin eventually led Lark back to Auden. She'd believed—hoped—that he'd come back Wednesday night, but he never had. She'd gone to his house and ridden across town but hadn't found him there either.

And she missed him.

She didn't mind being alone, but this new life of hers was better with him around. Plus, she needed to talk to him in person about the Mirror Keeper. But when she thought about how there was someone else pulling the strings, her best option was to see what Leni was up to. Because maybe she and Ridley were the ones in charge of the curse? It made sense to Lark.

Musical beats from Prince played through the air. Paloma danced with Cheryl and Leni—a whole new clique. Paloma's shitty love interest, Craig, shuffled through the crowd making his way to her sister. He was tall and stocky with deep brown skin and inky black hair—short on top and curly in the back.

Imani stepped inside, dressed in jeans and a Blondie T-shirt. She appeared melancholic as she scanned the crowded room. At first, Lark thought she was there to browse, but then her gaze stopped with intent on Leni.

"Imani," Lark called. As usual, no one heard her.

Lark pressed away from the wall and followed her friend. Imani halted in front of the tall music speakers and tapped Leni on the shoulder.

"Yeah?" Leni answered in a bored voice as she turned to face Imani.

"Can I talk to you for a minute?" Imani's sorrowful expression switched into a slight scowl.

"I guess."

What's going on? Were they mad at each other or something? It shouldn't have made Lark want to listen to "Safety Dance" with joy, but it thrilled her to know that was a strong possibility.

"Outside?" Imani asked.

Leni let out a huff of air and rolled her eyes but trailed behind Imani, Lark directly on Leni's tail.

Imani whirled around as soon as Leni shut the door behind her. "What's the matter with you?"

Leni furrowed her brows and lifted her chin as if she was better than Imani. "The matter with *me*?"

"Yes! We were originally supposed to ride to the party together but after Darrin…" Imani paused for a moment, swiping her right eye with the heel of her hand. Taking a few deep breaths to gather herself, she finally started talking again. "After Darrin died, I asked if we could watch movies at your place instead, and you said yes. I didn't feel it was right to come party—we were just with him the other weekend. Then when I get to your house, Beth tells me you went to the party with Paloma and Cheryl."

"Can I not change my mind?" Leni shrugged and cocked her head.

"You could've at least called me!" Imani shouted. "And what about Auden, huh? Don't you think he needs someone right now?"

Lark surveyed the area because things were growing intense. She expected to see people staring, but everyone seemed to be inside the house or in the backyard.

"Cheryl's going to drop me off at his house after the party." Lark wanted to scream that Leni didn't need to be comforting the fake Auden at all—especially not in Auden's or Lark's bed.

"And see, you couldn't have picked up the phone and made a call that would've taken less than a minute? And what about us scheduling to meet up with Jimbo?"

"It slipped my mind," Leni said with a dismissive wave, as if Imani was trash. "I already told you I haven't seen anything again and Jimbo says that happens a lot."

"Fine, but what is this?" Imani motioned her hand up and down beside Leni. "Why do you look like Paloma's actual twin all of a sudden?"

"Maybe because I'm tired of dressing like shit and wearing all black."

Lark's fists clenched at her sides, wishing her blade would've ended the doppel a long time ago. This was a disaster waiting to happen.

"No, that isn't it. Even when you've worn color, it's a whole different style." Imani reached forward and tapped Leni's arm covered in bracelets. "And you hate Madonna."

Jerking her arm back, Leni rotated a large cuff bracelet around her wrist. "Maybe I like her now."

"Seriously, are you forgetting a boy we were with at Rocky Horror just *died*?" Imani's eyes glistened, which caused Lark's to tear up.

"Are you just upset because you couldn't bring yourself to screw him? Too busy obsessing with the opposite sex?" Leni smirked and flicked her hair, which looked stupid since it wasn't even that long.

Anger boiled inside Lark, and she lunged at Leni but passed right through her.

"You know what?" Imani took several steps back, holding up her hands. "I don't even know you anymore. This Lark... *this* Lark, I wish didn't exist at the moment."

Grinning, Lark nodded. "That's right, Imani. Keep it up." Then Lark thought about the incident between Ridley and Darrin and how that had ended. She reached forward and tried to pull Imani back and tell her to stop. She cursed herself when her hands didn't connect with her friend.

Leni reached forward and clamped a hand on Imani's wrist. "Look, I'm sorry, I didn't mean any of it. Let me go inside and mix you a drink. I'll be right back."

Imani's eyes narrowed as the door closed behind Leni, angry tears springing from her eyes. "You know I don't drink alcohol," Imani said aloud to herself.

"Yes, keep thinking that! I'm right here. But please don't say anything else to her," Lark begged.

Imani turned and stormed away, and Lark's shoulders relaxed.

Lark hurried back inside the house, cutting through people and finding Leni alone in the kitchen right as she was finishing up mixing a drink for Imani. The doppel flipped open the flap of her small rectangular purse and drew out a tiny bottle. Lark frowned in confusion.

Glancing up, Leni flicked her gaze around the room, then poured something into the cup from the small glass vial. She hastily placed the bottle back into her purse before stirring the drink.

"What do you think you're doing?" Lark demanded. Was she trying to poison Imani or drug her? Based on what had happened to Darrin, she could guess the answer.

She stayed on Leni's heels. The doppel stepped outside, noticing Imani was already gone, then stared down at the drink. "What a waste."

"Hey!" Paloma yelled, grabbing Leni's arms. "Come on, Lark! Dance with me until Craig comes back. He's doing shots outside with the guys." Paloma lifted the full drink from Leni's hands.

Lark pushed forward, trying to shove the cup from her sister's hand, but her ghost-like position prevented the contact. Her heart beat erratically in her chest. "Just dump it out!" she screamed.

Following the two girls into the living room, she watched Paloma place the drink on the counter and started dancing with Leni. Lark snatched the cup up and poured the liquid down the sink, but the original still remained.

Leni either forgot about the drink or didn't care as she and Paloma danced next to the couch. Lark slouched beside the counter, knowing she would stick around, but desperately wanting to hunt Imani down at the same time.

If she were to go to Imani's, Lark would only become more frustrated because she wouldn't be able to do anything or tell her that Leni was a piece of shit who didn't know what she was talking about.

After two full songs, Paloma shouted over the music to the girls, "I'm thirsty!" Leni continued to dance with Cheryl and didn't even glance at Paloma as she walked to the counter and stopped in front of Lark, picking up the cup the doppel had set down earlier.

"Don't be an idiot, Paloma! You don't just grab drinks that've been sitting out!" Lark shouted in her sister's face, spittle flying.

But Paloma didn't hear her and drank half the cup before staring hard at it. She shrugged and went outside with Lark right behind her. Craig hovered near the keg, making a sexual thrust with his hips and arms. The four guys surrounding him all laughed and tried to cover it up when Paloma pulled up to the group. Lark had a pretty strong feeling Craig was talking about her *virginal* sister, who would probably be dumb enough to give it up to the guy.

At least with Scott, Lark knew she wasn't in love with him. She did it because she wanted to. Paloma would most likely have sex with Craig thinking they were going to get married one day—she probably thought that now—but then he'd toss her out like yesterday's trash.

"Oh, hey, Paloma," Craig said, straightening and becoming the perfect fake gentleman. "I was just telling the guys what great dance moves you have." Lark rolled her eyes at the imbecile.

Paloma tossed her hair. "Yeah? I watch a lot of MTV with Cheryl."

Craig draped an arm around Paloma's shoulders, and she pressed closer to his broad chest. Not even two seconds later, his hand veered down to her butt.

Lark would've walked away right then, but her stupid twin had drunk from whatever skull and crossbones venom

Leni had poured into that cup. And no matter what their differences had been in the past, Lark didn't intend to leave her alone. But Paloma still appeared fine.

Although, beads of perspiration gathered above her sister's lip and brow. It wasn't that hot outside—slightly warm with a light gust of wind drifting around them.

"It's too hot out here. Let's go back inside," Paloma whined, tugging on Craig's arm.

His meaty legs stood still with his feet planted on the ground. "I'll meet you back in there, babe... unless you want to go somewhere more private."

One of the guys with a dimpled chin, the sort that made it look like he had a butt on his face, tried to hide his snicker like he was an immature sixth grader.

Tossing her head back, Lark sighed and rolled her eyes. Her sister started to say something, but Paloma's knees suddenly buckled and she slumped to the ground. Lark dove forward and tried to catch her, but Paloma slipped right through her arms, hitting her head against the concrete.

Lark's angry gaze ripped from her sister and bore into Craig, who picked Paloma off the ground. How had he not caught her? Was he too busy holding the damn beer still in his hand? She got her confirmation of his idiocy when he didn't even bother to set it down before lifting Paloma back up.

"What's wrong with her?" one of the other guys with auburn hair and freckles asked.

Craig set down his beer—finally. "I think she's had too much to drink." He placed his hand on Paloma's jaw and gently shook her face. "Babe? Are you all right?"

"No, you idiot!" Lark yelled. "She probably has a concussion! And you shouldn't have moved her!"

Craig tapped Paloma's cheek and looked at one of the guys. "She's not waking up. Go get Shannon."

"Is she breathing?" Lark screamed into the void. "Does she have a heartbeat right now?" Worry coursed through her —maybe her sister wouldn't be all right. Why hadn't Paloma just stayed home? Why did Imani have to come? Why was Leni such a bitch? Why did Lark have to be cursed?

Shannon tore through the door into the backyard, locating Paloma, and placing two fingers against her throat. Pausing for a moment, she finally said in a frantic tone, "I can't feel anything."

Leni and Cheryl burst through the door and joined the group. Lark kept her anger in check as she studied Paloma, waiting for her eyes to open.

"She doesn't have a pulse," Shannon cried, turning to Leni.

"You don't even have your fingers on the right spot!" Leni shouted. She bent down, pressing her fingers against the blue vein on Paloma's neck—and waited. "It's there but it's faint."

Did Leni even know that Paloma drank her cocktail of death? Lark wanted to scream, to throw a tantrum like a two-year-old and kick all these idiots out of the yard and hold her sister. Her *moronic* sister.

"I'm calling 911," Cheryl said and ran inside.

"What?" Shannon yelled, taking off after her. Lark stayed close behind. "My parents are going to flip out, especially after last time. Maybe she'll be fine."

"Maybe?" Lark shouted at Shannon. "Are you more concerned about what your parents will think over Paloma's life? Maybe you should've thought about not having a party after getting in trouble a few weeks ago!"

"No, I'm calling," Cheryl snapped, placing her hands on

her hips. "Would you rather be grounded or risk Paloma dying?"

Shannon didn't answer. Lark couldn't believe she was actually contemplating the issue.

Cheryl dialed the number and waited for someone to pick up on the other end. "Yes, I have a friend who just collapsed." Lark wasn't fond of Cheryl, but at least she was a good friend to Paloma.

Lark ran back outside. The guys were drunk, and Craig looked wobbly as he carried Paloma inside to the couch. She was afraid he was going to drop her sister and make Paloma hit her head again. Leni knelt beside Paloma and held her hand, making Lark go mad.

Cheryl hung up the phone and looked at Shannon and Craig. "The ambulance is on their way."

In that moment, Lark could finally find time to breathe steadily. Her sister still had a pulse. People around them were hightailing it out of there, including all of Craig's friends.

Craig's eyes darted around the living room, and Cheryl noticed too. "You have to stay—you were a witness."

If Lark made it back to the real world and Paloma survived, she was going to tell her to drop everyone except for Cheryl, not that her sister would listen.

After maybe five minutes, loud sirens wailed from outside, drawing closer. Shannon flung open the door, allowing two paramedics to come inside with a stretcher. They rattled off questions that no one could give any answer to—besides Craig who said she'd just fell—as they placed Paloma on the stretcher. Lark knew every single answer, but everyone was deaf to her words.

In a hurry, she followed the paramedics outside just as a police cruiser parked at the end of the street. Shannon and

Craig panicked. *Good. I hope they get in trouble.* Cheryl appeared stricken and started to sob, her blonde hair falling into her face. Leni silently hurried behind the paramedics into the ambulance.

Lark didn't stay to see what would happen. She hopped into the back of the ambulance and rested her hand over Paloma's. She avoided looking in the doppel's direction, who was the cause of all this. Even though Lark couldn't feel Paloma, she hoped her sister would somehow know she was there.

# CHAPTER 23

To Auden:

Lyrics from "Time After Time" - Cyndi Lauper

Auden pulled to a stop behind a police car in front of Shannon's large house. Someone must've put a halt to the party from the look of things—no other cars were lining the street. Lark's bike sat propped against the trunk of a pine tree. But which Lark?

He stepped out of Jenny and strode toward the bike. His hand gripped the handlebars—so it was Lark's set of wheels. She had to be there somewhere.

As he drew closer to the house, Shannon, Craig, and Cheryl stood outside talking to a police officer in her late twenties. The cop's hair was pulled back into a tight braid, and she jotted things down on a notepad.

Shannon's body trembled, tears streaked Cheryl's cheeks, and Craig looked as if he wanted to be anywhere other than there.

"I don't know," Shannon answered. "Paloma seemed fine when she was dancing."

"Paloma?" Auden asked aloud to himself. Did something happen to her?

"We were dancing," Cheryl started, "and then she mentioned how she wanted a drink. After that, she headed outside to Craig."

"She was fine," Craig added. "Then all of a sudden she

passed out and hit her head on the ground. I think she may have been drunk."

"No." Cheryl's eyes bulged at him. "I didn't even see her sip on anything until she went off to get something to drink before finding you, Craig."

"She'll be tested for all that at the hospital," the police officer noted.

Something wasn't right here—he had to find Lark. Auden shot past the small group to get inside the house. "Lark!" he called. "Lark!" He went into each room, the backyard, then to the front again.

The police officer had mentioned the hospital. He assumed Lark must be at the one where Paloma had been sent. *Dammit, I should've been here.*

Jogging down the drive, Auden loaded Lark's bike in the back of his van and sped off in the direction of the nearest hospital as "Time After Time" blasted through the speakers, reminding him of his urgent need to get to Lark. He could only think of two reasons why Paloma would be in the hospital—Ridley or Leni. The curse was doing too much damage, and he could do nothing to stop it.

Just past a row of trees, the hospital slid into view. Auden turned in and skidded to a stop at the curb in front of the tan building. No other invisible people would be asking him to move his vehicle.

Yanking open the glass door's duplicate to the hospital, he flew inside like a bat straight out of hell to a waiting room with a dozen or so people. Some were coughing and another held gauze against a knuckle, staunching the blood from what looked to be a missing digit.

Where should he go? The hospital was filled with so many rooms that he didn't know where to start looking. A woman, smelling as if she'd just smoked a whole pack of cigarettes, rushed past him and stopped in front of the receptionist at the desk.

"I need to find my daughter." Her voice came out raspy and frenzied.

The receptionist with dark frizzy hair set down her pencil. "Slow down. What's her name?"

"Paloma Espinoza."

Auden's head whipped to the woman with tightly permed curls. *She must be Beth.* He inched closer to the desk, leaning over to scan the pages as the receptionist sifted through them.

"She was just brought in. You're going to have to go into the lobby and check in with them. They'll have paperwork for you to fill out." The receptionist rattled off to Beth the direction to another waiting area two halls down.

Auden followed Beth down the disinfectant-smelling, blinding-white hall, her fingers twitching as if she was desperately craving to light a cigarette right there. The thought of cigarettes reminded him of Darrin, and he didn't want to go there. The pain was still too raw. He had to focus on what was happening.

When they reached the open area, decorated with two fake potted plants and filled with patterned upholstered seats, Auden's eyes fell to Lark in the middle of the room, sitting alone in a chair. But when Beth rushed to her and wrapped her in a hug, he knew it was Leni. He should've known right away from how she was dressed. But his gaze had lingered on her face, and he'd wanted to run to her too.

"What happened, baby doll?" Beth asked, still holding onto her fake daughter.

"I don't know," Leni sniffed. "She was outside and then

passed out." Auden didn't believe a single word out of her mouth.

"I knew I shouldn't be letting you girls go to these parties."

"She wasn't drunk."

Stepping away from Leni, Beth checked in with the man at the front counter. He then took Beth and Leni to a short and wide hallway in the ER. A tall, lanky man with balding hair strolled out, pulling away his face mask.

"Are you the parent?" he asked Beth.

"Yes, is she okay?" Her hands were clasped in a prayer.

"Right now, she's stable." The doctor tilted his head to the side. "But we did have to pump her stomach. Has she ever been depressed? Ever attempted suicide?"

Beth straightened and shook her head, tears slipping down her cheeks. "No, not Paloma. She's never done anything like that."

"Maybe someone slipped something into her drink. If so, we can report it. We have to run tests, but it looks like she may have been poisoned."

Auden's gaze automatically went to Leni, knowing the answer. As soon as the doctor said the word poison, her face had shifted for a split second. A glimpse of guilt had been there in the way her eyes widened, but before anyone could see it, her expression became grief-ridden all over again.

"Poisoned?" Beth scoffed as if it were an impossible fate to think about.

"The two of you can go in and see her, but she probably won't be awake for a while." He pointed them in the direction of Paloma's room—down the first hallway on the left.

Leni wrapped her arm around Beth's waist as Lark's mother began to cry.

Auden moved ahead to where the doctor had pointed and spotted Lark right away. Her wild curls looked more tangled than ever. Her forehead was pressed against the window while her warm breath fogged up the cool glass. The AC inside the hospital was working overtime to combat the blazing Texas heat.

He wanted to fold himself around her, but he stayed at the edge of the hallway. Beth and Leni strode past him and entered Paloma's room.

Lark's head lifted from the glass, and she stared in the direction of Beth and Leni. Her shoulders fell, and she returned her forehead to the window.

Auden debated with himself whether to wait or go ahead and approach her. In the end, he did what he wanted—fears be damned.

She didn't even angle her head back from the glass to look at him, too entranced with the picture before her. Beth took Paloma's hand, and Leni held Beth's other one as well as Paloma's, forming their own inner circle. One Lark was painfully isolated from.

Leaning forward, Auden wrapped his arms around Lark's waist and settled into her. He nestled his chin onto her shoulder and whispered in her ear, "Sorry, I was late meeting you at the party."

"Lyrics," she breathed.

"Curses," he exhaled.

CHAPTER 24

To Lark:

Lyrics from "Behind Blue Eyes" — The Who

When Monday arrived, after Lark's Weekend of Hell, Paloma was released. Lark had stayed at the hospital every night, watching over her sister with Auden by her side.

At night, they passed the notebook back and forth and played almost every game with the deck of oddity cards that existed.

Lark had gone to Darrin's funeral on Saturday with Auden, and she'd pressed her bicep against his, letting him know she was there if he needed her. She'd also told him about seeing the Mirror Keeper, which she couldn't help but think about as Auden drove toward her home.

You know the Mirror Keeper?" she asked, stroking the edge of an oddity card on the hospital floor of Paloma's room, remembering the awkward Ouija board situation.

Auden's eyebrows furrowed, a hard crease appearing in between them. "Yeah? What about the jackass?"

She flipped over another card. "When you disappeared for those few days, I saw him in front of the laundromat."

"And you're just now telling me?"

"There's more to it than that. I talked to him."

Auden dropped his card and swung his hand up, his eyes shutting tightly for a moment. "Let me get this straight. You talked to the asshole, and you didn't tell me earlier?"

252

"*Yeah, that's what I'm saying,*" she said through clenched teeth, afraid of him hearing the words. "*You've only been back with me an hour, not days, and I wanted to tell you in person.*"

"*Go on,*" he said as he continued to glower at the stark white wall.

Taking a deep and slow swallow, she explained everything that had happened in full detail with the Mirror Keeper—most importantly, the part where he had no head and probably no body underneath all the black clothing. Then she told him how she'd brought out the notebook and Ouija board for the Mirror Keeper to use, and how the cloaked flute player was named Butterfly, but it was a nickname from the Mirror Keeper. But then the flute player took him away again. "*Apparently, there is someone else pulling strings, and my guess is that it's Leni and Ridley. How, you ask? I don't know yet.*"

He placed two fingers on the side of his head and didn't say anything.

"*When Butterfly played 'Space Oddity,'*" Lark continued, "*he went more than puppet-like this time—he's definitely being controlled by that music. For example, if you were holding the controller to a remote-control car and making it drive around, the car couldn't stop, even if it wanted to, only if you made it quit going. So he isn't totally to blame here.*" She felt awesome for coming up with that analogy all on her own.

"*I don't care. If I see him again, he's dead.*" Auden pointed at least ten times at the card on the hospital tile floor.

While Auden went to check on his family over the weekend, he'd driven by the laundromat, but he never encountered the Mirror Keeper and neither did Lark. It had still stood empty. Now, they pulled up in front of her trailer, and Auden put the van in park. A few seconds later, Beth eased to a stop in the driveway with Paloma.

"I'll be right back." She told him to wait for her, not only to be alone with her family but because she was secretly embarrassed for him to see the inside of her home. It wasn't a house like his, and her mattress was on the floor, for Pete's sake.

Lark stepped out of the van and followed Beth and Paloma inside. She wanted to make sure they got home all right.

Beth set down an overstuffed duffel bag beside her recliner and turned to Paloma. "Now listen, sweetie pie, you are officially forbidden from parties. Especially with Shannon. Cheryl told me how that girl treated you, and I don't like it one bit. I'm shoving my foot in the ground."

"You mean through the trailer?" Lark said with a smile— Beth, of course, didn't hear her. Maybe Beth was really stepping up her game. She hadn't left the hospital either—she'd slept in the cramped chair beside the bed. Leni came back and forth, accompanied by Ridley most of the time, causing Lark to shout her rage.

"That's fine, Mom." Paloma yawned. "I just want to sleep in my room for a while."

"Here, let me help you." Beth snaked her arm around Paloma's waist and guided her to her room as if she was an invalid. Paloma no longer needed the help, but she leaned into Beth anyway.

From the look of things, Paloma and Beth were safe with Leni, unless one of them happened to catch her without her reflection.

Lark's chest tightened as she spun around and headed out of the trailer. It was no use moaning and sulking that she couldn't be there for her family all day when she had bigger fish to fry.

"Hey," Auden said with the edges of his mouth tilting up when she took a seat on the passenger side.

"Hey," she replied with a small smile in return. "I'd say I'd invite you in the next time we're here, but I'm not sure when that'll be yet."

The smile slipped off Auden's face, and he gripped the steering wheel. "Again, I'm sorry, I shouldn't have just gone off like that."

She shrugged as if it was no big deal. "It's okay, though. We still have until 11:59 on Saturday."

His grip loosened on the wheel, and his gaze focused on her. "I think your optimism may be rubbing off on me a bit."

"You're here. I'm here. We'll keep doing the best we can." She always had herself, but the addition of him seemed to strengthen things.

Auden tossed the red notebook onto her lap and took off in the direction of Bubble's. She opened the notebook and read the lyrics from Blondie's "Call Me."

Closing the book, she turned to him. "Auden?"

He turned his head to look at her. "Yeah?"

"Just calling you."

"Anytime."

Her lips twitched and she sat back, tucking the small notebook into the front pocket of her backpack.

As Auden drove, she leaned her head back against the seat and closed her eyes, listening to "Behind Blue Eyes" through the speakers, Jenny's engine, Auden's minor movements— everything that gave her comfort. He pulled to a stop, and she opened her eyes to the parking lot in the strip mall of Bubble's.

She hoped to catch another glimpse of the Mirror Keeper, but he still wasn't there. More than anything, she needed to find a way to break this curse, not only for herself or Auden, but to protect their families.

Together, they headed inside Bubble's, finding Jimbo eating a sandwich and potato chips. On the counter rested a stack of Magic 8 Balls, along with two expensive-looking crystal balls atop golden stands.

"You want me to read your fortune?" Lark asked Auden.

"I'll read it for you." He rubbed his hand over the "magic" crystal ball. "Shitty."

"Sounds about right." Lark was mid-reach for a plastic Magic 8 ball when the cowbell rang. Out of habit, she turned around to look at the customer. In strolled Imani, striding toward the counter, her hair appearing disheveled for the first time ever. She had a sinking feeling it was because of what had happened with Leni.

Jimbo set the bag of Ruffles down, making loud chomping noises as he chewed the rest of the chip before speaking. "Imani, did you come back for more of the miracle remedies?"

"No, even the bubbles didn't blow right."

"You probably didn't use them correctly." He pushed his glasses up the bridge of his nose.

"Dip a stick in and blow." She forcefully air pumped a pretend stick into a pretend bottle of bubbles. Sheena had even complained about those bubbles when Lark had watched the movie at Imani's house the other week.

Jimbo scrunched his face in confusion, obviously thinking Imani was full of it. "Aren't you supposed to be at your new job?"

"I actually took the day off."

"Do you want to come back? I may open up on Sundays now since the business has been booming," Jimbo said.

Lark strummed her fingers against her thighs, wondering how Imani was feeling from the other night, wishing her friend could see her right then.

"Possibly in the future." Imani rubbed the side of her chin. "But first I have a question for you about Lark."

Lark perked up and shifted even closer, leaning across the counter. Auden stepped right beside her.

"Yeah?"

"Have you noticed anything odd about her lately?" Imani asked, her dandelion hair bobbing. Lark couldn't help but think again of the showdown between Imani and Leni, and her heart hurt about the things that were said to her friend.

"She still listens to her headphones up here." Jimbo shrugged.

She may be listening to headphones, but it's not the same music.

"She's been dressing differently though."

"They're just clothes—she told me she's been trying out new fashions. Besides, you used to show me new purses every week."

"Hmm."

"Don't hmm, like you're contemplating what he said!" Lark shouted while Auden toyed with his lip as he watched.

Jimbo squinted his eyes as if deep in thought. "Although, she has been more talkative. Normally, she's stuck in a book when she's not listening to her headphones, even though I have a music box right there." He pointed his thumb—as if he was about to hitchhike—at the radio.

"What about the haunting situation? She told me she talked to you about it when you got back."

Lark rubbed her hands together because now they were getting somewhere.

"Right when I got back, and she came in to the store, we discussed it. Said she thinks the ghost finished up its unfinished business. I told her that happens. Sometimes spirits just move on."

"Dammit, Jimbo." Lark ground her teeth.

Imani leaned forward and peered over the desk. "Well then, what about the mirror the man dropped off? Can I see it?"

"Lark said he already came back and got it before vanishing from her life."

"Tell her when, Jimbo! So she can add up the time frame!"

"Oh."

"Imani, keep digging around," Lark begged.

"It's probably just me," Imani continued. "People grow and change all the time. Maybe I'm the one who isn't changing," she said mostly to herself as she turned and headed out of the store.

Lark sidestepped as she followed Imani out from Bubble's. "No, don't give up. I'm right here. Right in your face. Literally one millimeter from my nose touching your eyeball. And you *hate* when people are that close. Also, Leni is a bitch for what she said the other night. You could marry a ghost for all I care. You know that! I'm the first one you ever told you were gay. So come on!" Lark shouted, growing more infuriated by the second.

But it was too late. She felt Imani giving up.

"And she was so close," Auden muttered as he came out a few seconds later and stood beside Lark.

"Not close enough," she whispered.

Shoulders slumped, Lark stared at the gravel and kicked at

the loose bits. She turned when the gravel crunched beneath Auden's feet as he took off running in the direction of the laundromat.

The Mirror Keeper was standing back outside with his boot propped up against the glass. *Finally!*

"Auden!" Lark hollered as his hands clenched around the collar of the Mirror Keeper's trench coat.

The man didn't try and fight as Auden's fist slammed into the Mirror Keeper's face.

"Stop!" Lark yelled as she finally remembered how to run.

With one fist grasping the trench coat, Auden stuck his other hand in his back pocket. He pulled out a knife and flicked it open—then he pressed it against the Mirror Keeper's throat.

Half of Lark agreed that Auden should stab the guy because of their predicament, but the other part of her was remembering her remote-control analogy earlier.

Auden didn't seem as set on it either as his hand shook against the Mirror Keeper's throat. "It's your fault Darrin's dead. You were there, you saw it," he growled in a low voice laced with venom.

Slowly, the Mirror Keeper's hand gripped Auden's, squeezing it until Auden let out a grunt. The Mirror Keeper took the knife as calmly as if he was removing his coat.

Lark yanked Auden back by his T-shirt, thinking the Mirror Keeper was about to stab him. With her other hand, Lark whipped out her knife, prepared to attack if she needed to.

When the Mirror Keeper held out his other empty palm to them, Auden rasped angrily, "What do you want me to do, asshole? Give you a high-five?"

"I don't think that would be a high-five, seeing as his

hand's not up high," Lark pointed out.

Auden scowled at her.

The Mirror Keeper brought the knife up and thrust it through his own hand. Auden's eyebrows flew up with shock and maybe a little thrill about him doing that. Lark just watched in horrified wonder.

Auden ripped the knife from the Mirror Keeper's hand.

"Can you take off your glove?" she asked, needing to visualize the situation.

He tilted his head up at the ceiling of the overhang above them, then removed his glove. There was no hand, just like the day with his head. And there was no blood. She thought it was better to have no blood than floating red stuff there without a hand. But the idea did make her want to see what it would've looked like.

"I get it," Auden said. "You can't be stabbed. But I still hope the punch to your face hurt like hell."

The Mirror Keeper didn't move any more.

"Where did you and Butterfly go off to last time?" Lark asked.

With his gloved index finger, he made a motion through the air. Lark opened her backpack and pulled out a pen and a scrap sheet of paper. The Mirror Keeper struggled to write like he had at first the last time but managed to scribble *Mirror Dimension.*

"Let me get the Ouija board again." She took off in a hurry, and when she came back, Auden looked unimpressed with the "witch board" she carried from Bubble's. They had around five days left, and they weren't getting any closer to answers—she needed them.

Lark handed the Mirror Keeper the triangular piece.

"Can you answer our questions better now?" Lark asked,

shoving the Ouija board in front of him.

With slow precise movements, he spelled out the word *MAYBE*.

"This is the most fucked up thing I've ever seen," Auden said. "Can you go ahead and break the curse?"

NO.

A muscle ticked like a heartbeat on the side of Auden's jaw.

"Who's in charge?" Lark asked.

OTHER DIMENSION.

"Are they here?"

NO.

That had to mean Leni and Ridley weren't in charge then…

"Do you want to be helped?"

YES.

"Tell us how."

NO.

"Can't have your cake and eat it too," Auden mumbled. Then he straightened his stance and asked, "So if our dimension is connected to your Mirror Dimension, why were we picked for this?"

The Mirror Keeper bowed his head as though he were sighing. Then he spelled out *MY FAULT.*

As Lark was about to jolt forward, the Mirror Keeper held up a hand for them to wait. Breathing deeply, Lark watched as he pointed at his chest.

"You," she said.

He pointed to his eyes.

"Saw," Auden grumbled.

Then he pointed at Lark and Auden.

"Us." Lark smacked the ground. "We already knew

this…"

He shook his head and made a rectangular drawing in the air.

"You saw us in the mirror?" Auden asked. "Are you meaning from your dimension?"

The Mirror Keeper furiously nodded. Then he pointed at Lark's backpack and at her ears.

"You like my music?"

He nodded again.

"So are you saying you chose us because you like what we listen to?"

The Mirror Keeper gave a hesitant shrug as though he'd expected them to yell at him, and Lark wanted to but she needed to get things moving along. Meanwhile, Auden's knuckles were white as his fingers dug into his legs, holding back.

Taking the planchette again in his gloved fingers, he spelled out *LENI*.

"I don't care about Leni right now. Can you please at least give us some sort of clue on how to break the curse?" she said in desperation before Butterfly made another unpleasant entrance.

The Mirror Keeper leaned forward and spelled out the word *INSIDE*.

"The store? The mirror?" Inside a car? *Inside* could be anywhere.

YES.

Quick notes floated through the air, faster than she'd ever heard "Space Oddity" be played before. Lark and Auden both cursed as their gaze fell on the woman in the cloak. The material swished back and forth with the light breeze, the butterfly pendant on her chest barely noticeable.

"The mirror?" Lark hurried and asked, already knowing what to expect from last time.

Shakily, as if he was having trouble, the planchette pointed to *YES*. He then pressed a finger to his palm as his body became jerky. Lark was sure if he had skin that she could see, it would be drenched in sweat. The flute tempo strengthened as notes were spun into the air.

Hurriedly, Lark kept her attention on the Mirror Keeper. "What with my hand?"

Then his body twitched, vanishing with a flash of silver light before he could spell anything else. And she wanted to scream. Butterfly, along with her music, was gone too.

"See, she definitely has control," Lark said, trying to catch her breath. "And we were chosen for what we listen to? I don't even understand that!"

Auden massaged the back of his neck. "What about what he said before he disappeared?"

Lark thought about him spelling out the word *inside* and pointing at his palm. "Maybe it's something sacrificial?"

Auden tapped the glass window of the store, as he studied Lark. "We can't touch anything, and the only living thing I can see is you. And I'm not going to gut you if that's what you think."

She pressed her back against the wall of the laundromat and gave a heavy sigh. "I'm not stabbing you either. I don't think that would help, and even if it did, I'm not doing it. I'd rather be trapped in the mirror. But we need to try for our families. We could attempt a blood oath or something. Nothing too crazy."

"Yeah, okay. Why not? I suppose the next thing we'll do is ritual dancing, am I correct?" he asked with sarcasm.

"Feathers and everything." She smiled.

CHAPTER 25

To Lark:

Lyrics from "Ring Of Fire" — Johnny Cash

Lark wandered back into the oddity store with Auden leading the way. The information the Mirror Keeper had given could be fake advertisement to drive them off course. Or maybe they were one step closer to breaking the curse.

Jimbo stood in front of the counter across from an older man with gray hair and brown spots around his temples, shaking one of the plastic Magic 8 Balls at the man's face.

"Do you want to buy three of the balls?" Jimbo asked, then shoved the ball forward. "It reads yes."

"That answers my question," the old man exclaimed, tapping his wooden cane on the carpet. "I didn't want to purchase just one for my three granddaughters to share. They fight over everything."

Lark remembered her younger days with her sisters and their hobbies—there was never anything to argue over since they didn't even share one of something. Lark had music, Paloma had invisible friends, and Robin watched TV.

"Well, it's your lucky day." Jimbo placed the three balls into a plastic bag. "I'll give you ten percent off your total purchase."

Lark turned to find Auden already gone. She hurried to the mirror, and it rippled and tickled her flesh as she crawled in.

"Hey, you left me behind out there," she huffed as he stood observing his empty mirror.

"Just setting up our new home for us," he said sarcastically, running a hand along the mirror that would be his, as if he was swiping off dust.

"Mirror, Mirror on the wall who's the morbidest one of all?" she asked, strolling up beside him. "I think we're tied."

Ignoring her, Auden pulled his knife out from his back pocket and set it on the table. "Your knife or mine?"

Lark fished out her weapon from her jacket pocket, placing it beside his. She tapped her lower lip. "Choices... choices."

He snatched her knife from the table, rotating it in his hand. "I think I'll use yours—it'll feel more... *intimate*."

"Quit acting ridiculous." She palmed his knife and closed her fist around the brown outer layer, tracing a thumb over the embedded ridges.

Lark had always liked dark things. But even though she'd always had the knife with her, she'd never thought about cutting herself with it. Faced with the option now, she realized it creeped her out even more than being invisible. *Get your priorities straight, Lark. Gotta break that curse!* Flicking the knife open, she sighed. "Same time."

"On the count of three," he replied, unenthused.

"How about four? I don't know who came up with three." The longer she could prolong cutting herself, the better.

"*Okay...* on the count of four."

"One, two, three..." She counted and stopped. Her entire body trembled as she gripped the knife.

He rolled his eyes. "Four."

Lark pressed the silver blade in just enough to feel a slight pinch and burn as the skin opened. Pushing back her disgust, she skated it diagonally across her palm, and watched as the flesh spread apart.

Red didn't bubble up. Instead, silvery fluid—that shone like mirror glass—flowed against her skin. Lark's breathing stopped, and her heart punched her ribcage at the sight. She tore her gaze from the sheen and locked her eyes on Auden, who was studying his hand.

"Not blood," he whispered, lifting his head, his eyes blinking.

"No." Why wasn't it red? It should be red! Even if she still believed they were ghosts, this would've broken that theory because ghosts couldn't bleed. *Stop with the ghost thoughts, Lark.* Were they already a part of the mirror—*their* mirror?

He shook his head and reached his hand toward hers. "Give me your hand."

Body shaking, she pushed her palm toward his and he folded his hand around hers while their eyes met. The feel of his hand holding hers stopped her trembling, but Lark was still focused on the liquid glass that filled up her body.

She held onto his hand for a long time, more than she probably needed to, before he finally released her. The wounds on both of their hands had already sewn their way back together, not even leaving a pale line.

"Maybe we should try burning one of those leaves in here at sunset if this doesn't work," Auden suggested, moving toward the main mirror and trying to shake it—it didn't budge. "That could be where we went wrong, by doing it outside."

That was a good idea. There were several things they could attempt.

"For now, let me try those rain sticks." Leaving Auden,

Lark climbed through the mirror. She waved at Jimbo, but he didn't notice her. So she went and found the group of various-sized rain sticks in the corner of the store, resting in a wooden barrel. She grabbed two that were the length of baseball bats but thicker around.

"Slicing our hands didn't work," she grumbled as she slid back through the glass and handed one of the rain sticks to Auden.

Trying to fight a smile, Auden brought the rain stick in front of the main mirror. He did a quick Irish jig.

Lark snorted, shaking hers furiously at the large mirror, wondering how awesome she looked because she couldn't see herself.

"Where's more of your dance?" Lark asked, pointing the stick at his red Converse.

"Where's the rain?" He tipped his rain stick over. "Oh, here it is."

She did a few kicks to the air that probably wouldn't be qualified as dancing, but that was the closest she was going to get.

"I'm not even sure what that was." Auden let out a deep rumble of laughter.

"We can't all do Irish jigs." Lark turned around and crawled out through the mirror, and yelled, "Jimbo!" Not the slightest reaction.

"Let me guess, no response," Auden groaned, smacking a few duplicate bottles from the miracle remedy wall after he crawled out.

"My dear Watson, you are becoming brighter by the moment." She struck a few of the remedies, too—it made her feel a little better.

"I think I'm going to go home for a while and check on

everyone. Make sure they are all okay. Do you want to come?" he asked.

"Nah, I'll meet you back here tonight with some herbs we can try along with another bay leaf. I'm going to go hang out in Paloma's room for a bit and see that she's still all right."

Lark never thought she would be saying that. They never stayed for long in either one of their bedrooms. It was always a forced togetherness at the kitchen table or living room. But Lark had rather been holed up in her room listening to music.

Now, she needed to investigate her own room and search for any clues Leni may have left behind.

Outside, Lark closed her eyes, thinking about how her life mirrored being trapped inside a ring of fire, and she slid in the tape of that song into her Walkman. Maybe it would bring her focus so she could eventually break out from these cursed flames.

She pedaled her bike in the direction of home, taking in her surroundings. She might not have that much time left in the world.

Lark stopped in front of the trailer beside the small amount of grass that was in need of mowing. Beth was home from her cashier job, and she wondered how long Beth had taken off from work for Paloma. Despite her obvious flaws, Beth's dependability at the job was on point. She always made it into work and never missed a day, no matter how drunk or drugged she'd been the night before.

Stepping inside, Lark found Beth nestled in her usual spot —the recliner—but there weren't any beer bottles or cans around her, only an ashtray and a pack of Camels resting on the small side table beside her. Lucy maintained her new position on the couch, and Lark stroked through her since she couldn't make contact.

On the way to the back of the trailer, Lark halted in front of Paloma's room but turned around when she heard whispers from her own room. Opening the door, she found Leni cuddled up beside Ridley with most of their clothing off. She would've set fire to her mattress without a second thought if she could've.

"I told you it was an accident," Leni whispered. "I made the drink for Imani."

Ridley straightened and grew serious. "Is she going to be a problem?"

"I don't think so. Imani called earlier to check on Paloma and didn't sound mad about the other night."

"We have to cool it, though," Ridley said. "We can't turn all Bonnie and Clyde. It's all about blending in."

"You're one to talk," Leni pointed out. Lark wanted to rip them into the tiniest of pieces. Ridley didn't appear the slightest remorseful about Darrin.

"I have to watch my impulsiveness. Maybe you should wear a little more black and not so much color," he suggested.

"Or a little less black," Leni purred, hauling her black tank top over her head. She turned over to kiss Ridley as her hand crept lower to places Lark didn't want to see. It was irritating her even more because they looked like her and Auden. "Our time is almost up."

"What do you mean your time is almost up?" Lark asked. "Don't you mean my time?"

Lark tried to ignore them as she searched frantically through her room for a sign of anything. She came up empty.

Slamming the door so hard the walls shook, she went into her sister's room.

Paloma lay curled on her side in bed with the comforter pulled all the way up to her chin. She appeared much younger without her makeup hiding her face, her mouth partially open, softly snoring.

Lark crawled on top of the bed and lay down beside her sister. "I think we've always been different. People used to say because we were twins, we must be the same, even though we were fraternal. But we never were, were we? You always went to the left while I went right. I don't even know if we ever really liked each other. We just had to deal with the same shitty things. But I'm here and will always be here if you need me. Even if I have to watch you through Leni's mirrors."

Lark slid her headphones on and listened to music. She even took a Madonna cassette from Paloma's terrible collection and placed the headphones between the two of them while cranking the volume up all the way. After two songs, Lark couldn't tolerate the nice gesture anymore, and she tossed the cassette back. She could be nice, but not *that* nice.

After a long while, Leni and Ridley left—the rumble of original Jenny's engine booming from outside. She couldn't help feeling better, knowing Paloma and Beth were safer since Leni was gone for a while. Lark stretched as she stood from the bed and headed into the kitchen to get ready to leave. Beth slid a glass container with chicken into the stove right as the phone rang.

Beth set down her oven mitt, and Lark watched as she answered the phone hanging on the kitchen wall. "Hello?"

Beth paused on her end as she listened. "Robin, I know you can come down for *one* day. Your sister almost *died*. I waited and waited for you to show up at the hospital, and you never came."

Lark didn't know Beth had even called Robin. She'd thought Beth had been too wrapped up in everything to call her.

So why hadn't Robin shown up?

"What do you mean it's my fault she was at the party in the first place?" Beth pressed her hand against the wall and leaned her head on her shoulder. "You went off to parties, too, when you lived here, so don't act like you're holier-than-thou."

Beth grabbed a clump of her permed hair. "I don't care if you're mad at me. I don't care if you hate me for the rest of my life. I know I've made mistakes and am trying to atone for my actions. But what did Paloma ever do to you? Nothing, that's what! All she and Lark ever did was stick up for you, and how do you repay them? By abandoning them. If you hate me so much, maybe you should take a look at yourself because you're doing the exact same thing to them."

Lark's chest tightened and she needed air. Robin wasn't Beth, but she wasn't the sister she'd known before, either. Lark and Paloma were nothing to Robin now—only people she wanted to forget.

There must've been a click because Beth said "hello" two times before slamming the phone down. Lark was almost sure the base could've been ripped off the wall.

The anger on Beth's face quickly turned to something that resembled regret mixed with sadness before she began to cry, slumping to the floor right there in the kitchen. She banged the back of her head against the cabinets before she leaned forward and sobbed into her hands.

Beth had been a crap mom, but maybe she just didn't realize how terrible she'd been. Was it really possible for people to change? People changed from good to bad all the time. Couldn't it be the same to go from bad to good? Lark felt that even if a person tried to change, they would still have that seed of what they once were buried deep underneath flesh, muscle and bone, hidden far down in the sea of blood. The thing about seeds was that they could always grow back. Harder, faster, and worse than ever before.

The seed that was now planted would always be lingering and waiting inside Beth, and she would have to continuously battle it. But maybe Lark should try helping Beth fight the battle, because two were stronger than one, and with Paloma's help that would make three. If Robin was a lost cause, that was her choice, and Lark didn't blame her for not wanting to talk to Beth. She could even handle her sister ignoring her, but Robin should've been there for Paloma.

Beth stopped sobbing and stood up, opening the refrigerator to grab a beer.

"Come on, Mom. Don't do it. Don't do it!" As she watched Beth staring at the metal beer can, Lark realized she'd just called Beth "Mom." It surprised her, but it also felt right in that moment.

Beth pulled the tab of the can, cracking it open. Lark sighed in disappointment. The seed had already started to grow back. But to Lark's astonishment, Beth poured the contents of the beer down the drain.

Then she walked back to the fridge and reached for another and another and another, popping them all open and emptying them. Lark helped by scooping up the cans and tossing them into the trash. Even though the real cans were still on the counter, she wanted to help in what seemed like an epiphany for Beth.

Afterward, Beth shuffled down the hallway to Paloma's room. Lark watched as Beth whispered, "I love you, sweetie pie."

It no longer seemed like some stupid name. For the first time, Lark felt as though Beth meant it.

Beth returned to the living room and slumped into her recliner, pulling a cigarette from her pack. Lark took a seat on the couch next to Lucy and decided to stay for a while longer to comfort her mom, though Beth didn't even know Lark was there. She was a ghost—but ghosts could help too.

After making it through one of Beth's favorite television shows, Lark rode her bike back toward Bubble's after stopping to get the bay leaf and herbs she needed. The sun would be setting soon, so she pedaled faster as she listened to the music from her headphones drumming its way into her ears.

Auden's van sat in the parking lot, but neither the Mirror Keeper nor Butterfly were in sight. Disappointing. She still had too many questions and not enough answers.

The oddity store was now closed, and Jimbo had already left. She padded her way toward the mirror with the bay leaf and herbs in tow before crawling through the glass, feeling like Alice once again. Instead of meeting the Mad Hatter, a white rabbit, or the Queen of Hearts, her gaze latched onto Auden with the sleeping bags on the floor and a picnic of food strewn across.

CHAPTER 26

To Auden:

Lyrics from "Crazy On You" - Heart

Auden finished spreading out the sleeping bags. Opening the plastic sack, he took out cheese, bread, lunchmeat, and lettuce. From the other bag, he pulled out chips, desserts, and drinks. Next, he set the record player and box of vinyl on top of the table beside the Mirror Keeper's jeweled box.

He'd visited his mom and brothers briefly but spent the rest of the time at the gravesite, giving Darrin a proper goodbye.

Darrin was someone he'd taken for granted, thinking he'd always be around and would show up even when Auden hadn't asked him to. Never again would he see the new color of his Mohawk, or what kind of hat he'd use to cover it if he didn't feel like styling it.

Auden's emotions teetered on the verge yet again, and he bit down on the inside of his cheek, staring at the blanket and trying to shake his feelings away.

A scuffing sound came from the mirror as Lark spilled out into the room. His first thought was how perfect she looked in that moment with her windblown hair and reddened cheeks.

"Lyrics," she said.

"Curses," he replied.

"Are you trying to woo me?" Lark asked, her gaze falling to the blanket with food spread out like a picnic. Then she moved to the table and skimmed through the box of LPs, pulling one out.

His eyebrows furrowed in confusion. If they needed to figure out things inside of the mirror, he thought they might as well sleep here. But was that what he was doing? Trying to woo her? Maybe it was. "I suppose I forgot the candles and 'Crazy On You,' but there are flames above us to give off the smolder."

Gently, he took the vinyl from her hand and placed it on the record player. He let the needle press down, allowing the music to share the space of the room with them.

Her smile grew as she padded to the blankets. "Just keep bringing me chips, and you have my steady attention."

"I didn't know exactly which ones to get, so I grabbed four different bags." He watched her body dip low, her delicate fingers wiggling before she plucked the bag of Cheetos from the mix. The bag's crinkle echoed through the room. She took a seat and lit the bay leaf with a lighter, smoke wafting upward. And he pretended for a moment he didn't feel anything, but he did—every time he was around her.

After the bay leaf went out and after unsuccessfully attempting to talk to the cursed mirror again, they built sandwiches, layering them as high as they would go. While Lark ate and read, he tore off a piece of paper from a notebook inside his backpack and scribbled down what he'd been wanting to say before setting it flipped over on top of her knee. There was more he wanted to say, could've said, should've said, but he wasn't good at expressing himself out loud.

She turned over the paper, careful not to get cheese residue on it. Then her gaze landed on the words he had written. *I don't want you to be another addiction.*

Her eyebrows furrowed and stayed there. "I don't know this one." She turned to face him. "You didn't put the artist."

"Because they're my words," he said softly.

"Oh."

Auden couldn't tell by her expressionless face or voice what she thought about it. It felt like the two times she'd said "thanks" after they'd had sex in his van. Maybe he should've just written another song lyric instead.

Lark lifted her book and started to read again. Feeling like an idiot, Auden grabbed the oddity cards and set them out to distract himself with Solitaire.

After one round, his fingers tapped the smooth surface of the sleeping bag with anxiousness. He gathered the cards back into a pile and pushed them aside, then slid under the sleeping bag, turning his face away from her.

They still hadn't said anything to each other.

He couldn't fall asleep. It wasn't even the faces on the mirrors down the hall and beyond that bugged him—it was Lark's silence. The wall kept him entertained for maybe fifteen minutes as he stared at it, when Lark finally slipped in beside him. Somehow, he could feel her eyes burning into his back.

Several moments passed, then she tapped his back. He didn't roll over. She tapped him again.

This time he turned around to face her. "Yes?"

A harsh scowl was on her face. He lifted his hand and ran his index finger across her left eyebrow and then her right, attempting to straighten it back out. It fell back into a scowl.

"Well, are you going to say anything?" he asked, the right side of his mouth tilting up.

Her eyes narrowed slightly, but she still inched forward,

nearer to him. "What did you mean, 'I don't want you to be another addiction?'"

Did she not understand what he had written? "I meant I don't want you to be another addiction."

"That doesn't answer the question."

A lock of her curled hair had fallen into her face, and he moved it away. "You know better than I do—with lyrics—it's all about interpretation." He angled his body closer to her. "So what's your interpretation?" The thought of hearing the way she'd decode his words made him feel crazed—in the best way.

"You see me as an addiction and want to toss whatever the hell this is"—she pointed between him and her—"away."

Damn, it was the opposite of what I meant.

"A true artist never gives away the real meaning. But for you, I'll let you know this one time." Auden pressed his forehead against hers, and it was almost electric. "I mean, I want you to be more than my addiction. Addictions come and go— they can be treated... like a wound needing to be stitched, then a scar left in its wake. But I never want to get cured of you, Lark." He made sure to keep his eyes focused on hers, not wanting for a second for her to doubt what he said. "But with you, I'd never want the wound to be closed."

She blinked several times, not saying anything.

"Maybe showing is better than telling," he said, wrapping his arm around her waist and drawing her in until she was flush against him.

"Do show." She grinned.

His lips met the spot of her neck right below her jaw.

"Without a hickey on my neck, please."

He chuckled against her warm skin. Of course, she had to bring that up. Still smiling, he softly kissed her neck, lower and lower, but the collar of her shirt was in the way. "Other places instead?" he asked.

"I'm fine with that," she answered and lifted her shirt up and over her head. Auden kissed his way down her bare shoulder as he released the clasp to the back of her bra. He wanted her both slowly and quickly.

He didn't give a damn that they might screw on the floor in a place with thousands and thousands of mirrors around. *Let them watch.* Who knew how much time they had left?

Auden rolled onto his back, taking her soft body with him. He ran his hand through her wild curls. As he brought her mouth to his, Lark was the most beautiful thing he'd ever seen. She tasted of the spearmint Tic Tac she'd eaten after their meal, and he wanted to drink it in.

She caressed her mouth against his, and he nipped at her bottom lip before he tangled his tongue with hers. Even though this wasn't new territory for them, beneath his ribcage, Auden's heart thumped as though there were wings thrashing inside his chest. Maybe they were wings of an actual lark or some shit like that.

Not going as slow as he'd planned, their clothes had been pulled, yanked, tugged, maybe even ripped off, both too eager to feel their skin against one another's.

And she *would* know that she was more than just an addiction to him because he wanted to show her just how much he cared.

CHAPTER 27

To Lark:

Lyrics from "Once In A Lifetime" — Talking Heads

Lark looked at Auden's watch on the floor of the Realm of Mirrors, and it was still early morning. He lay asleep on his stomach, shirtless, with a lock of hair falling over his closed eye. Last night, they'd created their own music through each body movement, each touch, each word. Her heart was more than his, filled with the songs between them.

She continued to think about their night together—her skin against his, his skin pressed to hers—as she got dressed. Then she sat down and examined the mirror butterfly in her hand, rolling and rotating the silvery glass across her fingertips and palm. The sand ran down the hourglass. The bottom filled quickly. Almost as if someone had put a vacuum in the lower tube. Fourteen days had felt like an eternity. Now, there was little less than four.

No matter how much she wanted them to, the seconds never stopped ticking.

There was nothing to do but wait. She reached for a tomato and took a bite—she ate them like apples—but a bitter taste overtook her mouth. It was something more than the fruit bothering her as her mind filled with too many questions. She examined the butterfly again.

"Butterfly," she whispered. Somehow, she knew the

Mirror Keeper had once cared about the woman. Why else would he have had a nickname for her? When she thought about Paloma and Darrin, anger stirred within her. There was nothing she could do in this state to stop anyone else from getting hurt. She threw the butterfly at the mirror that had brought this destruction and waited to hear it shatter. The butterfly struck the glass with a soft *ping* and fell to the floor, still whole.

Her eyes widened and her hand flew to her mouth. *It didn't pass through the glass.*

She scrambled up from the blankets and scooped the unbroken butterfly from the dark floor, then pressed her hand, holding the object, into the glass. Her hand went through as it always did. She ripped her arm back and stared at the butterfly with her lips parted in fascination.

The pieces finally fell into place—what the Mirror Keeper had meant. *Inside.*

Whirling around, she shouted, "Auden!"

"What?" He jerked awake and scurried to stand. His eyes were wide, scanning the room as if he was ready for battle, yet still tugging on his jeans.

"Watch." Lark wasn't sure if she even believed what had happened, so she had to do it again to show him. Once more, she hurled the butterfly at the mirror. It bounced back and clacked on the floor.

Auden scratched his head, unimpressed. "Sherlock, you need to maybe find something more to do with your time."

Fiercely, she shook her head. "We need to try and break the mirror from the *inside.*"

He cocked his head and blinked at her. "And then how would we get out?"

"I think I'll keep you as my Watson." That was a good question. "Does it really matter, though? We have less than four days left. I want to risk it."

Auden released a long sigh, then said, "How about you crawl out, and I try breaking it from in here."

What if they *could* get trapped here if the mirror really did break? Then Auden would be alone in this Realm of Mirrors while Lark was inside the oddity store. It didn't seem right. Not after everything they'd faced together.

"I have a better idea. How about *you* crawl out, and I try breaking it from in here," she echoed.

"Move."

She stepped back as he grabbed one of the rain sticks propped against the wall. With his fists clenching it like a baseball bat, he swung the stick against the mirror—it passed through.

"Shit," he said. "I can't be holding the object, right?"

"Right." Lark picked the stick up and hurled it at the mirror, but it shot straight through the glass. Her heart dropped. Why didn't it work?

"What the hell?" Auden said. He grabbed the butterfly from her hand and examined it. "Butterfly… The Mirror Keeper gave you this"—Auden's head jerked up as he inhaled sharply, seeming to become aware of something—"but I think instead of focusing on only linking it to the flute player, we should've really been linking it to something else. He lifted the jeweled box from the table, showing Lark the bottom that read *For Butterfly*."

"The Mirror Keeper was telling us to use the box," she gasped. "And the scroll!" She pointed to the words across the page. *Do not waste time searching the halls past this room.* "It was here all along, Auden! We were supposed to search *this* room and use what we found here! We had to use an object that didn't come from our dimension because the mirror didn't come from here either!"

"Try it, Lark," Auden murmured, sliding the box toward her.

She looked at all the mirrors hanging on the walls, the ones that wouldn't come off as she cradled the box in between her fingers. *Please, oh please, let this work.*

Lark swung her hand back, praying so hard that it would work. Auden moved out of the way, and she flung the box at the mirror. A loud clang reverberated through the room as a crack skated all the way down the center of the glass.

"Again," Auden said with something verging on excitement in his voice.

Gathering the box up, she launched it, striking the glass again. Two cracks ran jagged diagonal lines. Any other mirror would've already been in pieces on the floor.

"Watch out," Auden shouted.

Lark shuffled backward, as he scooped the box from the floor. He threw it hard, and it pummeled the glass. Two large chunks fell—one breaking into three pieces when it hit the floor.

Auden picked up the jeweled box and repeated his movements again and again and again and *again.* The remaining pieces fell like flashes of light. Some broke into tinier fragments while others held their shape. All that was behind the glass now was a dark-colored wood.

A thumping pulsed through the room, rattling her teeth. Then came a light buzz like the first time they'd come in there. To her left, Lark studied the mirror with her name above it as a tempo of clanging streamed together.

Lark's lips parted, and her heart skipped several beats when her reflection in the glass appeared. "I think it's working." She turned her head over her shoulder.

"I-I don't think so," he stuttered.

A hand thrust from the glass of Auden's mirror, trying to tug itself inside the room. Auden ran to Lark and pulled her away from the mirror, right as a hand punched out from the one with her name above it.

"Try going through!" He rushed the words out and flung her in the direction of the main mirror.

She stared at the wood panel. "There is no mirror!"

"Go!" He shoved her forward anyway, and although she was ready to slam into the hard barrier, her arm went past it just as it had when the mirror had glass. She crawled out as Auden nudged her to go quicker, but the invisible curtain was thicker than before, like crossing through sludge.

After passing into Bubble's familiar room, she whirled around and hastily grabbed Auden's hands, yanking him out to the carpet.

"We did it," Lark breathed. She was about to high-five Auden when a hand came barreling out from the glass, Ridley's head poking through. The mirror was still whole on Lark and Auden's side.

"Grab something!" Lark barked, snatching a mace with sharp spikes off the wall, then cursing at herself because she wasn't sure if she could swing the thing without striking herself.

Plucking up the one baseball bat that hadn't cracked, Auden swung it at his doppel's head. It crossed through Ridley. *What the hell is going on?*

Lark's doppel was already in the room, slowly dragging herself up to stand. "Don't worry, *Lark*," Leni said. "This gets a little more amusing before you have to be put into the mirror."

Teeth clenched, Lark dropped the mace, because that was a dumb choice, and took the bat from Auden's hand. She started swinging it like a maniac. It passed through Leni, but Lark didn't stop her motions. Ridley pulled Leni back, but not far enough. This time when she swung the bat, it went through her doppel again, but not Ridley, as it smacked his arm with a sickening plop.

A howl of pain came from Ridley. *So I can make contact with him but not Leni. Interesting.*

Before she could bring the bat up again, Ridley lunged toward her. He thrust his leg forward in a weird-kick and knocked the weapon from her grip. Her hand throbbed from the contact.

"This is screwed up," Auden groaned as he grabbed the other cracked bat from beside the counter. He swung the bat right as Ridley slammed Lark to the floor, pinning her down.

Lark heard a whack and hoped to God it was Leni, and not Auden. Ridley struggled to keep Lark pinned as she bit, kicked, and went as crazy as she could, like a rabid dog. She caught a glimpse of Leni, gripping her head and seeming dazed.

Not Auden.

"Just stop moving, you little bitch," Ridley seethed with his lip curled, digging his fingers into her wrists. Lark kicked her legs like she was deranged, but she wasn't going anywhere.

"Hey!" Auden yelled. "I have *your* little bitch."

Ridley turned his head. Lark tried to knee him in the balls, but he was ready. He flipped her over, holding her hands behind her back.

Auden held his knife to Leni's throat—*good thinking*. She silently thanked herself for always having a knife to begin with, and for Auden wanting to carry the excellent weapon after seeing her with one.

"Whatever you do to her will happen to Lark," Ridley taunted.

Lark's eyes widened when they settled on a line of silvery liquid running down Leni's face. Lark whispered the word "liar" to Auden. There was a glimpse of fright on Auden's face before he masked his expression with hardness.

"Do it," Lark demanded.

There was no hesitation as Auden sliced the main vein at Leni's throat. A haunted expression crossed Auden's face as he dropped Leni's body onto the carpet. Her hand flew up to staunch the bleeding as she coughed up specks of glittery silver liquid.

"Leni!" Ridley let go of Lark as he rushed to the doppel's side.

Auden tossed the knife at Lark's feet, and she snatched it up. On impulse, she flung herself at Ridley, but his reflexes were too fast. With a hard shove, he pushed her to the floor. Her hand didn't release the knife, but his body was barricading her arm. This time, she was able to drive her knee between his legs.

Ridley let out a grunt, and Lark pushed him away. Auden pulled her quickly to her feet. The knife was now at the ready. Somehow Ridley had one of the baseball bats, swinging it. Two hands pushed Lark out of the way as Ridley jolted forward. The bat went right through Auden, but the tip still hit Lark's left arm. She gasped in pain and whirled around.

"Lark!" Auden shouted.

She ducked as Ridley swung the bat and hit a rack. A sea

of black skull candles fell to the carpet. Before the bastard could lift the bat again, Lark charged at him, driving the blade through the side of his throat. A single ragged breath escaped his mouth as he slumped to the floor on top of Leni.

Lovers united in death.

Horrified at herself, Lark dropped the knife covered in the mirror-shard silvery liquid. There was a sick feeling that lingered inside her for stabbing someone. Especially someone who looked like Auden.

Her bicep throbbed, and she winced at the pain. Then two arms lifted her from behind. Lark peered up at Auden who was chewing on his lip. His fingertips shook against her stomach, and she knew he was affected by cutting someone's throat who looked like her as well.

"Your arm?" he asked.

"It's fine."

"Let's try pushing the doppels back through the mirror."

She didn't want to see their bodies anymore, so she hurried to them. Auden's hands still couldn't connect with Ridley, but Lark was able to roll him over. Lifting Leni's lifeless body, Auden brought her to the mirror. It rippled as he slid her inside, inch by inch.

It was harder with Ridley, because Lark was smaller. "Why are you so big?" she grunted.

"I'm not that heavy."

"It sure feels like it." Red-faced and holding her breath as she pulled, pried, and pushed Ridley's body through the mirror. After minutes that felt like hours, the mirror stopped rippling once the doppel's feet were gone. Lark and Auden were then met with their reflections in the glass.

The cowbell to the store rang as the door was yanked

open. Lark's head twisted toward the sound, and her gaze settled on the Mirror Keeper.

Swathed in his usual black with his hat tipped back, he took long strides toward them and came to an abrupt stop. Lark stepped closer to Auden in case she needed to protect him.

"What do you want?" Auden growled.

The Mirror Keeper lifted his hat and pressed it to his chest. He bowed his head, then pulled the ski mask off. Lark expected to see the decapitated-looking person again, but she didn't.

Her breath caught in her throat. The Mirror Keeper was maybe only a year or two older than her with an almost boyish face. His hair was chin-length, brown and curly. A light dusting of freckles covered his nose and cheeks, and his eyes caught her attention—one brown, the other gray.

"I can see you!" Lark's jaw dropped.

To her astonishment, the Mirror Keeper spoke in a deep voice with a weird accent she'd never heard before—possibly Irish mixed with something else. "I don't have much time. I wasn't myself." He blinked one too many times as though he was trying to speak through his blinking. His eyes shifted in the direction of the cursed mirror. "I-I did this for her, for Leni."

"The *doppelgänger?*" Auden asked, his voice cracking on the last word.

"No, the real Leni." The Mirror Keeper sighed. "The real Leni is the Piper. I called her Butterfly." He paused as if looking for something. "Sorry, sometimes words are hard for me without writing them." Pausing again, he blinked several times.

"But as I mentioned in the scroll, our dimension links to yours through the Realm of Mirrors. We create the reflections, your souls, before you're born. To keep our dimension powered, our rulers must absorb souls every so often—because we don't have souls ourselves—so in return a filler is given to your dimension. And if our dimension dies, then no souls can be created for the Earth Dimension, and that can't be good either since yours would fade, too."

"*The fuck?*" Auden took a step back.

"I'm sorry, it was my fault for choosing you two, but it was because you two loved the music like I did, like Leni did. I first saw Lark's room filled with the things I liked through a mirror in my dimension... Once I got here, I tried to fight it, but once Phase One of the curse started, I wasn't always in control. It was hard at times to get to the laundromat, but that spot was easier for me to hide longer since it's the farthest from my dimension."

"What happens now?" Lark hadn't moved, just stayed planted to the carpet, not knowing exactly how to feel about dimensions being able to end and being noticeable enough for the Mirror Keeper to choose her.

"Don't worry, I won't be back."

"Now that everything is all hunky dory, right?" Auden scoffed.

"Nothing is ever completely all right." The Mirror Keeper rubbed his thumb across his hat.

"What's your real name, anyway? And how is Butterfly Leni?" Lark asked. None of it was making sense. Out of everything he just said, that is what perplexed her most.

His head flicked side to side between her and Auden for a second. "I... I'm Ridley. I didn't know she was going to use your bodies for us instead of the ones she was required to use from our dimension once the curse was complete. But as the curse started, the pre-filler, or as you say, doppelgänger, was part of you, part Leni, and part glass in between. The doppelgänger wasn't Butterfly yet. Same goes for Auden's. And while they had aspects of us, they didn't contain the same memories. However, I don't know everything either."

"You and her?" Lark spat, her insides coming to a boil. "You're saying once the curse was finished, you two would've been us?"

The Mirror Keeper tugged his ski mask back on and set the hat on his head. "I didn't know she was going to do this, and I don't know why. Before I became the Mirror Keeper, I was only Ridley. Leni had no control about being picked to be the Piper." His arm jerked forward. "The music, our song, is calling me back now." With that, his body straightened like that of a soldier and moved toward the mirror. As if someone was holding him by strings, he lifted the mirror, and it appeared to be light as a feather in his hands.

"Hello?" Auden asked, waving a hand back and forth.

But robotically, the Mirror Keeper turned away from them and walked out of the store, mirror in hand. Lark and Auden didn't chase after him.

There was a quick flash of silvery light as he stepped out the door and was gone, hopefully for the last time.

Lark didn't know what to think. After what he just confessed, and how he'd chosen them in the beginning, she still felt a pang of sadness for him. But it was obvious he'd chosen his path for Butterfly—Leni, who Lark knew nothing about. And that made her feel worse because Darrin was dead, and her sister could've also been dead because of the curse. Yet, there were also the clues he'd given to help them, even though it seemed like it could possibly affect his dimension.

She couldn't be his savior.

"Did you hear the music like he did?" Lark asked, turning to face Auden.

He shook his head. "No. But if I meet anyone from that dimension again, their ass will be more than grass."

"What does that even mean?" She never understood that lame terminology. At least it was a good sign they hadn't heard any music—a feeling of relief washed over her.

The cowbell clanged again—Lark expected it to be the Mirror Keeper coming back. Instead, it was Jimbo carrying a large box filled with trinkets. A skull with horns poked over the edge of the cardboard.

Jimbo stopped when he spotted the two of them. "Auden, do I need to put up a sign that says no shirt, no shoes, must go home?"

Lark stared at Auden's shirtless form and bare feet. Luckily, Lark had already been fully clothed before all hell broke loose.

"Sorry, I had an accident on the way to work," Auden lied, pursing his lips for a moment. "I spilled coffee on my shirt and then when I pulled over to clean myself off, I stepped in dog shit."

"I suggest figuring that out *really quick*." Jimbo shook his head and walked past them, placing the box on the floor in front of the counter. "You two are actually early anyway. I'm about to leave, just wanted to drop these things off. Price tags are already on them."

Lark's gaze drifted around the store, and nothing looked out of place. No fallen candles, no bats on the floor, and no mace.

"I was just about to go to my van and see what I have to wear," Auden mumbled, turning around and leaving.

"Let me help you," Lark said in a rush. Jimbo's left eyebrow rose all the way up, and she shot out the door after Auden.

Outside the store in the humid air, Lark let out a frustrated sigh. "My backpack!"

Auden patted the pocket of his pants. "My keys and record player are gone."

All of her cassettes were gone, too. They were her entire life wound up inside plastic cases. She wanted to cry—she was about to spill tears over it. She didn't care if they were material possessions. They were *hers*.

Her eyes fixed on the laundromat—empty. She assumed it was going to be a permanent thing from now on. But part of her wondered if the Mirror Keeper would ever come back there for someone else, or maybe it would be a different state or a different country.

"Lark." Auden nudged her arm.

"Yeah," she answered like she was Oscar the Grouch.

"Jenny's gone."

"What?" she squealed, finally noticing her bike was missing, too. No longer in front of the store window.

Auden gently gripped her arms, preventing her from collapsing to the ground and possibly breaking a window. That bike was her nostalgic transportation... and plus, her tapes!

"You know what I think, Lark?" He didn't wait for her to say anything. "I think the originals are back at home, where the doppels left them."

A part of her relaxed at the possibility. "If you're right, I'll take you in the back of Jenny right then and there, as soon as we see her." Lark bumped his arm with hers.

"One problem." He made a clicking sound with his

291

tongue. "Now we have to explain to Jimbo that he needs to give us a ride home to pick up my van as you explain to him what really happened."

"Cue 'Once In A Lifetime' to play right now." She cracked a smile.

# CHAPTER 28

To Lark & Auden:
Lyrics From "Boys Don't Cry" – The Cure

"I still don't know how this could've happened," Imani said over the phone.

Lark twisted the cord. Lucy was tucked into Lark's side and had started staying in her room again.

"Did you really believe I would've dressed like Paloma?" She shuddered, trying to get the image out of her head.

Two weeks ago, Lark had explained everything that had happened, but only to Imani and Jimbo. She hadn't known if Imani would believe her because it did sound a bit on the ludicrous side. If she had told Beth or Paloma, they would've either laughed or sent her straight to the psychiatric hospital. She would've been basically confessing that it was she who had poisoned Paloma, instead of Leni—or that was what they would've thought. That was not an option.

As for Jimbo, he hadn't known anything about a mirror dimension or an in-between realm, but he was going to try and do some digging.

"I know. I should've known with the haunting stuff you'd mentioned," Imani hurried on. "I knew some weird shit would go down from working at Bubble's with all that freaky awesome memorabilia Jimbo brings in. It's like a choice magnet for the strange." She paused for a moment, getting a little choked up. "But then there's Darrin."

"It's hard to think about," Lark murmured. "Also, I can't say it enough, but I'm sorry about that night." Every time she saw Imani's face, even though she didn't say those awful things, it still bothered her to have seen someone treat her friend that way.

"It wasn't you. Plus, I need to prepare myself to hear the worst. I plan on telling my parents about me and Emilia. It probably won't go over so well, so I'll need your support."

"I'll always be here, and I'll see you tomorrow. Auden's on his way here, to say goodbye, before I have to head into work." When Imani decided to tell her parents, Lark was going to be ready to give her a hug or a shoulder to cry on, depending on how it went.

"Glad you got your brooding prince in the end. See ya."

Lark hung up the phone. Not so sure about that, seeing as he was leaving for a bit. She headed out of her room, stopping by Paloma's doorway. "I'm off the phone now if you want to use it."

"Finally." Paloma's eyes roamed over Lark. "Still in black again."

"Copying Madonna as always," Lark drawled.

Paloma and Lark's bond, whatever it was exactly, had gone back to being like before. Lark knew they wouldn't be the best of friends any time soon, but she'd always be there for her sister if she needed her.

"And it's not all black... see?" She flashed her red-polished nails and left the room as Paloma rolled her eyes.

"Hey, baby doll." Beth set down her cigarette when Lark came into the living room. Her hair was styled in a fresh new perm that was tighter than usual.

"Hey... Mom." Lark hadn't been good at being the perfect

daughter like the doppel seemed to be. But she had attempted to be better by trying to be a little nicer to Beth.

There had been no phone calls from her older sister Robin. If her sister ever wanted to talk to her, Robin could initiate contact, but Lark wasn't holding her breath.

She looked at the clock and Auden should be pulling up at any minute. "I'm going outside real quick before work."

"I'm startin' lunch in a little while, so I'll save you leftovers."

"Extra crispy or extra crispier?"

Beth's eyes narrowed on her.

"Kidding." Lark's gaze shifted to the door. "Or am I?" She'd been eating the charbroiled goodness the last two weeks and was accustomed to the extra layer of dark.

"Stop being a smartass."

Lark grinned in return.

On the way outside, Lark avoided glancing at the living room mirror. In fact, she'd stopped looking at herself in them most of the time. She'd taken the mirror out of her room and tossed it in the trash, listening to it break, not worrying if she'd indeed have seven years bad luck. The luck she had before must've already been terrible.

But even the simplest things with a sheen had a reflection, and she couldn't avoid everything. Lark even wondered how the real Ridley was faring. Though she wanted to forget him and Leni, she couldn't help being curious.

The sound of Jenny roared through the trailer park, and the dark van came around the curve then stopped in front of her home.

Over the last two weeks, things had been different, yet somehow the same between her and Auden. They'd talked, listened to music, continued their lyric notes—done the deed in the back of his van, his bedroom, the beach.

Auden left the engine running and stepped out. "You sure you don't want to come?"

"I do. More than anything. But I still have to finish my senior year." She stared up at him. "Why did you have to be a grade older?"

"Why did you have to be a grade younger?"

Lark wanted him to stay, but she couldn't tell him that. If he had a chance to leave this town for a while, she wouldn't hold him back. Because one day, she'd get out of here too. And it wasn't as if he was going to stay gone forever.

Auden handed her the small notebook. "I got a new one in the van, and I'll be filling it up each day."

Trying to fight her sadness, Lark took the notebook. "I'll do the same."

He gave her a soft kiss that ached with goodbye. She wasn't sure when he'd be back from his road trip across the country. And she itched to go, but finishing school would ensure she'd get out of this trailer park one day—permanently. She'd been so close to losing her life, and now that she had it back, Lark yearned to truly live it. Auden had wanted to get away from this town for a long time, and now he finally was.

The future awaited, but at that moment, Lark just wanted to cry.

Auden got back into Jenny, watching Lark standing on the steps. He could feel the red lipstick smeared over his mouth, but he didn't want to wipe any piece of her away.

Every part of him had been set on leaving, wanting to get out of this hellhole town. He put Jenny in drive and took off.

Thirty seconds later, he knew he was a fucking idiot. Darrin would've told him the same thing if he was in the seat beside him. Turning the steering wheel, he looped around the trailer park and stopped back in front of Lark's trailer. She was still standing on the steps, studying him with amusement.

"Just couldn't leave, could you?" She shook her head and smiled.

Placing his arm on the door, he set his chin on it and stared out at her. "Why didn't you just ask me to stay? Do I need to remind you of the two times you said 'thank you' in my van after we were together, or how you misinterpreted my lyrics?"

"I didn't say thank you, I said 'thanks' because I didn't want to ruin how, in those moments, everything had been perfect."

His head perked up. "So you do care?" If only she knew how many times she crossed his mind throughout the day.

"Seriously, just go already," she teased, strolling up to his door. "I know you want to leave."

But there was an even better reason to stay. "So I was thinking that maybe I have a different plan. Do you think Jimbo will give me my job back?"

"I don't even think he knows you were quitting. So, technically, you're still an employee."

He ran his middle finger across his lower lip. That was probably a shitty thing for him to do since Jimbo was a stellar boss.

"Anyway, I was also thinking we could go camping next weekend. And maybe a road trip next summer once you graduate?" They could go an hour or two away for now, and it would be just as good.

"You couldn't have thought about that sooner? Before packing all your shit in the van." She peered in and looked toward the back. "Okay, you barely have anything in there. How long were you going to last? A week?"

Auden hadn't thought that far, but for now, they could relax in his van before she had to go into work soon. "Hop in the back and pick a song free from curses."

As soon as the curse had ended, Lark had insisted on starting a bonfire at the beach, burning their blankets. It had been quite the show. Auden had also pricked their hands to confirm there was indeed blood pumping in their veins instead of the silvery liquid.

"Do you…" she said softly, avoiding eye contact. "Do you want to come in instead?"

Was Lark really asking him to come into her home? All the other times she'd insisted on coming to his house. He knew she was embarrassed, even though she shouldn't have been. He didn't care if she was a bum on the street—she was still Lark.

"I'd love to."

"Are you going to quit talking from the van and get over here?" she asked, taking a step back for him to open the door.

Shutting off the engine, he hopped out. Lark's dark curls blew back and forth, flapping in the air, and he wanted his fingers to get trapped in them.

With a smile, she moved toward him and wrapped her arms around his waist, placing her head on his shoulder. "You sure you don't want to leave? I don't mind waiting here. No guys do it for me the way you do, anyway."

"I think I may have to keep you," he murmured.

In answer, her arms squeezed around him tighter.

With his index finger, he lifted her chin from his shoulder and stared into her big brown eyes. "I wanted to tell you that I-I..." He struggled with saying the words aloud, but they were there inside his chest, aching to break through. And he knew he wasn't his father, but that worry would always be with him—he just couldn't let it control him.

"You don't have to say it, I know. All the proof is in here." She held up the spiral notebook and tapped it against his chest where his heart was hidden beneath. "I love you, too, Auden."

"Lark, if you ever sprout wings, maybe you can fly me away from here." He broke into a wide grin. "Was that a bit much? It was, wasn't it?"

"Sorry, the only bird I have in me is my name." She laughed. "But either way, one day, we'll both get the hell out of here."

A single tear slipped down Auden's face, and she wiped it away. "Remember, boys don't cry, Auden." Then she stood on her tiptoes and whispered in his ear with a smile, "Lyrics."

"Curses." He pulled her close and kissed her deeply, right before she guided him toward the inside of her home for the first time.

EPILOGUE

Music from "Space Oddity" — David Bowie

The music drifted through the air, the melody that always reminded Ridley of her. His hand fell to the mirror-glass butterfly back in his pocket and brushed his fingertips over it —she'd made it for him.

The task hadn't been completed because of him. He needed his pencil and paper to write down his thoughts because his head was always a jumbled mess.

He tried to control his movements, but the flute called to him, the melody floating in and out through all his nerve endings. Ridley was losing track of who he was, giving in to the song. Leni. He wanted to hate her, not for what she did to Lark and Auden—that was partly his fault too—but for how she'd treated him. Even after all she'd done, he couldn't bring his heart to hate hers, no matter how hard he tried. Leni was behind the flute, and she was the girl he loved. What he didn't understand was why she'd made the pre-fillers half her and half him, instead of doing like the kings and queens had requested.

As the Mirror Keeper, he'd had to choose two people from the Earth Dimension. He'd chosen Auden and Lark, but he shouldn't have. He shouldn't have chosen anyone. From the Mirror Dimension, he'd seen their bond through his cursed mirror and had wanted to know more about them. But his choices had been wrong—he should've fought for them earlier.

The music grew stronger, harsher, harder, the shadows calling to him, and he drifted farther and farther toward it, back to the Mirror Dimension, back to the place that was his home. He wouldn't be Leni's marionette ever again, but all he could do was blink, like he used to do when he'd first been created from mirror glass and had met Leni. Back when he was hers and she was his.

Leni shakily held the flute in between her lips and let the notes flow through. She wanted to break the flute, give it back, but she couldn't because it was hers. She hadn't chosen this path—it was attached to her, like the shadows were. The shadows serving the kings and queens had selected her. Still, she wouldn't have changed what she'd done because she had her reasons. Though she did wish things could've been different. Closing her eyes, she continued to play, drawing Ridley back to her—to their song. With tears sliding down her cheeks, her face hidden beneath her cloak, Leni remembered a time when she was happy with him and he was happy with her.

Did you enjoy Lyrics & Curses?

Authors always appreciate reviews, whether long or short.

Want more Cursed Hearts? Check out Leni and Ridley's story in Music & Mirrors, Book Two in the Cursed Hearts Duology!

Music & Mirrors

Before Ridley became the Mirror Keeper, he was just a guy in love who'd had a tough life before meeting Leni. Through Leni, he thought he'd found a way to truly live through the music they loved. But in the Mirror Dimension, everything can easily be broken—even their bond.

Leni has been haunted by shadows her whole life. She had kept the burden a secret from everyone, except for Ridley and her brother, and turned to music as a distraction. But those shadows are what led her to become the Piper, whether she wanted it or not. The only reason she continued on her destructive path is the secret she must protect at all costs.

Now back in the Mirror Dimension, Ridley and Leni must face punishment by the royals in charge of the curse. Music alone won't be enough to help them this time. In order for Ridley and Leni to save themselves, they must seek help from the two people they almost killed. If they can't band together to defeat the royals, Leni will end up dead and Ridley will become something he truly hates.

ACKNOWLEDGMENTS

This book! These characters! I've written a lot of things, but this one means so much to me. Lark and Auden have a huge piece of my heart, as does the '80s.

I'd first like to thank Midnight Tide Publishing for taking a chance on this story. Elle, you are such a wonderful human being and thank you so much.

To my Fairy Godmother, Carla, you seriously feel like one. You understood this story better than I think I did and knew exactly what needed to be done with it to make it better. Even with Lark and Auden you understood them perfectly! I will never forget all the help you've given me.

Brandy, you are amazing and helped so much in the construction of things and making my blurb into something wonderful. Jess, you were great at pinpointing things out that I didn't even think about.

Jena, holy crap, I couldn't have imagined a better cover and I want to sleep with it beside me always. And to Elissa, who made the inside just as excellent!

I'd like to give a special shoutout to all the people who

helped me early on! Amber H., Alexa, Gerardo, Vic, Kathryn, Donna, Sheila, Patricia, Kattie, Amy, Amber D., and Kristin.

Nate, you know what good music is, and Arwen you're discovering it as well! Mom, thank you for having me in the '80s!

And to all the readers, you're awesome for taking the time to read my story. Now, if only I could figure a way to travel back to this time.

ABOUT THE AUTHOR

Candace Robinson spends her days consumed by words and hoping to one day find her own DeLorean time machine. Her life consists of avoiding migraines, admiring Bonsai trees, watching classic movies, and living with her husband and daughter in Texas—where it can be forty degrees one day and eighty the next.

MORE FROM CANDACE ROBINSON

Cursed Hearts Duology
Lyrics & Curses
Music & Mirrors (coming soon)

Glass Vault Duology
Quinsey Wolfe's Glass Vault
The Bride of Glass

Laith Trilogy
Clouded by Envy
Veiled by Desire
Shadowed by Despair

Faeries of Oz
Lion
Tin
Crow (coming soon)
Ozma (coming soon)

Avocado Bliss
Bacon Pie
Hearts Are Like Balloons

Short Stories
Lullaby of Flames
A Layer Hidden
Dearest Clementine
Dearest Dorin

Something in the Shadows By Midnight Tide Publishing

For fans of Moon Called, True Blood, and Vampire Diaries.

You've heard their folktales-saw the carnage they left behind-those creatures, the things lurking deep in the shadows, watching and waiting until the right moment to ensnare its prey.

Four authors dared to tell their stories in this unique collection of wonderfully haunting and frightful thrillers, and even dark romance.

Inside, you'll discover tales of vampires, demons, and humans encountering spirits in these short stories that are sure to keep you up at night!

Available

10.28.20

The Girl in the Clockwork Tower by Lou Wilham

A tale of espionage, lavender hair, and pineapples.

Welcome to Daiwynn where magic is dangerous, but hope is more dangerous still.

For Persinette—a lavender-haired, 24-year-old seer dreaming of adventure and freedom—the steam-powered kingdom of Daiwynn is home. As an Enchanted asset for MOTHER, she aids in Collecting Enchanted and sending them to MOTHER's labor camps.

But when her handler, Gothel, informs Persi that she will be going out into the field for a Collection, she decides it's time to take a stand. Now she must fight her fears and find a way to hide her attempts to aid the Enchanted or risk being sent to the camps herself.

Manu Kelii, Captain of the airship The Defiant Duchess, is 26-years-old and hasn't seen enough excitement—thank you very much. His charismatic smile and flamboyant sense of style earned him a place amongst the Uprising, but his fickle and irresponsible nature has seen to it that their leader doesn't trust him.

Desperate to prove himself, Manu will stop at nothing to aid their mission to overthrow MOTHER and the queen of Daiwynn. So, when the Uprising Leader deposits a small unit of agents on his ship, and tasks him with working side by side with MOTHER asset Persinette to hinder the Collection effort, he finds himself in over his head.

The stakes are high for this unlikely duo. They have only two options; stop MOTHER or thousands more will die—including themselves.

Available

9.23.20

Made in the USA
Columbia, SC
18 December 2020